MEDICINE MEN

MEDICINE MEN

a novel by

ALICE ADAMS

Alfred A. Knopf   New York   1997

THIS IS A BORZOI BOOK
PUBLISHED BY ALFRED A. KNOPF, INC.

http://www.randomhouse.com/

Library of Congress Cataloging-in-Publication Data
Adams, Alice, [date]
Medicine men : a novel / by Alice Adams. — 1st ed.
p.   cm.
ISBN 0-679-45440-3
I. Title.
PS3551.D324M44   1997
813'.54—dc20   96-42001
CIP

Manufactured in the United States of America

First Edition

For Dr. Allen Wheelis,
who was always kind
and often brilliant

MEDICINE MEN

ONE

For a long time, Molly Bonner's strongest reaction to doctors was a fear that they would bore her to death. Seeing her come into their offices every year or so, and perceiving a visibly healthy (thin, clear-skinned, clear-eyed) youngish woman, and soon recognizing a good listener, they all began to talk. Molly had grown up in Richmond, Virginia, trained to listen to men and to laugh at their jokes—true of all women, of course, but even more so if they are Southern.

Her internist, Dr. Douglas Macklin, from Boston, talked about his impressions of San Francisco, contrasting the two cities; her gynecologist, Dr. Summers, talked politics—or, rather, he lectured her on the evils of Southern Republicans, which she was not. Dr. Gold, the dentist, spoke of travel, which in his case meant hotel prices and Frequent Flyer bargains.

These men all struck Molly as more than a little nuts, with their endless, not very interesting obsessions, but since she had no medical problem to contribute at the time, she let them go on talking. She also had some superstitious fear that if they talked about medical matters she would develop something or other, a fear that some years of working as a temp in medical offices had done nothing to allay. And all those men were a couple of generations older than Molly was; since each had been recommended by one of the others, they formed a more or less coherent group of middle-aged white males.

Contrary to received opinion, and prejudice, the doctor who seemed the sanest, as well as the least boring, was a psychoanalyst, Dr. Edgar Shapiro, whom Molly went to after the accidental death (in a helicopter crash) of her second husband, Paul West, a daredevil documentary filmmaker. For Molly, there was not only the shock and pain of Paul's death—she had loved him in many ways; Paul was wild and handsome and funny, intelligent and sexy—but there was also moral confusion. They had been on the verge of separating, and the death had left her rich. Paul did not like being married; they were both too young, he said. Molly disagreed, they were almost forty; how old did you have to be? She supposed he meant that, unmarried, he would feel younger, which was no doubt true. She also supposed that he meant that he hankered after younger women. In any case, she had not argued, but agreed to separate—and he so suddenly, horribly died.

The money complication came about because wild, crazy, adventurous Paul had a not wild brother, Matthew, who sold insurance. Who had sold Paul a policy that paid for an accidental death.

Grieving, and very confused, not sleeping well and given to headaches, Molly asked Dr. Macklin what to do, and he recommended Dr. Shapiro. "He's supposed to be the best in town. Probably charges a lot."

He did charge a lot, but he was both smart and kind, and sometimes even funny. He kept to the subject, Molly, and he managed to help. Molly came to feel that she was just a grief-struck and rattled person, not a permanently crippled one. In a practical way he pointed out that she now had a lot of choices, which they discussed—including giving away all the money. Or starting up a homeless shelter, something like that.

In any case, except for Dr. Shapiro, for a long time most doctors simply bored Molly. She did not share the medical panics experienced by some of her friends, for whom a mammogram was a major trauma. Nor, God knows, did she feel the sexual turn-on that doctors seemed to inspire in her beautiful friend Felicia Flood, who was for a long time involved with the famous heart surgeon Dr. Raleigh Sanderson, although she was not exactly faithful to him—but that is to get far ahead of the story.

And then, for medical reasons Molly was involved with a great many doctors all at once—and with another one in another way: he fell in love with her, obsessionally, angrily.

In the years since Paul's death, Molly had not "gone out" except with old friends: women, gay guys, sometimes couples. She had even imagined that part of her life to be over and done, despite what Dr. Shapiro and all her friends said to the contrary. She did not have much sense about men, was one of her conclusions, since her first very early marriage had not been a big success either.

But she did agree, one June, to come to a party at Felicia's at which Felicia admitted that there was to be someone, a friend of Dr. Sandy's, whom she might like. Since Molly did not much like Dr. Raleigh Sanderson, this was not promising, but she said yes, she would come.

"He's younger than Sandy, a little, and his wife died a year or so ago," Felicia said. "He's tall and thin, sort of handsome. You might like him. I don't know him very well, but he seems okay. Dave Jacobs. He practices in Marin."

This party took place on a magically warm star-sprinkled night in June—San Francisco is never warm at night in June. It was out in Felicia's careless, generous, and lovely garden, which smelled of jasmine and garlic, the garlic from Felicia's famous fish soup, the jasmine blooming everywhere that night. Arriving late, a calculation, Molly stood there for a moment, assailed by those scents, smiling but not recognizing anyone at first. Until

Felicia floated forward, in something pale and gauzy, and kissed her. "Oh, how wonderful, you're here." Felicia, smelling floral, her long hair loose, blond silk. She whispered, "And Sandy's here."

This was unusual. Sandy, married to rich fat alcoholic Connie, did not in a public way come often to Felicia's house, but every now and then he did. As though officially to stake his claim, Molly thought, which was probably unfair.

A long table, white-clothed, was set up at the end of the garden, near the azaleas and rhododendrons, the roses, around which people now clustered, drinking white wine and inhaling the soup's strong sea-and-garlic aroma. Felicia had announced that the soup was still too hot.

"I don't care what you say, I've never had a bad meal in Paris," a somewhat shrill, didactic male voice announced just as Molly was sitting down and greeting friends in a talk-to-you-later way. "And I've never had a really good one in London."

The speaker—an almost bald though still handsome man, big dark-brown eyes and very large strong white teeth—Molly instantly identified as the proffered David Jacobs; he must be, since there was no one else whom she had not at least met before. Her first thought was, Good, I'm not at all attracted, and I'm not ready for attraction, for sex and all that trouble. Also she thought he sounded a little like Dr. Gold, her travelling, sententious dentist. And though she and Paul had had at least a couple of bad meals in Paris, plus some very good ones in London, she said nothing at the time. "I thought you agreed with me, you were wearing that lovely amiable smile," Dave later told her, and she answered, smiling, "I just don't like to argue. Much easier just to be amiable."

Molly and Dave were introduced, and Molly was welcomed by several people, who complained that they hadn't seen her for a while.

Felicia announced that the soup was ready, and conversation

shifted from foreign food to praises of Felicia: just the right amount of garlic, everyone said, and Sandy Sanderson added, "And great fish. From Swan's?"

"No. The Cal-Mart."

Molly and Felicia had met and become almost instant friends some ten years back, when they were both office temps: Molly because she and her first husband, Henry Starck, a Portland (Maine) lawyer, had just divorced and she had not come out well. And Felicia because, though her parents were both rich and generous, she was basically lazy, workwise; she liked earning just enough to get by, and she liked even more the variety of people and circumstances that such work provided. Molly saw herself at that time as "deciding what to do," an interim period for her. As she saw it she would think and make plans— whereas Felicia generally succeeded in living from moment to moment.

Thus, all those years ago, Molly had been a witness of the first days of Felicia and Sandy, Dr. Sanderson. Felicia had gone to work in his office and talked about him quite a lot. And then, for a year or so, she talked about him all the time.

"He's terrifically attractive" was the first thing that Felicia said. "And wow, he really knows it. That swashbuckling walk. I've heard he was a football star at Harvard. The other surgeons all imitate the way he walks, it's funny to watch them crossing the street behind him. His team. He sure learned my name right off. Miss Flood. I've heard his wife is an alcoholic, and really rich. Doctors, honestly. I think he's sort of coming on to me, I don't know. I sort of hope not, I'm so weak that way, and I do have this thing about doctors, I know I do. All those med students when I was at Wellesley.

"Guess what? We had lunch together. I thought he meant just a sandwich someplace near the hospital, but no, down into the parking level where his Jag is—of course a Jag—and down to this quiet little place off Union Street. They seemed to know him, so I asked him, 'Do you always take your secretaries out to lunch?' He said, 'Not secretaries, beautiful women.' Which is kind of a snotty, sexist remark, if you think about it. But I guess he was being gallant—my dad sort of talks like that too. He's a lot nicer than I thought—Sandy, I mean. We talked about—oh, a lot of stuff. He's really very smart. For a doctor." She laughed. "But he did keep looking at me, you know? I was not entirely surprised when this great box of flowers arrived last night. I guess he got my address from Personnel, and he sort of knows my mom and dad. Just with a note about thanks for lunch."

And then more flowers. Another lunch. Or lunches. And then, "Well, you know, I couldn't fight him off anymore. I said I was weak. And Sandy's so—so powerful. So intense. He really comes on. Besides, by then I was in love."

By then Molly had met Paul West, and she too was in love, or nearly, and so she listened to Felicia with even more than her usual sympathetic interest. At first it was a way of not talking about Paul, which, distrustful of both their feelings, hers and Paul's, she did not want to do. She knew he was dangerous.

"Oh, I know," Felicia went on, and on and on. "Married, etcetera. Something bad to do to another woman. But I hear she's drunk all the time, and I'm sure I'm not the first extra lady in his life. Or probably the last. But in the meantime, I have to say, it's terrific. Sandy is really a piece of work. And he's interesting. I guess I like hearing about medical stuff. No good can come of this," Felicia said, with her sly cat's smile. "But in the meantime . . ."

Molly's own relationship with Raleigh Sanderson was lopsided. Odd. On the one hand, she felt that she knew him well, through Felicia; certainly he was a strong presence in her life. On the other hand, she had almost no personal contact with him at all. Two years ago, when Paul was killed, there had been a great sheaf of flowers, gladioli (Molly disliked gladioli, but never mind; it was the thought), and a card, engraved *Dr. Raleigh Sanderson.* And, handwritten, "I'm very sorry for your loss." That was really very kind, Molly thought, and at that time it occurred to her that Felicia must have talked a lot about her too. "Poor Molly, she's all broken up, she's just not herself . . ."

Well, by now she was herself again, or nearly; since early spring she had been extremely uncomfortable with what she assumed were allergies, or sinus problems—new to her, and seeming not to go away. However, the best way to deal with physical symptoms was to ignore them, Molly thought, and so she had, pretty much.

Now, at the party, anxious to impress Sandy with her general well-being (no matter what Felicia had said), she turned to him, taking up his remark about Swan's. "It is a great source, though," she agreed. "And so much fun to go there and eat oysters."

"If you still dare eat oysters at all." He grinned at her. "And I do."

There followed a brief, boring, but animated discussion of purveyors of fresh fish, with Molly and Sandy smiling and nodding most amiably at each other, as though in the process of notable discoveries.

Actually, Molly's allergies, or sinuses, or whatever, had lately taken the form of an extreme heaviness inside her head, and a general, overall physical lassitude. Frequent very sharp headaches, to which she was not generally given. Occasionally she would mention these symptoms to a friend, or even in a social group, although usually she did not make such complaints; often someone else would have initiated the conversation with his or her own symptoms. In any case, the invariable response would come: "Oh, this is the worst pollen season ever. The drought. The rains. The plants."

Dr. Macklin, her internist, had said more or less all this him-

self, interspersed with an account of his projected fall trip down
the coast of Maine to Boston; "I can't stand missing a New England fall," he said, as he said every year. He did add that his own
allergies had been at their worst this year, and he prescribed an
antibiotic that had helped his wife (an actress, a red-haired
beauty), also allergic, but that so far had had no good effect on
Molly. In fact, it seemed to her that she felt somewhat worse.

And tonight she felt even worse than usual; she wondered if
she could be allergic to some flower or flowering shrub in Felicia's overflowing garden. Or to garlic? or fish, or wine? Or could
this be some neurotic response to the presence of so many doctors? Molly smiled at this, aware that even Dr. Shapiro would
find it unlikely. Excusing herself from the table, she went back
into the house and into Felicia's downstairs bathroom, where
she found some Advil among a jungle of prescription pills,
which, as a decent friend, she did not examine—and lipsticks
and mascara, which she did.

Returning, coming back outside to the table, Molly thought
that she might just casually mention her malaise—introducing it
as a topic, so to speak. Taking advantage of the presence of so
many doctors. But of course she did nothing of the sort.

". . . for real climbing, I just don't think you can beat the
Tetons," she heard from the dark, gravelly voice of Sandy
Sanderson.

And then, somewhat testily aggressive, Dave Jacobs: "Mont
Blanc, in my book, is absolutely tops. The views, and the
food—"

Sandy: "Oh well, if you climb for food—"

"Of course I don't, but it helps."

Felicia's lovely voice broke in. "Oh honestly, you guys. Whoever wants to climb all those mountains, anyway? I'd much
rather go to the beach, and just lie there. But then I'm basically
lazy."

"The beach is hell on your skin," Sandy told her, as he must have before, and Molly thought, Oh God, doctors! How does Felicia stand it? I don't care what a great stud he is.

Her cold, and at times Molly decided that it could be just that, a pesky, lingering summer cold—in any case, whatever it was—was also affecting her hearing a little, she thought. It was hard to follow the general conversation, which seemed to have turned to the plight of Cuba:

". . . end the embargo . . ."

". . . punish that Commie Castro . . ."

". . . more AIDS coming in . . ."

". . . all could drown . . ."

Having her own strong views, Molly still found herself at some remove from the talk. She was almost relieved when Sandy, seated next to her, observed, "That's some cold you have."

"Well yes, I guess it is. I'm taking an antibiotic. I can't remember the name—"

"That's what's making you feel bad," Felicia told her. "Antibiotics. They really drag you out."

"Antibiotics do not make you sick," Sandy insisted. "That's just a myth."

"I think it's a myth that they don't," Felicia told him. "They make you feel terrible—you have to be sure to eat yogurt while you're taking them, or some health food pills. Acidophilus. Of course doctors never tell you that."

Across Molly's mind at that moment flashed a news photo of Rwandans, fleeing, ravaged. Haitians. Hopeless millions. How could it matter what she was allergic to, including antibiotics? "I think we have to end the embargo on Cuba," she said, more loudly than she had meant to.

"Of course we do. Those people are starving, that's why they want to leave. We've got to end it, but will we?" Dave Jacobs had directed this toward Molly, agreeing with her. At which she was somewhat pleased; these were not attitudes that she would expect from a successful, middle-class doctor. But still, his voice was so harsh, his teeth so large and aggressive. (And I am so hypercritical, Molly thought; it's as though I resent other men for not being Paul. Being here instead of him.) She blew her nose hard into a Kleenex, and in the next instant realized that blood was running down her face, and onto her white silk shirt. Getting to her feet, she began to hurry toward the house, the bathroom.

She was followed by Felicia, who called to her, "I'll bring you some ice."

In Felicia's warm, aromatic kitchen, which smelled of every possible spice, and fruit and coffee and sweets—having removed the stained shirt in the bathroom and put on the soft pink, too-large sweater that Felicia offered—Molly began to run cold water through the shirt.

She wiped at her nose: no more blood.

"Just leave it here to soak," Felicia told her. "I'll hang it up tomorrow."

"Thanks. You know, I think I'll just go on home now. I'll be okay but I don't really feel all that great."

Molly's small but rather grand apartment, with its views of the bay, and the bridge, and Marin, was just a couple of blocks up the hill from Felicia's pretty little house—both being in the neighborhood called Cow Hollow, which is above the Marina and below Pacific Heights, and is where in earlier, simpler (pre-Earthquake) pastoral times, cows used to roam at large. Molly had moved into her place shortly after Paul's death: she wanted not to stay where they had lived together, on Russian Hill—and she suddenly had all that funny money, the insurance. New freedom of choice. And the idea of being in walking distance of Felicia was nice.

"Oh sure," Felicia was saying. "I'll do good nights for you, and we'll talk tomorrow. You sure you'll be okay?"

But just then a loud voice announced, "I'll take you home."

Turning, Molly saw the strong white teeth, smooth bald

head, and the handsome, authoritative face of Dr. David Jacobs.

"No," she told him. "Really. I just live up the hill a couple of blocks. I'll walk. I'd rather, actually."

She began to put out her hand, to say good night, but instead he took her arm and began to guide her toward the door. "You need a doctor," he said.

He had spoken jokingly, but did he mean it? Were nosebleeds a bad symptom, of something serious?

"Honestly," she told him, "I'll be perfectly okay."

He gripped her arm more firmly. "You don't know, you may need me." He grinned.

There seemed no way to escape him without a minor scene, and Molly never made even those minor scenes. And so she did not now, only murmuring, "You could just drop me off and then come on back here." And, to Felicia, "I certainly didn't mean to break up your party."

The two women lightly kissed, and Molly thanked Felicia for the party; they exchanged smiles that promised further talk.

Dave Jacobs had parked about two blocks from Felicia's house ("No space," he explained unnecessarily; parking in that neighborhood was terrible), making him farther still from Molly's. She reflected that she could as easily and more quickly have walked in the time the short drive required for the fairly battered old Camaro he drove. Molly found it sympathetic; it seemed such an undoctorly car. But he apologized. "My wife's car," he said. "For some reason she really liked it, and I haven't been able to get rid of it. A combination of sentiment and thrift, I guess."

Moved by both the sentiment and the honesty, Molly at that moment liked him a little better.

In the car he asked her, "Do you have many nosebleeds?"

"Oh no, not really." Actually she had had several in the past few months.

"Come on, how many?"

"Oh, maybe two or three."

"And how long have you had that cold?"

"Oh, it seems like all spring. I think it must be an allergy or something."

"Could be. You should see a good ENT man, no point putting up with that kind of discomfort."

"This is where I live," Molly told him. "You can just let me off here. Really."

Propitiously (or perhaps not) there was a parking space just in front of Molly's building, into which he slid the car, then came around for her before she could let herself out.

"And now," he said, with a flash of all those teeth, "you can ask me in and give me a brandy. Return for all that good medical advice."

"I'm not even sure I have any brandy," she murmured, though she did know: Paul had liked a good brandy after dinner, and the bottle of cognac had come along with everything else when she moved—although she remembered a fleeting temptation just to throw it out.

She was tempted now to throw David Jacobs out, so to speak—to tell him that she was tired, he would have to go. Southern training as usual prevailed, however, and moments later they were seated across from each other in her living room, he with a brandy and Molly with a glass of orange juice.

"I suppose you're strong on vitamin C," he remarked aggressively.

"Actually I am. And of course you're not," she said as she thought, Is this a quarrel? *already?*

"Well, I don't think it can hurt you much." The grin. "And God knows Pauling was a brilliant fellow." He looked around, dismissing Linus Pauling, and vitamins. "Great place you have here. I'm really impressed."

Molly started to explain, as she sometimes did: I had all this insurance money, Paul bought it almost as a joke to help his younger brother, I've never lived in such a fancy place. But she stopped herself, and only said, "Thanks, I like it here." She added, "I just bought it a couple of years ago when my husband died."

"That was really smart." He stared at her with faintly too much interest. "I should have done that," he said. "I thought of it. Moved out when Martha died, I mean. But I didn't, and there I am with all that stuff. Reminding me."

Molly heard such genuine feeling in his voice that she was moved: he had truly loved his wife, and he missed her. And she probably was fairly young to die, these days, Molly thought. She put Dave's age as late fifties, early sixties. But then, Paul had been barely forty. She asked Dave, "Where do you live?"

"Mill Valley. Down in the woods. I'm used to the darkness, but when I see views like these, I wonder."

Molly suddenly, uncontrollably began to sneeze. She sneezed once, twice, three times, four. She couldn't stop. At the same time, she tried to smile and to signal with her free hand that she was all right. And then she stopped.

He asked, "You do that often?"

She lied, "No. I must be sort of tired." The truth was, she was very tired indeed. Standing up, she said to him, "I'm sorry, but I think I have to go to bed now. But thanks for driving me home."

He quickly got up too. "Maybe we could have dinner sometime." An awkward smile; he was probably unused to asking women to dinner.

"That would be nice." She spoke without enthusiasm, she knew, but she smiled as though she had meant it.

"And watch that cold," he cautioned on the way out, once more in control. "Call me if you need the name of a good ENT man."

"Oh. Thanks."

TWO

Since he had always laid nurses, Dr. Raleigh Sanderson felt that laying nurses did not count; it did not constitute infidelity to Felicia, his official (and unofficial) lady. And "lay" is the word that he would have used for his encounters with nurses. "Fuck" in his mind was a dirty word; making love was what he and Felicia did—although sometimes they fucked, dirtily, on a sweaty afternoon. What Raleigh used to do with Connie, his wife, he thought of as simply that, as "doing it." But he laid nurses; Sandy did not think of himself as "getting laid," even though more often than not these days it was he who lay down, allowing the bouncy nurse to bring him to climax with her hands or her mouth, or both. He much disliked the vulgar, graphic expressions for these activities. Even "oral sex" was too explicit for Sandy.

Like so many people, Sandy was convinced that his sexual drives were exceptionally strong. As proof of such strength, he cited (to himself; he was not given to even semi-public boasting) the extreme and compelling arousal that he often experienced at the end of a successful operation, and almost all his operations were successful; his record was world-renowned. His skill was indeed quite fantastic; sometimes Sandy himself was amazed at what went on beneath his hands, the incredible speed and precision with which his fingers moved, all racing toward the instant at which he knew: This heart is all right now, I've repaired (or replaced) the valve, I've saved it. Of course he could not know absolutely for days or weeks, even months, that the heart was really functioning on its own. Still, there was always the moment when, within his own heart, he *knew,* and he lived for that moment, that peak. Further recovery on the part of the patient was anticlimactic, and basically uninteresting to Sandy. It was boring to have to keep seeing those patients again and again, listening to their parade of minor symptoms, their major gratitude. But the operations themselves—they thrilled him still. No other word for it, he was thrilled. It was thrilling work that he did.

Small wonder, then, that after such an exciting, deeply felt triumph he should feel himself excited in a sexual way, as well as in his own heart.

Not surprisingly, Sandy thought considerably about that organ, that marvelous muscle: his personal heart. He admired its strength, and its clear superiority to those lesser hearts that he operated on, and fixed: hearts enlarged or those with leaking valves, those damaged by early rheumatic fever, or simply born bad, defective. As his heart was born strong and good. A superior heart.

And he had kept in shape. Played racquetball and tennis at his club, swam at Tahoe in the summer and worked out on an exercise bike almost every day. Made love to lively Felicia a lot, in recent years, and sometimes laid nurses.

No wonder that even his hair was still so enviably thick and lively. He wondered about those guys, like Dave Jacobs, who went bald.

A long time ago, when Sandy was an intern at Mass. General Hospital, he and some of his doctor friends had a shared bachelor apartment down on Chambers Street. Connie Knowles was a tall, blonde Boston deb, and she had seemed the perfect girl for him, with her family house on Chestnut Street, Louisburg Square, and the summer place in Magnolia. She was even fairly smart. Unlike most of the debs who only dabbled in some kind of social work, Connie went to Radcliffe, where she studied sociology (well, that did seem a little eccentric; he might have known there was some sort of trouble ahead. Why not fine arts, or French?—something that would come in handy in later life). But she was very wellborn, and beautiful and rich, and to cap her perfections she fell madly in love with Raleigh Sanderson, out from Iowa. "Raleigh." Connie always called him that, turning his name into a beautiful Boston word, the first syllable long and drawn out, the second light, barely there. (Raleigh never told anyone that he got that name because his mother came from that town, Raleigh, North Carolina, and made it worse by naming his brother Durham. Jesus! But she missed it there.) Connie was crazy about her tall dark Dr. Raleigh; she wanted to get married and have a lot of children as soon as possible. Maybe even then she drank a little too much—"tee many martoonies," as they said on Chambers Street. But she let him do it to her, she was very passionate. First in the back seat of his car, parked behind some dunes, at Crane's Beach, in Ipswich. And then quite often, every chance they got, in the upstairs room on Chambers Street, even if the other guys with their dates were all downstairs.

That is how Sandy thought of what happened between them, her "letting him do it to her." He more or less discouraged active participation from Connie; it didn't seem right, especially once they were married.

In any case, Connie got her wish. She got her Dr. Raleigh Sanderson, in a huge June wedding with a big outdoor garden reception up in Magnolia. And, within the first six years, four children. All born out in San Francisco, where they moved for Raleigh's residency at Presbyterian Hospital—and bought a big house, in Pacific Heights, and stayed.

In the years since then Sandy successfully attached the phrase "Fetal Alcohol Syndrome" to explain his children, none of whom had turned out well, or even reasonably all right, by his standards. None of them are speaking to him just now, and he has disinherited them all. He has even been known to murmur that acronym, FAS, in response to inquiries about his family. This not only lets him off the hook, or covers his ass (to use a phrase that Sandy himself would never employ), it glosses over the fact that Connie as a pregnant woman and then as a very young mother drank almost not at all. She started up drinking in a serious way about the time of the first drug arrest of their youngest child, who was twelve and dealing LSD at the Town School for Boys. For Connie, that was the last straw. She began to go a little crazy after that, drinking and gaining weight, of course, and developing these crazy, irrational jealousies. Making scenes. Seeing shrinks, thousands of dollars on shrinks.

These days Connie still describes herself as an alcoholic, although she does not drink, not at all. Just Perrier, and other ridiculous expensive waters. She is still quite fat, although a recent accusation was that he had not noticed her loss of twenty pounds, some crazy so-called spiritual spa she went to. God knows what she does with her time all day: probably women's meetings, nature and animals and refugees, the things she mentions briefly at dinner; they do have dinner together, usually; they go to the requisite parties, they give the occasional obligatory reception.

But do not talk to Raleigh Sanderson about the sixties. These were the years that wrecked his family, finishing off the work of FAS. Since then it's been a series of drug arrests and crazy marriages, divorces and bastard children. (He has three half-black grandchildren, probably in Oakland; he no longer even asks Connie where they are.) Most recently, there have been lawsuits; they want his money.

What Sandy feels worst about is the grandchildren aspect of

all this trouble. He adores little tiny girls, even half-black ones. He is completely nuts about them, he admits it. When he sees one in a store or on the street, with her fat little cheeks and her big wide innocent eyes and her little ruffled panties, Sandy feels the most terrible pangs of longing, and of loss. Even, his eyes tear up.

And then he reads in the paper that some man has molested one of those babies—has actually done it to her. Sandy feels his blood pressure dangerously rise, and rage grips his throat. Those guys should be castrated, Sandy thinks. The chair or, God knows, lethal injection is too good for them. Just cut it off, without anesthetic, let them bleed to death. He can't even think about child molestation, it makes him crazy.

Felicia. What a woman! That was Sandy's first thought on seeing Miss Felicia Flood walk into his office. A classical big blonde woman, built like the Varga girls in the *Esquire* of his young manhood. But with a classier face, and a kind of style about her, and as soon as she spoke he could tell: real class. (Sandy is dead accurate on accents, an expertise fueled by ferocious snobbery. When a couple of other doctors suggested that Dr. Dave Jacobs might not be Jewish, despite the name, Sandy countered, "Of course he's Jewish, just listen to him talk." And of course he was right.) Sandy is also snobbish, and accurate about Midwestern accents, forgetting his own origins. No more Cedar Falls.

But Miss Flood, Felicia, his new temporary secretary, was something else. He read sexual compliance in her lively smile, but not right away, he knew that. She was too good-looking for anything immediate; old Sandy knew the rules. She liked him a lot, though; he could tell. She kept those big dark-blue eyes on his face (true sapphire eyes, like expensive jewels), and she smiled at his smallest jokes. So interested. She seemed intrigued by anything he had to say, fascinated by surgery, hospital politics. By professional tennis and water problems at Lake Tahoe and the general decline of life in San Francisco.

Strangely, their first time together was on the day of one of Sandy's worst surgeries: the old bastard (the patient) expired on him. A bad aortic, but Sandy had done a lot of bad aortics before, no need for this one to die. He was sitting in his office an hour or so later, feeling terrible, too terrible even to call in a nurse, as he had meant to do (had even thought of doing when he was right there in the OR; he had one all picked out, a plain girl with enormous cans), and suddenly there was Miss Flood, Felicia, who took one look at him and said, "You poor guy, can I feed you some lunch, for a change? My house isn't far from here."

And although he had carefully never touched her before, there was no playing around once they got inside her house. *They fell upon each other.* Knowing these words to be trite, that was still how Sandy described (to himself) what almost immediately happened with him and Felicia, that day, as she reached to close her front door. He grabbed her toward him, she turned and grasped his neck; his mouth plunged down to hers, which instantly opened for him. Wild! For a moment he thought they would have to do it right there, on the bright hall rug, but then Felicia jerked away, pulling him into a room where there was a bed, both of them ripping off clothes. As they fell upon each other.

Jesus Christ. The greatest experience of his life, bar none. Making love with Felicia was like—was like nothing else he could possibly imagine. Maybe like reaching the top of Mont Blanc—and then some.

For a while after that—in fact for quite a while—Sandy felt that his life was perfect. His work was going well—actually it always had: he was about the best in the business, well paid and well known too. And he had a lady in his life, the sexiest woman alive, probably, and also very intelligent and *nice,* and the most fantastic cook; often Felicia would bring him a pretty little bowl of soup in bed, always something amazing, sorrel or hazelnuts, mussels and spinach. And sometimes when Connie was out of town, back to Boston to see her family or some women's meeting somewhere, Sandy would boldly take Felicia out to a well-known restaurant—he favored the old ones, Jack's or Trader Vic's, or even Ernie's. Whereas she always had heard of a new place, with handsome boyish waiters, a lot of fruit and vegetables mixed in with the meat, or fish.

"I suppose this is where you come with your other boyfriends," he sometimes teased her.

And she would laugh. "Sandy darling, how would I possibly have the energy? You know I'm basically lazy."

It was certainly true that he kept her satisfied (that was a word he liked; it seemed both accurate and understated, in Felicia's case and in his), but he did feel an occasional pang at the thought of all the nights that she necessarily spent at home alone. When he was with Connie and couldn't even call her. Sometimes Felicia did go out to a movie or a restaurant or a party, and she had explained that she didn't like going alone, so she usually called a friend—warm, gregarious Felicia had lots of friends. Mostly women, of course. And queers. She didn't like it when Sandy used that word, so he kept on doing it, to tease her.

Once he saw her at a party, an enormous museum do, an AIDS benefit. (Connie had really twisted his arm, insisting that they go.) Felicia was with a handsome guy, even younger than she was, it seemed to Sandy. And so the next day (in bed, in the early afternoon; she had made a terrific lunch) he quizzed her—teasing, of course: "What's all this going out with good-looking younger men behind my back?"

She gave it right back to him: "What do you care? Charlie's only what you would call 'some queer.' " She added, "And a party like that is hardly behind your back."

She had him there, on both counts.

Rarely, he would come to a party that Felicia gave, at her house. He liked the sense of sharing in her life, being part of it; he liked meeting her friends, he liked to know who they were, and what they talked about (although he secretly disliked quite a few of them, including her good friend Molly Bonner and most of the queers). But he wanted her friends to know that he was there, a large, important presence in Felicia's life. She was not just some woman alone. And she was most certainly not "available."

Felicia's fidelity, then (to be fair about it), would seem implicitly to require his own—and for quite a long time Sandy took that unspoken demand quite seriously. No problem with Connie: he hadn't touched her for years, didn't want to touch her; nor did she want him, although occasionally she made some gesture that could have been interpreted in that way. But he could hardly believe that they ever had. Done it together. And look what came of that unhappy coupling: four really rotten human beings, his progeny.

Too bad he and Felicia would not have children. He sometimes had fantasies of their plump blonde little baby girls, all frolicking in the bathtub, bare bottoms and dear little vaginal slits among the bubbles. He could help them wash.

But with nurses the fidelity thing was a little different. Sex with them was something he was used to. Laying nurses, whenever he felt the need. For one thing, there were certain women, nurses, who were used to him—who expected it of him, so to speak. Who would think it was really strange and maybe be hurt if he never called them into his office. And smiled, and locked the door.

And so, without giving it much thought, or guilt, Sandy got back into the sex-with-nurses habit, although perhaps less frequently than before; after all, if he was going to see Felicia later that same day, there was really no need.

One of the nurses he was most used to—and she to him, probably—was his surgical nurse, Jane White, as plain as her name but with beautiful bazooms. And, incidentally, exceptionally quick and smart in the OR. Certainly Jane would have been hurt if many months passed without those particular calls. Without her getting laid. By Dr. Raleigh Sanderson, the Chief of Surgery.

On Fridays of every week there were so-called surgical conferences held, although in fact the cardiologists talked as much as if not more than the surgeons did. (It had struck Sandy quite often that the cardiologists, including the interns and residents, were usually Jewish; the surgeons were not. Sandy dimly felt that this was as it should be, although he could not have said quite why.) Cases were presented and discussed, procedures argued. The cardiologists, naturally, wanted to medicate forever—until death itself, it sometimes seemed; the surgeons often favored a more aggressive approach. As Sandy himself liked to put it, and often did: "A life like that is simply not worth living." By which he meant that if a given patient is in the terrible shape just described, the possible risks and discomforts of surgery are well worth it.

And so it went on the Friday following Felicia's party. One of the cardiology residents, Dr. Bluestone, from Brookline, Massachusetts, and Harvard, and with that *accent,* those Harvard vowels (despite his name)—Dr. Bluestone described a sixty-year-old woman, a Mrs. Miller, a widow with a history of problems: possible childhood rheumatic fever, and the familiar litany of symptoms—dyspnea on exertion, mildly cyanotic, etc. The only original feature in all this was what sounded like a classic surgery phobia: something about a botched hysterectomy, way back. Though what that could have to do with repairing her mitral valve Sandy could not quite see, and he felt that Bluestone was making too much of this woman's fears. She sounded to him like a very good candidate, just healthy enough to withstand the surgery, and sick enough to need it.

Sandy said, by way of summing up and to indicate that he didn't want to prolong the discussion, "She sounds like an excellent surgical candidate to me. And as far as her symptoms go"—he smiled; his audience knew what was coming—"a life lived like that—"

"But the point is her life is very much worth living." That pushy young Harvard kid had the nerve to interrupt. "As I said in my presentation, running the cat shelter keeps her very happy, if we could just make her even a little more comfortable. And she's convinced that an operation would kill her."

Seriously annoyed, both by the interruption and at the mention of cats, which he loathed, Sandy asked, as mildly as he could, "Since when have we taken the superstitions of patients into account?"

"Mrs. Miller is an intelligent woman," this Bluestone had the presumption to argue. "I take her fears seriously."

"I have yet to hear of a patient dying of fear." Saying this, Sandy recognized it as a lie; people did die of fear, children did. Not often, but it happened. Nevertheless, he then shrugged as eloquently as he could, by which he meant: I have spoken, and to argue further with you would be beneath my dignity. I am Dr. Raleigh Sanderson, and you are, so far, no one.

The hour was over in a moment that could have been awkward, with Bluestone sounding off again; instead, people began to get to their feet and to start casual conversations with each other. To move back toward their respective offices.

Not speaking to anyone, and ignoring the bunch of interns and residents who tended to follow him around, Sandy stalked out into the hall and down the long passageway to his own office, his head held high, his heavily starched lab coat rustling as he strode.

Inside his sanctum, alone, he removed the coat and sat there in his pale-blue shirtsleeves, and glared at the knots in his walnut panelling. Somewhat to his surprise, he became aware of a familiar stirring in what he thought of as his loins; he recognized at least some degree of sexual arousal.

He considered calling Felicia; he could be at her house in less than ten minutes. Then he remembered that in an interval between jobs she had gone up to Seattle to visit an old college friend (she had too many friends, such a waste of time). And so he called Jane White.

In the fifteen minutes that it took Jane to get there (so much time was unusual for her; she generally made it in five, after surgical conferences), Sandy had to recognize that whatever excitement he had felt was now in fact gone, he had lost it. Could something be wrong with his prostate? He would have to have it checked. But Jane could take care of him as she had before. He began to smile with relieved anticipation.

She came bustling in at last, still in her lab coat and carrying her clipboard, and Sandy saw trouble almost instantly on her large plain long-nosed face. What she said was "I don't have a lot of time. I'm really busy."

Having risen to his feet, Sandy smiled and came around his desk to where she stolidly stood, and he said, rather jovially, "Then we'll just have to make do with the time we have, okay?"

She did not smile, but frowned, and backed off. "Don't you get it?" she asked him. "I don't feel like fooling around today."

"Fooling around." He did know what that meant, and it was to Sandy an especially unattractive expression, and one that Jane knew he did not like.

Perhaps for that reason he made an unfortunate joke. He said, though with a smile, "You know I could get you fired for insubordination." And he laughed to show he was kidding.

But to his surprise—and horror; Sandy was genuinely horrified—Jane reacted as though he had meant what he said.

Narrowing her intense strange blue-gray eyes (her one good facial feature), Jane in a menacing half-whisper said to him, "And I could have you up for sexual abuse, do you know that?

You've heard of it? You read about what happened down at Stanford, and at the big law firm in Palo Alto? Well, don't think for a minute I couldn't do it, and I can think of several other nurses who'd be very happy—"

"But, Jane, come on. We've always been—I've always thought—"

"You always thought I'd come in and give you a blow job on demand."

Sandy winced. He hated, hated, *hated* that expression. "I thought we were friends," he said stiffly. "Colleagues, really."

"Colleagues!" She bore down hard on the first syllable, making it harsh and loud, accusatory. And she looked as though she had a great deal more to say along those lines, but she was interrupted by a heavy fit of coughing.

Sandy knew enough not to pat her on the back—or to touch her at all: God knows what her response would have been to any touch at this point. He felt that she was about to cry, and that when she did it would be all right to touch her, he could put his arms around her in a comforting way. Let one thing lead to another.

But Jane White did not cry. Or if she did, Sandy was never to know that she had. Still half coughing, choking a little, she just stammered out, "You stupid old shit!"—and hurried out of the room.

Alone (abandoned!), Sandy sat down again. He reached up to stroke his hair, a familiar and usually reassuring gesture, but noticed that his hand shook. (Lord, could he be getting Parkinson's too?) Everything felt awry. His stomach clenched. He was hungry, but the very idea of food was revolting, impossible. Even his heart, that strong reliable organ, seemed to ache.

Various bad words came to his mind. Fear—but how could he possibly be afraid of a nurse? Loneliness—but he wasn't lonely; he had Felicia, and in a way he had Connie. Old age, impotence, failure. Cold, hunger. But none of those words had any application to his life.

THREE

"She has the soul of a courtesan," Molly once said to Paul, by way of explaining her friend Felicia. "She loves to please people, to be loved, and she's so intelligent, so realistic that she knows what she wants. She's learned to be infinitely pleasing. Being with her is a delight, almost always. For one thing she really lives in the moment, so when she's with you there's nothing, no one else on her mind."

"I can sort of see that," Paul told her. "Plus which she's a dish. But Sandy. The guy's an old shit. I don't get it."

Molly laughed, partly because she had heard a tiny edge of competition in Paul's voice. "She knows he's a shit, although she never quite admits it, how could she? She does say that she's hung up on older men, preferably doctors. Married. She likes men she can't marry. She's probably right. For her, I mean."

This conversation took place early on in their marriage, when Molly, bedazzled, thought (when she thought at all) that they would be happy forever.

Paul said, "But Sanderson, Jesus. As you know I'm crazy about Felicia, I'm an easy prey to her charm. But I'm glad we don't have to see a lot of that guy."

"Me too, actually. And I don't think he likes me either, much. But I'll still bet on Felicia. She'll end up doing him in."

"Do you think she plays around?"

"Well, again she's never said so. But, lately, there've been some things she's said that make me wonder. And only a moron would be faithful to someone married."

Paul laughed. "I love the way you women have it all worked out. The new rules. I'll remember that if I'm ever inclined to stray."

"See that you do."

He added, "And for all we know old Sandy still fucks nurses."

"That's possible. It would be just like him, wouldn't it."

"Are all doctors terrible guys, or do they just get that way in med school?"

"I don't know. Felicia and I've talked about it, and she doesn't know either."

This was shortly after Felicia and Sandy had started their relationship, and not too long after Molly and Paul were married (in the tackiest chapel they could find, near Reno). Felicia thought Molly and Paul would last forever—and Molly, like Paul, gave the Felicia-Sandy affair a couple of months. And both women were wrong. Paul opted out of the marriage, and then he was killed, and for whatever curious reasons Felicia continued for several years, not months, to be the lady friend of Raleigh Sanderson.

Paul was remarkable-looking. More striking than handsome, but very, very striking. For starters he was very tall, and thin, but good shoulders. His face was long and thin, high-boned. His eyes were what one remembered, though: a very pale, very bright light blue. Like certain skies in the early dawn on a day that will be very hot—Molly had thought that, remembering summer beach days in Virginia. Paul had very gray, almost white hair, obviously premature.

Since he was a screenwriter (later a documentary filmmaker), when they first met she had asked the obvious (silly) question, "How come you're not an actor?"

"Because I'm too smart," he told her, somewhat dismissively. By which she understood that she was about the hundredth person to ask him that.

So she said she was sorry, and he said that was all right; the real reason was that he couldn't act, was too shy, and really not very smart.

But he was still, always, amazing-looking.

They had met, or picked each other up, in a bookstore on Fillmore Street, in front of the travel shelves. "Talk about meeting cute," Paul said later. "It was worse than Neil Simon." At the time he had said to her, right off, "I like your hair. Are you going to Mexico?" They were standing in front of Guides to Mexico.

"Not particularly," she told him. "But I do think about Mexico." And then, "Actually I like your hair too."

They laughed, and became good friends, and then lovers. And then they got married. As simple and as infinitely complex as that.

A long time ago, long before Paul, as a very young just-out-of-college woman, Molly had married Henry Starck; they met in college, Bates College, in Lewiston, Maine. Molly had chosen Bates for being small and excellent, coed—and far from Richmond. Henry had gone there because all the men in his family had, for generations. Henry was from Portland, a splendid old gray-shingled house on Cape Elizabeth, and a large, rich and parsimonious, discreetly alcoholic family. Henry and Molly married, and moved down to Cambridge, where he would go to Harvard Law. This was regarded as an aberrant move by the family, which they managed to blame on Molly, the Southern parvenu in their New England ranks; traditionally all the Starck men were doctors, a fact to which Molly only gave some thought, a lot of thoughts, some years after her troubles with Henry and his family were over, and those with doctors had just begun.

"It was sort of like being in love with an Easter egg," Molly once explained to Felicia, trying to describe that marriage. "This perfect smooth surface, but brittle and hollow. Maybe dyed blue. But an attractive, very fragile egg."

"And holy? Easter?"

"Oh, very. Groton, all that. They all wanted to be more New England than Down East. More Bostonian than really from Portland."

"God, I'm glad I'm from California."

Molly had fallen in love with New England, along with Henry, or perhaps the other way around: she loved Henry because she loved Maine and all of New England that she saw— the weather (it was always such definite weather, days in Virginia could be so blurry, ill-defined), the landscape, the rocks and birches and firs, the coast and lakes and marvelous vistas of blue mountains. And local accents, like the weather and the landscapes, clear words with a definite end. In Southern talk she had often found no closure and quite often no meaning, hidden or otherwise.

They drank a lot, Molly and Henry. They used to drive out to Bailey Island with a shaker of martinis, climb down to a rocky beach and drink, and watch the waves. Drink often made Henry loquacious, and occasionally amorous, but never slurring or sloppy, like certain Southern boys. And drinking out there on the coastal rocks seemed much more romantic than smoking dope on the edges of the hockey field, at St. Catherine's School, in Richmond, with boys from St. Christopher's.

Henry's kissing was restrained, was pleasant but never pushy; he did not try to shove her into bed. At first she thought him chivalrous, later just unenthusiastic. The problem was that she herself was aroused; she was very excited by Henry's very light kisses. She wanted to go to bed with him, to make love, screw, fuck—to do anything and everything that they were not doing.

When Henry remarked one night in a casual way that maybe they should get married, Molly instantly agreed—mostly by way of getting him into bed: Now he'll have to make love to me, she thought. We'll sleep together—every night!

Henry did make love to her, and Molly enjoyed it very much. But sex made her greedy, she found, she wanted to do it more and more. At least every night, and preferably twice. Whereas Henry seemed satisfied with much less, and down in Cambridge Molly came to feel, as months went by, that Henry made excuses not to sleep with her. Ostensibly studying late, he would fall asleep in the big chair in his study. Or he began taking long solitary walks around Harvard Square in the evenings. "I'm in classes all day, I've got talk and people coming out of my ears." She knew that he was doing exactly what he said he was, he was walking around alone, but still she was hurt. Was it too much to expect that he would look forward to going to bed as much as she did? Molly supposed that it was.

In a way that she could not explain to herself, she continued to be in love with Henry. She longed for him.

"I kept thinking someone wonderful would emerge from that shell," she told Felicia—and her shrink, Dr. Edgar Shapiro. "I had to keep reminding myself that it was empty."

"An excellent image," he kindly murmured.

"Am I your first patient to fall in love with an Easter egg?" Molly had a tendency to make a lot of bad jokes to entertain and possibly to throw him off—she later realized.

He laughed, the smallest sound. "Probably."

. . .

Also, Henry really drank a lot. Molly was used to heavy drinking; civilized people had a couple of martinis every night and then some wine with dinner. She had been taught this by her own parents, her Republican (still somewhat unusual in Virginia) ex-VMI football-star father, Boyd Bonner, and her ex–Sweet Briar May-queen mother. They drank a lot at home, and then more rowdily on Saturday nights at the Country Club, out in Westmorland. (And they fought a lot drunkenly; they were living disproof of the romantic adage holding that couples who yell and scream a lot are basically loving and sexy.)

But Henry and all his family drank and, though enormously, they did so with great discretion. At Molly's wedding reception, which was naturally held at "the club," there was considerable talk about how much these Yankees drank, and how well they did it. (Molly's own parents were known for not holding it well at all.) "Those folks can really put it away. I never saw or heard a one of them give any sign" was the Richmond post-wedding verdict on the Starcks.

Except when you get to know them, was Molly's inward response to that remark. Intimate exposure to the family soon taught her to read certain signs: when Henry's mother said she was tired, was getting a headache, was going up to lie down, she meant that she was plastered, about to pass out. And when Dr. Starck, the father, shifted accents within the same sentence, Portland to Boston and back, that meant he was drunk. He was like an old railroad, Molly thought, the Boston & Maine.

"What happens if your father has to leave a dinner party for some emergency surgery?" she once asked Henry.

Stiffly: "I'm sure he could always perform as he should," Henry told her.

Which is more than I can say for you, she did not say.

But such moments of malice directed at Henry were rare for Molly, which in a way was too bad; they might have had a certain saving quality. Mostly she was very confused, and hurt. "I must truly be crazy," she said to Dr. Shapiro, later on, referring both to Henry and to Paul.

"I really don't think you are."

Before Henry, though, there had been a few other "unwise" choices; even at St. Christopher's, Molly managed to find ostensibly nice Southern boys who were seriously deranged. She wished that she could blame all those boys and later men on Boyd, her cold and raging, lethally handsome father, who was often incredibly charming, often drunk, and almost never warm. Or even on Angelica, her lovely, silly, and loveless mother, also a drunk, who during the sixties, the years of Molly's adolescence and Angelica's early middle age, took up smoking dope in a serious way. Dr. Shapiro, whose orientation was generally Freudian, took more than occasional swipes at both those parents. Molly's own conclusion was that she simply had very poor judgment in terms of men. She was not at all smart; in that way her needs far outstripped her intelligence.

In any case, young as she was, and foolish, she knew better than to marry Henry; poor reader that she was, she could still read danger in his drinking, in his sexual diffidence, but she married him anyway. Perhaps she had meant to rape him, and certainly their marriage was a form of rape for Henry.

Despite the confrontational habits of their generation, Molly and Henry were quite unable to talk about sex, nor were they able to talk about their other, possibly more pressing problem, which was lack of money. Molly's father, the hotshot lawyer, in the course of their many Vietnam fights, took the view that Molly was close to retarded in worldly matters, and he monkeyed around with a trust fund from Molly's grandfather, Angelica's parent, so that instead of getting her money at twenty-one she would have to wait until she was forty.

She investigated auditing courses at Harvard or Radcliffe, but even auditors' fees were high. Since Henry already ranted about their expenses, she did not dare to cross him in that way, but she found a cheap secretarial school in Belmont, a six-week course, after which temp jobs were guaranteed.

Which is how Molly Bonner became an ace secretary. She was very fast, and extremely neat (she could not have dared be otherwise); even Henry admired those perfect pages, almost as much as he admired her immaculate kitchen floors. She got a few jobs around Cambridge then, and in Boston, for more money. And, more importantly, she began to think of herself as self-supporting.

Henry was offered a job in a firm in San Francisco. A large, old, and excellent firm, he was told.

And Molly, who had never been anywhere west of West Virginia, was deeply excited. She looked at beautiful pictures of that most photogenic city, and romantically, youthfully, hopefully she imagined that such a shift in scenery would profoundly change their lives. Thousands of miles from Henry's parents, his brothers (all those doctors) and his sister, and from Portland, Henry would be a new strong and free man. And Molly, on another coast, would be a more independent, liberated woman.

Inspired, perhaps, by sexy visions of San Francisco, their sexual life did indeed improve. Temporarily.

But then Henry decided that instead of San Francisco he would take a job back in Portland, with a good, big, and very old law firm there.

"San Francisco is probably ridiculous," he said, by way of partial explanation. "All those silly cable cars and Victorian houses all painted up like tarts. And all that dumb flower-drug-love stuff in the sixties. Nothing like that ever went on in Maine."

"That stuff isn't happening anymore," Molly told him firmly, as in secret she hoped that to some extent it was.

"We wouldn't feel at home out there," he told her.

But I would, I know I would, Molly's inner voice insisted.

Curiously (or perhaps not curiously at all), Molly at this point came down with a serious case of flu, chills and fevers and aches and intestinal miseries. Odd, in that she was truly never sick. Her great good health from infancy on had always been a given, a source of pride for her parents, and for Molly a pleasant fact on which she could count, like clear skin and healthy teeth.

This illness, then, seemed to Molly to impart some message, and at first she thought, It's simple, I am sick with disappointment, not going to live in San Francisco, which I imagined would solve everything.

She went to a doctor to whom she imparted this theory; he laughed. "I suppose you've been reading some feminist literature on the subject?"

"But no one in my family is divorced."

Under the circumstances, which included in her case a serious fever, Molly could not laugh at this upright statement from Henry. Only later—when she told herself, He actually said that—did she laugh.

At the time, she only answered with the truth. "No one in mine either, but that doesn't seem relevant, does it? We're just not happy together. Neither of us is, I think."

"I suppose you think you'll be happy in San Francisco."

"Well, I hope so."

Despite the content of what he was saying, Henry's voice still was compelling to Molly, the flat vowels of New England, and the very slight hoarseness (probably from too much booze). She was powerfully moved by his voice. Henry the eggshell, whom she had truly loved.

True to form, he was a perfect gentleman about the divorce; he and Molly competed as to who could be most accommodating. About possessions, all those silver and crystal wedding presents, they said: "You take this. Oh no, I couldn't possibly use it. *You* have it."

. . .

And Molly moved to San Francisco, where she found a very small apartment on Sacramento Street, near Fillmore, with a pretty view of gardens, and for quite a while she was happy.

Her half of the money she and Henry had saved would keep her going for a while; nevertheless, Molly registered at a temporary agency, took the requisite tests, and performed impressively. And despite her intentions to the contrary, she was given an offer she wouldn't quite refuse, an immediate job in what was described as a hot new law firm, down on Union Street.

"But I've never done legal typing."

"It's okay. There's one other woman, and she's supposed to be a whiz."

The other woman, the whiz, was Felicia Flood. Very tall, very blonde, with corn-silk hair, Felicia was what Molly had imagined as a Californian.

Her eyes were what you first noticed: amazing eyes, the most translucent azure, a dark, dark blue with long thick black lashes and lazy, languorous lids. Her smile was lazy too, slow and shy, somehow surprising; she was so very—so conspicuously attractive that Molly would not have expected either the shyness or the smile. A big blonde beautiful woman—who was also nice.

"The point about this place is that really there's nothing to do," she told Molly, right off, in the Ladies Room. And since there were only two ladies in the office any conversation at all was possible. "You just have to look busy, make them feel important."

"They're not?"

"Oh no, not at all. Just rich." Felicia peered nearsightedly into the mirror at her perfectly pointed nose. "Shit, I look more like Pinocchio every day." She sounded genuinely discouraged.

Doesn't she think of herself as beautiful? Molly guessed that she did not.

"They split off from a much larger firm to go out on their

own," Felicia went on, instructively. "Out on their own with gunnysacks of money. They don't need two secretaries, they need maybe half of one."

Which left a lot of time for Molly and Felicia to talk, which they did. They liked each other very much, from the start. Although they were in many ways very unlike, each might have described the other in similar terms. "She's very smart and really funny, very up-front." Felicia might have added, For a Southerner, she's unusual.

Molly was on the whole happy, then. She knew she needed a much better, more demanding job, and eventually a larger place to live, but in the meantime it was good to be living away from Henry. Without his often-depressed and censorious presence she felt younger and lighter, stronger and smarter and funnier. (Henry had not much liked her jokes.)

Molly's insurance company wrote that a change of residence and work required a new physical, and so she made an appointment with an internist recommended by Felicia.

Dr. Douglas Macklin was very tall and thin, very Bostonian-sounding; his voice awakened various nostalgias in Molly, even a little for Henry—at least she had always liked his voice. Seated in his office, she was asked the usual questions. Family illnesses? Really none. Her own health problems? None. And then he asked how she liked living in San Francisco.

"I like it, but it's an awfully self-conscious city, don't you think?"

"Oh, indeed I do. And parochial. Provincial."

They continued in that vein for quite some time, going on about the terrible newspaper, inadequate bookstores. Kitschy postcard views. Molly was aware of exaggerating the negative aspects of her response to the city, and perhaps he was too (after all, he had lived here for quite some time, she gathered), but this more or less set the tone for later encounters. Since Molly was always in perfect health, they continued this rather self-congratulatory city-bashing—even after Molly had to a great extent changed her mind, or her feelings—after she had met Paul in that (very good) bookstore, and fallen in love and married. They went on and on, she and Dr. Macklin, amusing each other, Molly mostly listening—until she was really sick, and attention had to be paid.

Paul had grown up in Montana—to Molly, more distant and exotic than California had ever been. His father had been a professional guide. Both parents had recently died; there was one brother, Matthew, about whom Paul only said, "He's sort of a problem for me. He's really what we used to call square, and he married this awful Joanne, a lawyer. He lives in Chicago and sells insurance, if you can imagine. But sometimes he goes scuba diving. I think he's a little confused."

Paul spoke of the sweeping Montana plains, and the colors of the light. All the greens. The beautiful west fork of the Bitterroot River. The trees, the trout. The *space*. Big skies, wide-open highways.

In San Francisco, Paul lived on Russian Hill, one huge booklined room with a narrow view of Coit Tower, Treasure Island, the bay, and sometimes Oakland. Molly moved in with him; unable to control the impulse, she tidied up, which seemed to enlarge the space—but they were hardly there. Paul at that time was writing a film on the Spanish Civil War, and so they were often in Spain, in Madrid and Barcelona, in Saragossa, Guadalajara. Their life was fairly frantic, and often romantically beautiful, in those settings. They were very sexually charged; always, whenever and wherever possible, they made love.

And more or less incidentally Molly learned Spanish.

In all their time together (later, it seemed very short to Molly), they shared a high, exuberant energy, and splendid health; neither of them had much patience for sickness.

Looking for bad signs, combing through those months and years, Molly saw in Paul much impatience, small tolerance for delay, postponement, for any form of enclosure. Crazy in heavy traffic, for example. But wasn't that normal in a man who had grown up in great open space?

And, seemingly unrelated, he was hyper-friendly (you could have called it flirtatious) with waitresses. Once, noting some flicker of discomfort (call it jealousy) on Molly's face, he had laughed, "It's the Montana way, babe. Get used to it, you're not with some tight-ass Easterner anymore." All true enough; also, some Southern men, in their fashion, did that too. Boyd had liked to kid a pretty waitress—infuriating Angelica, embarrassing his young daughter, shy Molly.

And Paul did mention quite often strong feelings about turning forty in a year or so.

But did any or all of that add up to wanting out of a marriage?

"I did something funny today," Paul told Molly, during one of their rare times in San Francisco. "I may have made you a millionairess."

"Oh, really? Good." They had been on the verge of sleep when he spoke; Molly wanted to go back.

"Yes I did. I told you that I had lunch with Matthew?"

"Yes." Molly had forgotten even that Matthew was in town.

"I took out a policy. If I die in some accident you'll be really rich."

"Seems hardly worth it." She laughed. "But thanks."

He mused, "I hope old Matt has one for himself. With all that diving he's a lot more in accident range than I am."

"He must have insurance," murmured Molly, not caring, and caring even less for Matthew's wife, the dread Joanne.

"It won't cost much. My policy, I mean. At my young age."

"Oh, good." Her emphasis was ironic; what she meant was, Now can we sleep?

"And if we break up I can always change it."

"Terrific. Now can we go back to sleep?"

He whispered, "I love you a lot."

"I love you too. Don't die in an accident. It wouldn't be worth it."

But he had, and though he had wanted out, insisted on their separation, he either forgot or neglected to change the insurance. And later that silly, smart-ass, heartfelt conversation played and replayed in Molly's battered brain.

And she was rich.

FOUR

"He wrote me such a nice note that I had to give him your phone number."

Felicia spoke that on-the-surface illogical remark to Molly a few days after her party. Knowing Felicia, Molly saw what she meant: the nice gesture of David Jacobs' thank-you note had made it harder than usual, even, for her to say no, and so she had given him Molly's phone number, presumably asked for in the note.

But Molly told her, "I wasn't exactly attracted to him."

"You don't like bald?"

"It's not bald so much as those teeth. But actually it's not his looks at all. Something else about him, I don't know. I don't think I'm very receptive now. Yet."

"You're really not. I think he's sort of cute."

"Oh Felicia. You and doctors."

This conversation, like most between these two friends, took place on the phone. They generally spoke every day; their actual visits were far more rare.

"Oh, I know." Felicia sighed, but happily, self-approvingly. "You'll be happy to hear I met this really attractive guy in Seattle. Not a doctor. A professor."

"But you've done that. Professors."

"But this one's not even married."

"I suppose you'll tell Sandy he's gay. If he comes around."

She laughed. "How'd you guess?"

"Felicia, he'll catch on, and he'll kill you."

She laughed again. "I don't think so. He thinks, Why should I want anyone but wonderful him?"

"That's what O.J. thought."

"Oh, *please.* What I need is a new line of work, I think. I'm trying to get more hours at Open Hand."

Felicia did volunteer cooking and delivery at Open Hand, the organization that takes food to people bedridden with AIDS. Molly asked, "You'd like that? That would make you almost full time."

"I'd love it. All I'd need would be someone to support me. Anyway, how's your allergy or whatever?"

"Not so great. When he took me home the other night, your friend Dave Jacobs said I should see an ENT person."

"You probably should. Ask Macklin. Do you think you'll go out with Dave, when he calls?"

"I don't know. Maybe." It was true that Molly didn't know. She thought she would wait and see how she felt when he called. If he called.

"He takes a little getting used to," Felicia told her, adding, for no reason, "He was really crazy about his wife."

"This is Dave Jacobs. Dr. Jacobs, we met the other night—I took you home from Felicia's party? I was wondering if you were free for dinner on Thursday. There's a nice place here in Mill Valley, if you don't mind driving over . . ."

Having received that message on her machine, Molly called back and got his tape, and said that she was busy on Thursday. She said to Felicia, "And I do mind driving over—it's too far for someone I don't even know. And then the drive home."

The second call came a week or so later, and this time he caught her at home.

"You'd really better see someone about those sinuses," he said after Molly had said she was busy again, on the night that he suggested.

"I guess I should."

"You sound terrible. Who's your internist?"

"Douglas Macklin."

"Oh, a very good man. Not the best, but very good."

"Well, even if he's not the best, I'll call him."

Surprising herself—she did not usually follow orders— Molly did call Dr. Macklin, who agreed that she should see someone. She should be seen, is how he put it. He would call a Dr. Beckle, and then she could call Beckle and make an appointment.

Dr. Beckle turned out to be away at a conference for the next two weeks, which seemed very long for a conference; Molly wondered about that. But in the meantime her allergy or whatever seemed in mild remission.

Dave Jacobs called her again, and again she was busy. And that was a fact that they were to argue about, among many other facts and opinions: his having called Molly three times before she could (or would) go out with him. "I'd never call anyone again who turned me down three times," he swore. "Never. I've got too much pride."

But he had, Molly knew that he had. She remembered remarking to Felicia, "Wouldn't you know. I'm not at all interested, and so he calls and calls. Sometimes I think men are very predictable." Making such negative generalizations, Molly always automatically exempted Paul—who indeed would not have called, not have been turned on by someone who was clearly not turned on by him.

"Especially doctors," Felicia told her. "Egos like armored trucks. I often wonder which came first, the ego or the doctor."

"That's a good question."

The next call from Dave Jacobs mentioned concert tickets, and then dinner. On a Sunday. Since Paul, Molly had found Sundays the hardest days to get through; also, a concert sounded like a proper date. What the doctor ordered, so to speak. And she was free. She said yes.

She wore a red dress. "You knew red was my favorite color," he later told her, grinning and pleased.

"No, of course I didn't." From the start, almost, Molly was driven to combat with Dave, no matter how frivolous the issue.

Driving to the concert, Dave asked about her health, and she said that it seemed to have improved, but that she had made an appointment with Dr. Beckle, the ENT man.

"*Alfred* Beckle?"

"I think so."

Dave Jacobs began to laugh—an actual chuckle. "Must be the same one. He got into an interesting malpractice case a few years ago. Some patient who was a homosexual claimed that his throat was ruined. You know, for sex. He wasn't Deep Throat anymore."

"Oh, really?" Molly could not bring herself to laugh at this, early training (laugh at men's jokes) notwithstanding. Nor could she understand, either at the time or later on, just why he had told that story. She guessed that some gay-bashing was intended: those dirty people who do dirty things. But also a more general bashing of patients: crazy people who sue over crazy issues.

The concert, however, was a joy: chamber music, Schubert and Boccherini, Mozart. Dave Jacobs had liked it less. "I only really go for Bach," he confessed. "My wife and I used to go down to Carmel every year. The Bach Festival."

Getting the car out from the parking lot, fumbling with the ticket, getting onto the street and off to the restaurant, parking it there—all that seemed unusually difficult, and when Dave Jacobs said, "You wouldn't believe how long since I've done all this. Martha did most of the driving in town," Molly again felt a certain sympathy—even as she thought the word "dependent." Obviously he and his wife had things worked out in some way, as had Molly and Paul, who took cabs to most concerts and walked home. This was in its way Dave's "first date" too, as awkward for him as for Molly, and he did seem to be working at it.

"Sunday night a lot of places are closed. I'd forgotten that," he said, and Molly was touched, as she imagined him calling around. Taking trouble.

His final choice had been unlucky: a bright new on-the-waterfront brasserie-type place, lots of high polish and white linen. Already very popular with very young people. Molly was the oldest young person there, so to speak—and Dave was simply old.

Maybe for that reason, their combined advanced ages, the greeter seemed to take pity on them, seating them in the quietest possible corner window table, with a view of the bay and the new tall palms that lined the Embarcadero.

"How about a nice martini?" Dave asked, and before she could say, No, a glass of white wine, please, he added, "You're not one of those white-wine-only Yuppies, I hope?"

"Actually, a martini sounds good. Straight up, with a twist." That was how Molly had drunk martinis with Henry, all those years ago, and it did sound good.

"Good for your health," the doctor said, with that grin. "Cure your cold, or whatever it is that you've got."

Whatever it was that Molly had was coming back on her in full force, and it occurred to her to wonder if it could be doctors that she was allergic to—a thought that she was to continue to have for a very long time, in various forms. She felt, then, terrible. Heavy in her head, especially her nose. Heavy everywhere. Exhausted. It was comforting to have a doctor so close at hand, in a way; it would have been much more so if she had liked him more.

And obviously this needs some explanation, the fact that Molly continued to see and eventually to be involved with, to go to bed with, a man whom in many ways she did not like. She castigated herself for that involvement, hating to use illness as an excuse, which sounded so wimpy. But that was certainly a part of it, and more so as she got sicker, and sicker. Also, Dave did come along fairly soon after Paul, and although with the kind strong help of Dr. Shapiro (and maybe some inner strength of which she was occasionally aware), Molly had been getting stronger, oddly enough that made her lonelier. Or maybe just more aware of the lack of human (male) touching in her life. Sometimes she had thought that just a mouth to kiss would do it, or a large male back to hold in the night. Sex was almost secondary, though she surely missed that too, a lot.

And so, although at first she certainly did not want to do any of those things with Dave Jacobs, eventually she did.

Another way to put it would be to say that it is hard to say no to a doctor, when you are sick.

The martinis were very good. "I'd forgotten what a good drink," Molly told Dave.

"I'll make you some that are even better." His grin. "Martha always said I could retire and be a bartender." From the start, he had this way of quoting the most trite remarks from Martha as though they were gems, which Molly found both touching and boring—finally.

He talked a lot about Martha during that first dinner. About

ways in which he missed her, still. More things that she said. Her
cooking. Her sadness that they had not had children. Molly did
not get either then or later a sense of what she was like, what
kind of woman, really, she had been. She thought it quite possible that Dave did not know either, and eventually she developed
quite a few theories of her own about the character of Martha,
which she kept mostly to herself. She never told Dave much
about Paul, but then he didn't ask.

"It was actually sleeping together that I missed so much.
Next to each other," Dave said, leaning forward to lower his
voice. "Not just sex, although that too. But not having her with
me in bed—that was the hardest to get used to. I honestly
thought I couldn't."

"I felt that way too," Molly told him. "For a long time I
couldn't sleep. Do you take pills or anything?" A doctor, he
might have some great new surefire pill that she hadn't heard
about.

But, "Hell no," he said. "I play tennis, and run. How about
you? You don't take sleeping pills, do you?"

"Not usually," she lied. She knew that every night indeed
was usually. But she was remembering the night when she found
herself pushed over onto her side of the bed, and she realized
that she didn't have to do that. There was no one on the other
side to make room for.

"Exercise beats pills or any so-called psychotherapy," Dave
told her, and she did not argue. "For a long time I wished I'd
died too," he said. "I don't mean I was suicidal, I'm not a depressed person. I just wanted to be dead along with her."

It seemed somewhat confused, this death wish coupled with
a censoriousness concerning depression and suicide, but his
very confusion was touching. What came through to Molly was
genuine human pain, human love, and terrible loss. Molly felt
that possibly she should clarify her own confusion, too: in her
case it was not just mourning a loss through death; she was also
hurt, still, that Paul had wanted out of their marriage. And so

they sat there, she and Dave Jacobs, a mismatched pair of mourners, swilling white wine and eating good fresh salmon.

It was still early when they got out, and so as they drove up in front of Molly's building, she asked him in. He accepted, and then accepted a brandy, telling her with approval, "This is good stuff."

As he not too subtly inspected her living room, some wayward instinct informed Molly that he was weighing her as a possible replacement for Martha, checking out her taste and especially her housekeeping habits. She wanted to say, Look, in some ways you're a very nice man, but you shouldn't bother with me. It won't work out. I am not meant for you, nor you for me. Go and find some nice doctor's widow, who will think you're wonderful and cherish you into old age. Which I won't.

But of course she said none of that, and only thanked him when he said how nice it all was.

"You do all your own housework?" A rather nervy question, really.

"No," she told him. "There's someone who comes in once a week. She's not a very good cleaner but she's so nice, I can't fire her."

"Martha wouldn't have anyone, she was always worried about stuff getting broken."

"I guess I don't have anything that I care about that much."

Their conversation, such as it was, then languished.

Looking at Dave's face, his large strong nose and those exemplary teeth, so white and healthy, Molly had a very odd thought, which was: If he tries to kiss me good night I'll probably hit him. Very odd: never in her lifetime that she could remember had she hit anyone, unless possibly as a small child— and she was by now surely old enough to say no without resorting to physical violence.

What was even odder was that within a few weeks she had developed a sort of sexual fix on Dave Jacobs; she really liked their kissing, when once it happened. Although in many ways she did not like him, still, and had even thought of hitting. And only men did this, one used to think; only men had sex or wanted to have sex with women whom they otherwise disliked. But of course that isn't true; like so many things, including hitting, women do it too.

But at the front door, that first night, Molly and Dave quite formally shook hands. No kissing, or hitting.

She thanked him, saying how much she had enjoyed the concert.

"Lucky that Carl gave me those tickets," he said. "I'm glad you enjoyed it."

"Carl?" Molly was not sure why she asked this.

"New man in the office. Johns Hopkins. He's very good, and always buying tickets to concerts he doesn't go to. His kids get sick or something. Lucky for me, I almost always use them."

"Oh. Well, thanks."

The news about the free tickets had been just slightly dispiriting, she realized. Irrationally (what difference did it make?), she had been pleased by the small trouble he had gone to, and now she liked him just a little less. She wished that he hadn't told her.

FIVE

"I can't have people coming in late!" screeched Dr. Beckle's nurse. Her small angry pale-blue eyes darted around the crowded waiting room as her flimsy yellow-gray hair flew out in all directions.

Uncharacteristically, Molly argued, "But I'm really not late. It's exactly two-thirty now."

It was only then that the nurse seemed to focus on her. "Oh, I didn't mean you. It's everyone, and doctors running late. You're for Dr. Morris? Mrs. Winter?"

"No, Bonner. Dr. Beckle." Molly had said his name, and her own, about four minutes earlier.

"Oh yes, you're the one with the ear problem, right?" Her voice seemed to fade in and out, like a defective radio.

"No. Sinuses. I think."

There was no place in that room to sit down, so that at first Molly thought, Indeed, a bad season for sinuses. Later she guessed that all those doctors had simply overbooked. Greedy bastards, she thought.

After about fifteen minutes more, the nurse told her, "You can go right in now," ushering her—almost shoving, in fact—into an examining room, as Molly wondered if she was really the right patient for this doctor, this room—which was small, bare, all sterilized. Nothing there to read. On one wall was a large poster of the interior of the nose, nasal passages, ears and their passages—all that. It was a little scary, and, never having felt anything like fear in a doctor's office before, Molly thought that she was truly not quite herself.

Certainly, lately she had been feeling like some other, very sick person. The self with which she was familiar was never sick. But her head had been weighted, and she had frequent very sharp headaches. Quite out of character, she had fantasies about brain tumors. Galloping hypochondria, she thought. But still, she was both very uncomfortable and scared. And the longer she stayed in that room alone, the more uncomfortable, the more scared she got.

"All doctors do that to you," Felicia told her later. "They strip you of any possible sources of comfort—often, of course, including your clothes—and they leave you alone for one hell of a long time." At least Molly was fully dressed, but in Dr. Beckle's case, that day it was forty-five minutes that she had to wait. "They make you wait so you'll be ready when they are," Felicia said. "But I don't know why they can't time it a little better than they do. It doesn't seem fair to make a patient wait fifteen or twenty minutes so a doctor won't have to wait for two. But I don't think they see it that way. They don't care about fair. They assume that a patient's time has no value, whereas all of *their* time is priceless. God knows how often I've argued this with Sandy. Sometimes their time is really valuable, I know, but it's not as though they spent even most of it saving lives, it really is not."

And all that time in a room by yourself can be very scary for a patient, Molly realized, that day; you sit there contemplating your illness, whatever it is. In forty-five minutes she had almost everything. Including AIDS: just how unfaithful had Paul been, she wondered, and with whom?

She also had time to think a lot about Dave Jacobs, and the strangeness of their connection. He had wanted to come to this appointment with Molly, and in a way she wished that he had. But some inner voice continued to insist that really she did not like Dave, and that for that reason she should not use him, not for anything. Including sex, which by now she almost recognized that she looked forward to, although so far they had not even kissed. She wished that she could lighten up at least a little about both sex and her silly sinuses. For a woman of her generation, Molly thought, she was sort of a throwback, a relic of earlier, more inhibited times. Some of which she put down to being Southern, Richmond, St. Catherine's, all that, and some to the special craziness of her parents. But everyone grew up in a place with some peculiarities, and when you get to know them everyone's parents sound fairly nuts.

Felicia on the whole, though, handled those things better, Molly thought. She spent considerable time in bed with Raleigh Sanderson, whom in many ways she did not like, but she liked the sex quite a lot, Molly gathered, and she evened things out by occasional sexual forays elsewhere. These days Molly suspected someone new on the horizon, the man from Seattle, probably— and she looked forward to whatever Felicia would say about it. Felicia was never literal or explicit—her delicacy was a quality that Molly valued.

"Well now, let's see what's the matter with you." Dr. Beckle entered talking loudly, and not, either then or later, apologizing for being late. "What seems to be the trouble?" he demanded, frowning.

Short and stocky, with no neck and no bodily tapering, he was built like a bullet, Molly thought, and he moved aggressively, speaking in a rapid-fire, unstoppable way.

Molly tried to describe what was wrong, but she felt that she did a poor job of it. She sensed that Dr. Beckle had already come to his own decision about her case, from whatever Dr. Macklin had told him, and that she merely bored him as she spoke. He only half listened; the rest of his attention was waiting for his own speech.

When Molly stopped, feeling that her time was up, Beckle started in with what sounded like a set speech. Which she was soon able to forget, only that it was extremely frightening at the time.

He explained in detail and with some vividness the various problems that could be causing her "condition." Tumors, aneurisms, a long and horrifying panoply of ailments. And as he spoke he pointed at the big ugly picture on the wall, locating sources of trouble.

After maybe five minutes of this he said, "Well, let's have a look."

Punchy with fear, Molly repressed her impulse to run out of there, to find the nearest acupuncture clinic, or maybe just a friendly drugstore, with some over-the-counter, proven remedies, and a kindly druggist.

He looked up her nose and down her throat and into her ears, with his small mirrors and long sharp steel instruments. For about three minutes.

"Don't see a thing," he finished. "We may have to go in there and look."

"Go in there?"

"Surgically. No big deal. I do it every day."

"But—"

"Well, that's my recommendation. Of course you can get a second opinion."

"Of course I will."

The nurse glared as Molly left. "Good-bye, Mrs. Steffins."

Dave Jacobs had taken to calling Molly every day, just to see how she was, he said. Thus, from the beginning, his role as potential lover (Molly could not call anyone over fifty a boyfriend) and as doctor were confused. Since she was not feeling well she welcomed all that attention, and also she had to admit to the rise of other feelings about him. To put it most simply, he turned her on. She observed with a horny pleasure the very good shape of his body: tall and lean, broad-shouldered, slender-hipped.

One day he called and asked if she wanted to take a walk; he had a free couple of hours, it would do her good, he said. They walked from Molly's house up to Pacific Heights, and back. At every corner, in a protective (or dominating?) way, he took her arm, which led to their holding hands for the last few blocks of the walk. Molly recognized in herself the small rush of specific heat, which she had not felt for some time. Not since Paul. Dave had to get back to his office then, and she wished that he could have stayed. That they could at least have kissed.

Once inside her house, though, alone, she castigated herself. Did she really want to involve herself with a man whom she did not much like, with whom even the most minor conversations included arguments? They had argued over everything from vitamin C to the Grand Canyon, where Molly had never been and did not much want to go.

"You're crazy!" Dave told her.

"What a horrible person!" she told Dave on the phone, the night of her visit to Dr. Beckle. "Going out of his way to scare me. And keeping me waiting all that time with no apology, ever. I really hated him and so did his nurse. I think it's an awful office. I think you can tell a lot about doctors from the tone of their offices, how their nurses are."

"Good Lord, Molly, I never heard anything so silly. How their girls feel is so totally irrelevant—"

"Girls! Can't you even call them nurses? Jesus, Dave. Anyway, why do they try to scare you? Does it have to do with malpractice suits? I just feel so much worse after seeing that guy, I'll never go back to him."

"Whether or not you like the doctor has nothing to do with anything. He probably kept you waiting because he was in surgery."

"He could have said that, I'm not really unreasonable. If he'd said he was sorry it would have been okay. Or if he was in surgery the nurse didn't have to put me in that room for all that time."

"Well, I always apologize to patients when I'm late. But it's not all that important. You make such a point over manners. That Southern stuff. The point is his competence as a physician."

"I can't stand short men."

"Oh for Christ's sake."

Her conversation with Dr. Macklin, in his office, was considerably less heated. More rational and coherent.

He said, "I'm sorry you had such a bad time. I probably shouldn't have sent you there. He does overbook and I've heard from other patients who didn't like him, including my wife. She couldn't stand him. The problem was, Stinger was out of town, and he's where I wanted you to go. And I do think whether or not you like a doctor is relevant. After all, communication is important, and if you hate a guy you can't exactly talk to him easily."

"Next time I think you should listen to your wife."

"I'm sure you're right."

Molly had the occasional fleeting thought that Dr. Macklin was, if anything, too pleasant. How would he handle some hard, unpleasant situation? She wondered, but at the same time she told herself that he was highly intelligent. That was why she liked him, wasn't it?

Dr. Stinger, to whom she went next, was also short.

Molly asked Dave, "Does something about ENT attract short men?"

"Christ, only you would generalize from two examples."

He probably had a point, which of course Molly did not admit. (Dave always brought out her most childishly defiant qualities, which cannot have been entirely his fault.)

Dr. Mark Stinger, then, was short but dark and handsome, and while Molly did not agree with the received opinion holding that handsome men are generally bad (she rather preferred that they be handsome), still she did not like him much, and at the time she was not at all sure why. He was polite (God knows more polite than Dr. Beckle had been), and he seemed intelligent—what more did she want?

Dr. Stinger prescribed some antibiotics, which he assured her would work. (Was that it, his assurance, just short of arrogance?)

And they did not work. Molly felt worse and worse, more heavy in her head, and in her veins. The smallest tasks, like making her lunch, seemed difficult, and reading was almost impossible. She could not believe that she could hardly read; always, she read enormously.

"Call Stinger and tell him how you feel," said Dave. "You patients don't tell your doctors enough, and then you blame us."

Molly did call Stinger, and she told the nurse how terrible she felt; she would call her back, the nurse said (she, not the doctor). She did call back, with another antibiotic prescription.

"I don't like doctors whom you can't even get to talk to," Molly told Dave.

He hesitated, then said, "Well, it's not the way I do things, I always get back to patients eventually. But maybe he has it worked out this way." A meaningless defense, Molly felt.

Dave asked her out to dinner. "No free concert tonight," he told her, with a laugh. "Worse luck. We'll probably even have to pay for dinner."

On the way to the restaurant he made several small jokes about their possibly going dutch, which he understood was what people did these days. But when Molly said, "Sure, fine with me" (in fact she would have liked it much better), he bridled, as though scandalized, and he told her, "I guess you don't know when I'm kidding."

Which was true enough, both at the time and later on.

At dinner they talked again about how much they missed, respectively, Paul and Martha. And they argued. That was the first occasion of the Grand Canyon argument.

"Look," Molly told him, "I'm almost forty. Old enough to have gone there by now if I'd wanted to."

"And too young to be so rigid. It's the most glorious experience of nature in this country."

"I like Maine. New England. Lakes, the Atlantic coast."

"But you won't even try?"

"I'd hate it. I hate looking down from heights. Or even up."

They drank martinis, and had a bottle of Beaujolais with their steak, that restaurant's specialty. Molly hadn't had steak for several years, and she had to admit that it was good.

They went back to her house and then, as they both must have known that they would, they went to bed.

Sex with Dave was pretty much just that, sex. At first Molly liked it, and responded happily to something she had not done for so long, and had missed. But after the first few slakings of thirst, she began to feel drowned.

Many women complain, with reason, of too little sex in their lives, as Molly had privately done about Henry. With Henry more and more often it was she who initiated sex, as some therapists say you should, and more and more often he turned her down, which made her feel terrible. Ugly and unloved—rejected.

But Dave overdid it, so that Molly began to feel that he was engaged in some contest with himself. She was sure that he was counting: four times, not bad for a guy almost sixty. Try for five? But that was several too many times for Molly; she could not, was not thirsty anymore.

Love with Paul was not exactly perfect, whatever perfect love would be, but for quite a while it was perfect enough for Molly. Until (another sign that she should have read) it slacked off to almost never. But in the good days, early on, she surely never thought of numbers, nor of being drowned.

Invaded is actually what she felt with Dave. Assaulted. He almost never let her peacefully sleep; he kept waking her, prodding her, turning her over. And while he talked a lot about love, how much he loved her, how wonderful to find love twice in his lifetime, to Molly it did not feel like love but rather a form of aggression. She could have been anyone at all, Molly thought, and she often wondered, Why me?

She complained, "You've got to let me sleep. This is crazy. You don't listen. I need more sleep, and I need to be sort of alone to sleep."

"But you're so terribly attractive to me. Aren't you glad?"

Actually she was not glad, but she did not feel that she could tell him that, and so she only repeated, "I've got to get more sleep. I'll never get well with no sleep."

"Love is the greatest cure," he told her, sententiously. "Haven't you heard that? It's what your friend Dr. Freud always said." Like many so-called "real" doctors, Dave disliked and distrusted any form of psychotherapy; he was full of anecdotes (patients of his who had had terrible experiences with shrinks, and *no help*) and of very old bad jokes.

However, playing up her illness was effective, Molly found. And besides, what she said was true: sleep deprivation made her feel a great deal worse.

Dave and Martha, his wife, had made love every night of their marriage, Dave told Molly. Taken literally, that statement struck her as impossible, or most unlikely. The certain truth, though, was that Martha was a woman who could not say no, and Molly tried to imagine that poor masochistic lady, who Dave had assured her was not a feminist. ("I'll bet not," Molly had said.)

"I don't remember her too well," Felicia said. "I just met her once, at that terribly dark-brown house in the woods where they lived. It was a big party, and Dave was all over the place being host. She was more like the maid, serving things. She had the most boring perfect hair and perfect flowered silk dress, I do remember that. A real doctor's wife, I thought. A fifties throwback. Of course that was early on with Sandy, and I was feeling a little hostile to wives, but still. That poor woman."

"Wasn't Donna Reed's husband a doctor? Remember 'The Donna Reed Show'?"

"I think so. The paradigmatic doctor's wife, anyway."

"Poor Martha. Is Sandy's wife like that, do you think—poor Connie?"

After the tiniest pause, two beats, Felicia said, "Actually I don't think so. I've heard lately that she's doing really well. She went to AA, stopped drinking. And she's fighting City Hall about the homeless." Another pause. "I really don't know what to do."

"Neither do I."

They laughed. Then Molly said, "I have a new theory about men like Dave who hate cats. They're bullies, you know? And you can't possibly bully a cat, that's why they hate them."

Molly called Dr. Stinger to say that these new antibiotics did not work either. She felt worse. Dr. Stinger was out of town, his nurse informed her. Perhaps Molly would like to see some of his residents? Molly thought that she would. Any doctor would—or might—help, she thought. Any doctor but Dave. She realized that in a very irrational way she was confusing her illness with Dave: I'm allergic to Dave, is what she more or less thought, as she made more and more excuses not to see him.

The two residents were both Chinese, both small. One plump, one thin, and both very courteous, shy, and thorough. They examined Molly gravely, with a small air of apology for invading her head in that way. They smiled a lot in her direction—a form of reassurance, she thought.

But then, at the end, with a tiny frown the thin one told her, "We found some small polyps. High up."

"Well, that would explain quite a lot, wouldn't it?"

Evasively, their looks consulted each other. "We have to talk to Dr. Stinger."

Dr. Stinger's nurse told her that Dr. Stinger would like her to have an MRI, whatever that was.

Molly told Dave, "I really don't like all this communicating through his nurse. He could call me. Dr. Macklin does. I'm not going to keep him on the phone."

"His girl is good at communicating with patients, I'm sure. She's trained for that."

"Why do you insist on calling her a girl if she's so highly trained? She's a nurse. I met her, and she's a very smart woman."

Carping at Dave had become a way of complaining about her whole situation, for Molly. Otherwise she was really too enfeebled to protest. Her sense was that Dr. Stinger thought her a neurotic, hypochondriac woman—and she was not entirely sure that he was wrong.

"Everyone calls them girls," Dave snarled.

"Not anymore. Besides, why didn't Stinger find the polyps?" Molly had suddenly thought of that, another indictment. But it was a reasonable question, to which Dave had no answer.

The MRI.

Molly had to lie in a long white tube, with a lid fitted over her head and her legs strapped down. The nurse, Dr. Stinger's "girl," had asked as she made the schedule if Molly was claustrophobic, and Molly had said no, not especially, but lying there, locked in place, she thought that she really was claustrophobic, very. And what would she do if she was: would she kick and scream her way out of there?

Later, when various kind friends remarked that she had been such a good sport about everything, even that she had been "brave," Molly thought that really she had not had much choice—as she had no choice in the MRI white tube. She just had to lie there. Enduring.

Almost the worst of it was the noise. The young doctor who put her in the tube had warned: "There'll be a sort of pounding in your ears. If you're really uncomfortable with it let me know." He did not say how she would let him know. But before each bout of noise his disembodied voice would announce, "This first will take about five minutes . . . this will take seven . . . fifteen minutes."

All those long sequences involved a pounding near Molly's ears, as though someone were tearing through the next room with a jackhammer, Molly's most hated noise; to her it sounded like a giant's dentist drill. Sometimes in the intervals there was music, once a Haydn "Sinfonia Concertante" that she especially liked, so graceful, so literally full of grace. Superstitiously then, she thought, Oh good, a good sign, this will be okay.

So much for superstition.

Until that MRI, Molly had no idea how long seven or eight or fifteen minutes could be. Just lying there, with that terrible noise in her ears. Later, she had no idea what she had thought about during those endless minutes, nor for that matter how she had managed to get through it without some childish display.

At last the doctor, a dour and sallow young man, released her, and Molly sat up. "I can go now?" she asked, not believing it possible that she could.

And—right: she could not. He said, "I just have to look at these pictures a little."

Scowling hard, he held a series of what looked like X-rays up against a light—all images of shadows, all dark and terrible.

But the sheer relief of being out of that tube had made Molly manic. She was mildly hysterical. "I suppose you're finding lots of brain tumors." That was her notion of a joke, at that moment.

"We're not allowed to give diagnoses." He frowned more deeply. "Well, I guess you can go now."

SIX

As a small child, near the banks of the James River, in Richmond, what Molly liked best was the game of doctor—and "like" is not the correct word; this was an obsession, a major passion. She played that quite unregulated game with various other children, often new ones, but later she was unable to remember how the activity was ever proposed. Was it always she who made the suggestion? Molly was a shy, on the whole very inhibited child, and so she found it unlikely that she should have been so bold. She remembered her intense eagerness for the game, but maybe all the children involved felt the same. They were like a bunch of addicts among whom a lot of verbal communication was unnecessary.

And calling what they did a game is misleading: the doctors that those children played at did nothing but examine, and that not very thoroughly. They only looked at each other, they showed themselves off. No mutual touching, and God knows nothing more advanced like "foreign objects."

Molly played doctor with many children, then, but for several years her best and most interested companion in that pursuit was a handsome, blond, and green-eyed little boy named Craig Stuart. His parents were friends and drinking companions of Molly's parents, and the Stuarts lived in a large, white, and somewhat forbidding house on a bluff above the river, with an ancient mysteriously laid out garden, full of inexplicable and wonderfully secret nooks and glades. And so that is where Molly and Craig exhibited their small pale-pink genitals to each other, among the sheltering, giant pre–Civil War boxwood, the magnolias and crepe myrtle. Their parents were pleased that they were friends, and that they liked to play together so often, and so contentedly.

Craig's was the first penis that Molly ever saw, and she thought it was marvelous. Tiny and a pretty peachy-pink, it sometimes stood straight up. Craig could make it do this just by thinking about it, he said. So interesting, Molly thought. A sort of magic.

When she told Felicia about playing doctor, after they had become friends and were talking about what they were like as children, Felicia said that Molly was the only person she knew with a genuine case of penis envy, but Molly said that was not true. She didn't envy Craig's penis, she only admired and wondered at it. It was much more interesting to look at than a girl's tiny fold, she thought.

Craig was also very interested in something that he persisted in calling "poopoo," a minor obsession that Molly considered babyish, unworthy. He liked poopoo jokes, and he told Molly that once he had "made poopoo" in his sandbox; proudly confiding, he giggled with pleasure.

"Didn't they find it and punish you?" Molly was frightened at the very thought of such a discovery by parents. Horrifying!

"They thought it was a dog!" Triumphant laughter from Craig.

Molly did not find it all that funny but she laughed enthusiastically anyway. (Southern female training kicks in early.)

On the other hand, Molly was interested in kissing, and Craig was not. Molly did not think that doctors kissed their patients, and certainly they did not kiss each other; still, making some obscure but definite connection, she felt that playing doctor should include an occasional kiss. Sometimes she would kiss Craig, her small mouth pressed for the one instant he allowed it to his cool smooth cheek. Molly especially like the smell of his shirts when she did that, a clean ironed boyish smell.

Actually, as Molly later came to think of it, Craig was more tolerant of her wishes to kiss than she was of his poopoo talk—which proved she was not sure what. Several things, probably.

Craig grew up to be a doctor, just as he always said that he would do; he is now a well-known plastic surgeon, living in Richmond. Molly did not think of him much in her grown-up life, except when she arrived at that time of overinvolvement with doctors, and then she wondered if lots of doctors started out like that, smart little boys who liked to play doctor with little girls, who retained a lingering interest in poopoo, in the form of fecal jokes.

Certainly jokes of that nature seem more popular with doctors than with most other groups (this is the sort of wild generalization from Molly that drove Dave wild), and such a joke, and a vast divergence in their notions of what is funny, led to the first of Molly's final schisms with Dave.

Molly disliked going to Dave's house, in Mill Valley, and usually made excuses not to. This presented a problem in that Dave liked to cook; he was enrolled in a cooking class in Sausalito, and he often mentioned new dishes that he wanted Molly to try. But it never worked out very well. Two true gourmet San Franciscans, two foodies, they both recognized that his stuff was really not first-rate. Poor man, he always overdid the salt, or the cooking time, or something; and he tended to leave out the crucial garlic, or the lemon rind.

It was not really the dubious cooking, though, that made Molly not want to go there; it was rather the house itself, which she found depressing. Set in its deep dark glade of huge shadowing redwoods, the house was always dark and, as though to underline this effect, everything inside was dark brown. All "practical" fabrics. Draperies, upholstery, rugs, and heavy family portrait frames—all brown, no bright cushion or pot of flowers anywhere to relieve the gloom.

"I'll even come to get you," Dave offered, "though it's not much of a drive."

"Honestly, I don't mind the driving," Molly told him. "I just—I don't know." I just hate your house, she could not exactly say.

Dr. Macklin told her that her MRI was okay. Showed nothing much.

"That's very good news," Dave said when she told him. "I was a little worried." A remark that at the time Molly (wrongly) considered merely hostile.

But since she continued to feel so terrible, and since no antibiotics helped, Dr. Stinger wanted to "go in there and have a look." Which Molly understood to be very minor surgery, easily postponed for a couple of weeks: Dr. Stinger was off somewhere ("out of town" seemed to cover everything from scuba diving in Cozumel to a hot ENT conference in Brussels).

As she listened to the pleasantly familiar New England vowels of Douglas Macklin telling her all this, it struck Molly that in him she had found a new and improved edition of Henry, her cold and detached first husband, over whose unwilling head and broad shoulders she had poured so much warm, unwelcome, inconvenient affection. Which is not to say that she had a crush or anything like that on Dr. Macklin. She simply liked him a lot, and she wished (she still wished) that Henry could have been warmer.

And she wished that Dave would stop putting Macklin

down. You just envy his hair, she sometimes (not really) considered saying, envisioning Dave's shining bald dome. She assumed them to be about the same age, and she thought that hair envy might well be an issue among older men.

Since Dave's practice was in Marin County, and since they were (she hesitated to use the word "lovers") "friends," there was no question of Dave's becoming her actual primary-care doctor, but instead he carped from the sidelines, which did no good. Macklin should not have sent her to Dr. Beckle, Dave said; everyone knew Beckle was a shit—and Molly had to agree with him there. Also, further back, Macklin should not have prescribed Halcion after she and Paul broke up and then Paul died, and she couldn't sleep. "But that was before all the fuss about Halcion," Molly told him. "And nothing bad happened to me. I didn't get addicted or crazy, and I could sleep." "He was just lucky," Dave muttered sourly.

It was Molly's impression that Dave was a very take-charge, authoritarian doctor, commanding his patients and judging them in terms of obedience. Whereas Dr. Macklin seemed to take a less parental approach. "She was a wonderful patient," Dave used to say admiringly of his wife, poor woman, in her final illness. "All her doctors said so." And Molly imagined this passive, obedient woman, docile and uncomplaining. Following all the doctors' orders without question. A pre-feminist fifties doctor's wife.

Unsurprisingly, since on almost all fronts they got along so poorly, their sexual relationship had also deteriorated: whatever early (horny) enthusiasm Molly had felt diminished. "Come on, you're not even trying," Dave sometimes whispered loudly, angrily, scaring the cats. "I can't," Molly would whisper back.

She felt—she knew—that she had to get rid of Dave. That is, stop seeing him altogether. But in order to do this somehow it seemed to Molly necessary to convince him that they did not in fact get along, which was curiously difficult, if not impossible. In her mind she argued and argued, but only convinced herself—

talk about preaching to the converted. The truth is that I really don't love you, she would end by saying in her mind, which for Molly just about summed it up.

But she did not for the moment say that to Dave, and for two very bad but to her compelling reasons. One, she did not like the idea of being alone. Again. And, two, even less rational, she had a superstitious fear that without Dave (the doctor) she would get even sicker, as though in some mysterious medical way he was controlling whatever was wrong with her.

"Actually you don't have to dump him," said Felicia. "Just use him. See him as much as you want to. Have sex with him if you enjoy it. This is not a moral issue."

Molly liked what she had said, especially that last—but she continued to fret as though it were indeed a moral issue. And she guessed that for her it was: she did not believe that she was supposed to "see" (meaning sleep with) a man she did not especially like.

"You've got to come to dinner," Dave said. "I've learned to make the greatest bourguignon in the world."

How could Molly tell him that her mother, too, had learned to make a great bourguignon, from Julia Child in the fifties, and that they had had it at least once a week, for months, unimproved. And that she did not like it much in the first place. Probably she could have told him if she had not felt so generally guilty toward Dave, so aware of her non-love, which came out as surliness, and besides, supposedly everyone likes a good beef stew; it is not a dish you can legitimately take against, like tripe, which, eccentrically, Molly preferred to beef.

And so she only said a rather weak "Good for you."

"Okay, then, Saturday? And Sunday morning I'll make you a really great old-fashioned breakfast."

. . .

Certainly he had gone to a lot of trouble over dinner. With the early evening martinis they even had little puffs of cheese, nice and hot.

"Now if this isn't the best bourguignon you've ever had—" He grinned, sitting down and serving it out. He tasted his. "Super, if I do say so myself."

After all that, it was hard to make the appropriate remarks, and so Molly only said, "It's very good," with what she hoped was strong emphasis; she did not add that the meat was a little tough and gristly, which it was.

But his very desire to show off and to please was touching in its childish intensity. Molly was always hard on Dave, intolerant; she knew that and could not seem to control it.

And in bed she had to say to him, "Look, I'm sorry, but I just don't feel like it. I don't feel sexy. Actually I don't feel very well at all. It may sound like a joke but I do have a headache. *Please.* Please, Dave, come on, please don't."

Molly realized that it seemed a little exaggerated to call it date rape, an almost-sixty doctor whose house you have knowingly gone to for the night. Nevertheless, she did give in to superior force. She got tired of fighting him off.

In the morning, as he had said he would, Dave made breakfast. Bacon and eggs and frozen waffles, which he had just discovered. "As good as my mother used to make," he assured her, with a jokey grin.

"Your mother's waffles were good?"

"Of course."

Molly had not had any of those things for breakfast for so long that they all tasted very good, as she told him. She asked, "You don't worry about cholesterol?"

"It's a fad. No one with any sense takes it seriously. I suppose your Douglas Macklin does."

Molly wanted to go home early. She wanted to get into bed, to take some aspirin, whatever. She wanted to be alone with her cats.

Of course this entailed an argument, though less of one than she had feared; Dave recalled some household chores and gardening that he had wanted to do. "But remember about next Thursday," he instructed. "The concert. And then next Tuesday week."

"I'd better write all this down." Lately Molly had forgotten or confused a couple of dates. Her head was not itself, she thought. Maybe her problem was not sinuses but Alzheimer's? She asked Dave, "Could I have some paper? I don't have my book along."

"Here." He handed her a small pad, on which she noticed two printed drawings.

Following her glance, Dave seemed to recollect something, and he made a gesture to take back the notepad, but then he said, "That's just an old joke. Something I had printed. I'd forgotten. Just use the other side."

Curious, Molly first looked. The printed drawings were of human figures, both naked, without visible gender. The first was in a crouch, ass upward, one arm reaching up toward the anus; some small object was in that reaching hand. The second picture showed the same naked person lying down, also reaching around toward the buttocks.

"Dave, Jesus Christ, whatever?"

He was chuckling. "You don't know what that is? Lucky you! It's the directions for Fleet enemas, you give them to yourself—"

Molly said again, "Jesus Christ." (She knew that he hated it when she swore.) "You really thought that was funny?"

"I guess I did. You make such a fuss about nothing. Just turn the pad over, use the blank side of the paper."

"We have entirely different sensibilities," she told him furiously. "Anyone who would ever think that was funny for a minute—" Declaiming, she still felt that in a way he was right: she was making a fuss, and doing it on purpose. But she did think the "joke" was quite disgusting.

She collected her toothbrush, her moisturizer and nightgown. "Don't come out to the car with me," she told Dave. "I can manage perfectly well." Meaning, as he must have known that she did, Who needs you?

Muttering "Good God," with a heavy scowl Dave went off into his dark and overgrown garden.

Indeed she did not need Dave, Molly thought later as she lay in her sunny view-filled room, with the beautiful cats stretched out on her bed, near her feet. She could get through the operation on her sinuses, two weeks from then, and soon she would be all well, she would be herself again. And that would be pretty much the end of doctors in her life.

Just for a moment then she remembered, for the first time in many years, Craig Stuart and his poopoo jokes, and his darling little cock. Viewed in the mote-filtered light between giant Virginia boxwoods, ancient magnolias.

SEVEN

Felicia, out in her garden, deadheading the blowsy white roses that stubbornly bloomed on, even now into the fall, still could hear her telephone if it rang inside her house. Although there was no one, really, whom she wanted to hear from at that moment, sheer habit kept her poised for the phone. And besides, there was the answering machine.

The garden smelled richly of loamy earth, more faintly of roses, and of overripe pungently rotting apples from next door. Last week it had rained, and now small harsh weeds sprouted here and there. Seeing, registering the presence of weeds, Felicia continued with the roses, and tried to imagine an alternate, doctor-less life for herself.

In all the years that she had been a medical secretary, she speculated, she could have gone to medical school; in this fantasy she ignored the fact that at no time did she even consider medical training. Besides, she next thought, I never wanted to be a doctor, I only wanted to have sex with doctors.

Did it begin with the handsome pediatrician, Dr. Jack Chandler, whom all the little girls and all their mothers had crushes on? ("I called Dr. Chandler, Felicia has chicken pox, and he came right over!" boasted Susie, Felicia's mother, to an envious friend.) Felicia's crush, she felt sure, was stronger and deeper, more real than anyone else's, including her mother's. Dr. Chandler had gone to Andover and to Yale; he liked to say both those names. He was interested in child psychology; he encouraged his patients to talk. Without instruction, Felicia still knew the sort of thing he wanted to hear about: problems with parents, or guilts over some early form of sex, kissing games, masturbation, whatever. And Felicia, aware of none of those troubles, really, considered making them up—and considered too just saying: I really just want you to kiss me, and touch me, *here.* Dr. Chandler, perhaps advisedly, did not see adolescents, and Felicia was very upset when her mother told her, at thirteen, that she was now too old for Dr. Chandler. (Susie too was upset: the boys had outgrown Jack Chandler several years ago—but she might always run into him at a party somewhere; they were on more or less the same social circuit.)

Felicia's first serious boyfriend—if you call endless dope and sex serious—was a very tall (six four), very handsome pre-med student, Sloan Jeffers. One summer at Tahoe somewhat accidentally Felicia, at fifteen, had the big house on the lake all to herself, for a month. Her grandparents' house, solid timber and stone with great stone fireplaces and a broad surrounding porch above the rich green spreading lawn—and lovely big bedrooms, all with views of the lake. And huge soft beds.

What happened was that Susie, tired of the hereditary house, decided that Sun Valley might be more fun. And that she could leave Felicia and her brothers, who were students at Stanford, eighteen and twenty-one, with the summer live-in maid, Eileen, from Truckee. The Stanford boys decided to go camping up in the High Sierra, along with their girlfriends, an arrangement that no one's parents knew about. And Eileen really wanted to be with her boyfriend, who was working in Reno—so Felicia told her to go ahead, she could easily cook for herself. If

Eileen would just come back on Mondays and clean up the house. Felicia easily covered both for the boys and for Eileen. Her brothers were always out fishing on the Truckee River when their parents called, and they would not have asked to speak to Eileen. Everything was fine, Felicia told Susie, they were all fine. The summer of love. By the time her parents and then her brothers left, Felicia was on the verge of meeting Sloan, at a party in Squaw Valley.

Felicia was quite a big girl, back then, and she did not much like her size, although she noticed that all the boys seemed to like her, anyway. But in those years of Twiggy, and the onset of eating disorders in many young girls, Felicia, untrendily interested in cooking, ate healthily, and did not get fat, but she was big. Her mother told her, "Never mind about being thin. You have that ravishing skin, and those eyes, and if you'd only brush your hair more often—" At which Felicia smiled, and widened her eyes, and tossed her hair. "You can diet when you're middle-aged," her sensible mother told her.

At the Squaw Valley party, to which she had elected to come alone, and late, she stood out on a balcony, looking into and casing the party, until this very tall young man came out to stand beside her. For a minute he only stared at her, then broke into a huge (stoned) grin. Reaching for her face, which he then held between two large hands, he bent to kiss her lingeringly on each cheek.

"I had to see what you tasted like," he explained unapologetically.

She laughed at him—the nerve! "Was I okay?"

"Peach ice cream, only warm. I know I'm very stoned, but you're still the most beautiful girl I ever saw. Are you?"

"Stoned?" she laughed again, a little nervously. She was not used to boys quite so much taller and older than she was.

He had very straight, very dark-brown hair, long hair that fell across his high white forehead until he pushed it back. "I'm Sloan," he said. "Silly name. I just got up here this afternoon,

I was supposed to stay with these people. Here, have a toke."

He held the fat joint to her mouth, fingers grazing her lips—
so sexy!

Felicia inhaled, and held it, and then on the outbreath she
told him her name. "Felicia. My parents' house—"

He gestured at the bare-patched, steep surrounding mountains. "Out there?"

They both laughed, and then Felicia said, "No, back on the
lake."

"Oh, good."

They laughed again.

"Actually this is not a very good party," Sloan said, maybe
twenty minutes later (or maybe two hours). "Could I take you
home? But actually I don't have either a car or a place to stay."

They spent the rest of that night and most of the rest of that
month, that August, in Felicia's high, carved queen-sized bed,
sometimes looking out the wide-open window to views of heavy
trees and the brilliant broad lake, shimmering in the sunlight of
high noon, and the far distant, shadowed pink Nevada mountains. Or the slate-dark evening lake, the black trees of night.
They raised their heads from the pillows to look out at all that,
occasionally, but mostly they endlessly kissed, made love every
possible way (they both were inventive). They sometimes slept,
they smoked dope, and, sometimes starving, they went downstairs to eat.

They made, necessarily, an occasional foray out to the Tahoe
City Safeway where, hunger-inspired, they would buy almost
everything in sight, most of which they managed to eat. And Felicia, who had never really cooked before (or, for that matter,
never really made love before), turned out to have enormous
natural talent—everything they ate was incredibly good, the
fresh trout and lamb chops, the glorious salads, fruits, and garlic mashed potatoes, the muffins and cookies, the pies.

. . .

Later in her life Felicia would try to remember what Sloan was really like. To reconstruct him. But she could only remember certain smells—all his personal ones were lovely, including sweat, and sperm. And the tiny faint snores that he made on going to sleep. The strong bony-muscular feel of his back. His beautiful, magical cock.

They did not exactly have conversations. They exchanged a few plans, Sloan's to go to Harvard Med, where he had been accepted, in the fall, and Felicia's to start at Stanford. But mostly they were too stoned, or aroused, or just plain busy screwing for much talk beyond exclamations of love and praise. Neither of them sentimentalized the connection, though, and they accepted its end in September with regret but no tears or foolish promises. Whenever Felicia thought of Sloan, and of that summer, what she experienced was arousal rather than nostalgia, and very likely it was the same for him, soon to be a busy doctor—an orthopedic surgeon, very successful, in New York.

Felicia sailed happily through Stanford and came back to San Francisco where with some cash from a very nice trust, and graduation presents, she bought her small house on Green Street, in Cow Hollow, down the hill from the family home, up on Broadway.

She let it be known that she was looking for a job, and one afternoon a friend of her mother's called—Dr. Fredericks, Edwin, a very "social" psychiatrist.

"I find that I'm spending too much time doing silly things," he told Felicia. "Writing a couple of letters, answering phone calls, sorting my magazines. If you felt like doing that for a couple of afternoons a week—well, maybe three—you've got yourself a job."

Fredericks' office was up in Pacific Heights, not far from Felicia's parents' house and, for that matter, not far from where she herself now lived. Ideal, from the sound of it: an undemanding job that would pay a few clothes bills, that would not take too much of her time and energy.

It turned out, however, to involve more work than she had thought. The "couple of letters" were more like a couple of dozen a week, plus case summaries, a few articles, and an occasional book review for the local paper. All to be *perfectly typed.* "And since you're here," Edwin Fredericks further instructed, "Dr. Allen, in the next office, wondered if you couldn't do a couple of letters for him sometimes. And there're some simple books to keep, I'll show you how. And when you're free, if you wouldn't mind, a little tidying-up, just the ashtrays and stacking up the magazines in the waiting room. Oh, and I like my coffee strong, the coffeemaker's in the closet."

Somehow the money involved turned out to be less than Felicia had thought; she must have misheard what he said in the original conversation, or miscalculated.

After a few weeks of this work, Felicia thought, This is impossible. But she was in an awkward spot; after all, he was a friend of her parents, and of many of her friends' families. A gray-waved eminence, graceful at parties. And he was a doctor: who was she?

Also, some aspects of his practice interested her. Contrary to what she had always heard, Dr. Fredericks hated to talk about sex, and he discouraged his patients from doing so. There was one couple whom he saw in joint sessions, the transcripts of which Felicia typed—the Powerses. Mrs. Powers mentioned sex from time to time; she implied (she murmured) that they were not getting on well in that regard. Each time she did so, Dr. Fredericks quickly—and not very adroitly, in Felicia's view— changed the subject to money. Mr. Powers had made some bad investments, it seemed—here Fredericks sounded very judgmental, accusatory. And so poor Mrs. Powers retreated, probably embarrassed to have mentioned such a dirty, forbidden topic.

Felicia scanned Dr. Fredericks' files to see if there was anyone she knew, but alas, there was not. Nor anything of striking interest—again alas, just a lot more money-investment talk. She did not have time to go through them all with much care. She felt only the smallest guilt about her snooping: who could resist the private files of a "social" shrink?

She heard then about another job, in a hospital, a children's psychiatric clinic. It would take more time than this one, but would also pay more—and would be more interesting, Felicia thought. At least shrinks working with children could not talk about money all the time.

Edwin Fredericks took the news of her departure with a frown, and offered her more money, a very little more.

"It's really not the money," Felicia told him. It's more that you bore me to death, she could not say. "I just think I need wider experience," she improvised.

She did, however, remark to her mother in the course of explaining her move, "Edwin Fredericks is very hung up on money, you ever notice?"

Surprisingly, Susie laughed. "I've heard that. We know his broker, you know, Al Green, who is not exactly discreet."

The Child Guidance Clinic turned out to be more interesting indeed than life with Edwin Fredericks, though not in a way that Felicia would have imagined.

The director, Dr. Murphy, was in the throes of a midlife crisis, which he sometimes referred to as an anxiety depression. He had a tremendous, out-of-control crush on the pretty red-haired receptionist from Boise, Idaho, who in turn had a great, unrequited crush on a handsome black social worker, a devoted and faithful husband; his uxoriousness was a torture to the receptionist, who was further plagued by the unwelcome attentions of Dr. Murphy, as well as of still another aging psychiatrist. Another social worker had been having a noisily and extraordinarily public affair with still another psychiatrist, doors barely closed on lunging desktop encounters.

The children were mostly all right; they suffered, most of them, from fairly mild disorders, such as bed-wetting. There were a few adolescent girls with eating problems. But there was one family, the Farwells, who were gothic in the depth and scope of their trouble. There was a mother, a stepfather, two children, boy and girl, both adolescent. The boy and girl were known to be having sex with each other, also the girl and her stepfather, and the stepfather with the boy. The collective mind of the clinic reeled with voyeuristic pleasure—this was in the eighties, somewhat before child abuse and "recovered memories" became such major public issues. It took the health workers out of themselves, so to speak. Someone for everyone, they all said, amid unwholesome giggles.

Felicia decided that she hated it there. The staff was doing more harm to its own members than to the children, she very much hoped, but in any case she was doing no good at all to anyone, and the atmosphere was bad for her, she felt, like breathing brimstone.

Edwin Fredericks was having a hard time filling his job, Felicia's mother reported. "These girls are feminists now. They don't want to wash out ashtrays and make his coffee." And Susie laughed happily.

Raleigh Sanderson, Sandy, was not a friend of Felicia's parents, although they knew each other—San Francisco being the small town that it is. They greeted each other at the opera, at certain large parties. Susie and Josh Flood rather distantly disapproved of the way Dr. Sanderson lived; they would not have used the phrase "life-style"—the phrase whispered among Susie and her friends was "flagrant infidelity." Thus, Felicia had not

met him until the temporary agency with which she signed up
sent her out to his office.

Although she did not admit as much to Molly, Felicia knew
on first meeting Sandy that there would be sex, and trouble
ahead. She was unable, though, to gauge the weight of either—
the intensity of the sex, the severity of the trouble.

She did not really think that the early invitations to lunch
were in any sense innocent, nor even casually flirtatious.

That first afternoon, his orgasm, seconds after her own, was
so strong and so prolonged as to make her come yet again, and
again, as he shuddered to rest, still within her. They stared at
each other, both too shaken and too wise to speak. It was the
greatest sexual experience of Sandy's long sexual life, Raleigh
Sanderson knew that—but could he trust this new, very beautiful girl enough to tell her that? He also knew that there
would not exactly be a long line of girls succeeding Felicia; at
his age any one of them could be the last.

Felicia knew too that nothing so amazing had ever happened
to her, in a sexual way. But, being young, she imagined that life
and sensuality, her own especially, would go on forever—and although it would be many months before she was unfaithful to
Raleigh Sanderson, she was curious already.

And it was somewhat in a spirit of experiment—of wondering, Will this sex be as great as with Sandy?—that she first went
to bed with her good friend Charlie, who she had untruthfully
told Sandy was gay. And in a way sex with Charlie was just as
good; it was unlike what happened with Sandy but in its lively
way it was terrific.

Also, Felicia's basically logical mind informed her that being
faithful to a married man was silly—or, worse, it was masochistic. Furthermore, when Sandy admitted—or bragged; the sound
of it was boastful, very—that after the arousal of an operation he
would sometimes "bed" a nurse (he used that curiously inaccu-
rate and old-fashioned word), Felicia, in the course of asking

him about that (it was interesting, and she was curious), had strong intuition that he had not stopped doing it, that he still sometimes "bedded" nurses, although she gathered (more intuition) that these days he had a little more trouble doing so.

She asked him straight out, "But, sexual harassment? You're not worried about lawsuits?" She laughed to imply that of course no one would dare to sue the great Raleigh, but still she did ask.

He laughed too, of course, in his confident way, but she heard unease in the sound. "They wouldn't dare," and he laughed again.

By which she thought he meant that yes, he was still doing it to nurses—or secretaries, sometimes—but things were more difficult than they used to be.

There would only be trouble between herself and Sandy, as Felicia saw it, if one or the other of them began to feel a strong attachment for someone else, and most likely it would be she. She even sensed that she could be close to getting into this particular trouble with Will, the man in Seattle. But maybe not. And in the meantime, she felt that she and Raleigh Sanderson had made a very mature and sophisticated bargain, unspoken but surely there.

The trouble, in fact, began on the very day when Felicia was so peacefully and happily tending to her roses, out in the garden.

Like an omen, suddenly, then, with no warning at all in the quiet day, the blue air was rent with a horrible zooming sound, and there above, racing across the heavens, was a squadron of Army planes, small black malignant toys. The sound was dreadful, terrifying, even though Felicia vaguely remembered reading in the paper that a group called the Blue Angels were to practice that day. Practice for what, for God's sake? She had also read of the enormous fuel costs, and now she frowned with extreme annoyance at the whole procedure, especially the ghastly noise. It was fairly soon over, although the day seemed now less peaceful, the morning air less pristine. In the wake of war.

Felicia returned her attention at least in part to the roses.

Another area of her mind was preoccupied with Will, the nice and attractive professor from Seattle. A fantasy developed in which Will came down to stay with her. She would cook lovely meals for him, and they would make love. A lot. She smiled to herself at the thought.

Just then inside her house the phone began to ring and, still smiling, Felicia hurried into the bedroom, as though she had known who it would be.

And she had. "Will! How really nice. I was just thinking of you—no, I honestly was. . . . Next weekend? But that's terrific, of course stay here—"

At just that moment, though, they were interrupted by a return of the horrible Blue Angels, the furious, lethal sound that for those long moments filled the world. "Can you hear that?" she shouted into the phone. "It's this ghastly air show. Maneuvers, I guess they call them. Jesus, isn't the Cold War over? Can you hear?"

After an impossible minute or two the planes were gone again, and Felicia resumed: "Ah, thank God. But Will, it's wonderful that you're coming down, and of course stay here with me," she repeated, with emphasis. "I can't wait to see you."

"Is that so?" From behind Felicia came the heavily familiar, controlled-rage voice of Raleigh Sanderson. She whirled to his face, still holding the receiver in one hand.

"Well after all that you'd better say good-bye," Sandy told her.

More amazed than frightened then, Felicia spoke into the phone. "I'm sorry, someone just came in. But let me know, okay? Great, see you soon." And she hung up, and turned to face Sandy. "Now look," she began. "Now really—"

"Really what? Really you get to stand around making dates

on the phone? People coming to stay with you, and you can't wait to see them?"

His voice warned Felicia of danger, and everything in his face. But she had seen him angry before—he had a bad temper. She could always get around him, somehow mollify. Now, though, she chose rather to defy him, to ignore the danger signals. "I didn't think I needed your permission for houseguests. Do you ask me when you want to go out with your wife, or to take some nurse—"

In a split second he had lunged and hit her across the face, hard, so that Felicia fell backward onto her bed.

"How dare you—" she ridiculously began, automatically clutching at her face, which stung, and burned. And then, more ridiculously, she began to cry.

"Oh my darling—" His voice broke, a voice that she had not heard before. Could he be crying too? Dimly, still clutching her face in pain, Felicia thought, I don't care if he cries. The old shit.

In a minute she heard his steps leaving the bedroom, and then he was doing something in the kitchen. Ice. She could hear the click of cubes. He came back with a neatly towel-wrapped pack. "Just hold this against your face," he instructed, once more believing himself in charge, in control of himself, as well as of her. "Keep it there—reduce the swelling—nothing will show—"

"Just get out," said Felicia very clearly. "Leave the key. Get out. Right now."

EIGHT

"Of course I'm not going to sue him. 'Bring charges,' as they say. I doubt if I ever tell anyone but you. After all he just slapped me, you can't really call it assault. I mean, I know he shouldn't have, and it hurt, but it's almost worth it to get him so clearly out of my life, you know?" Felicia was very serious.

Molly laughed—although indeed one of Felicia's lovely eyes was swollen, discolored. "There should have been an easier way. You don't look so great."

"I know, and he's terrified. Sandy is. He thinks someone will see me and I'll tell. It'd be almost worth it to go over to the hospital and just sort of walk around. You wouldn't believe the flowers he's sent. The notes. Not to mention all the messages on my machine that I don't answer. And all that helps to get rid of him too. You can always say no to someone who's desperate. And in his case the desperation is all about legal stuff, not love."

"He does love you, don't you think?"

"I don't know. Not really. His major passion is always himself, and maybe his work, but that's himself too."

"Dave's like that. Are all doctors?"

"Maybe." Felicia mused. "No one's ever hit me before." She shivered, out there in the warm fall air of her garden.

Molly had arrived with a carload of goodies from Vivande, the prize Italian delicatessen—since Felicia was staying close to home, both to avoid being seen and to avoid seeing Sandy, who just might manage to be around, she thought.

"I wonder if he's hit many people," Molly asked, but it was not quite a question.

"I doubt it. He seemed as shocked as I was, in a way."

"I doubt if Dave's ever hit anyone, but it's great getting him out of my life too. Now if these goddam sinuses or whatever will just get cleared up."

"Surgery Friday, right?"

"Right, and that's the day Will arrives?"

"Yes, but don't worry, I'll be there—"

"Felicia, I've told you, you don't have to—"

"I know I don't but I want to. Molly, look, you're my *friend.*" Then she laughed. "I'll be the glamorous one in shades."

"That color could go away. It's sort of a lot to explain to Will all at once, isn't it?"

"Indeed. It can't be just what he had in mind. I more or less hinted that there was Sandy—'someone I'd just broken up with,' I said. Dear God, how often I've described him that way."

They both laughed, and Molly said, "Well, now it's true."

"Sure is. But lucky you're going to a different hospital. He'd somehow show up at your bedside."

"Waiting for *you.*"

"Yes. No more doctors for either of us, right?"

"Oh, right. As soon as I get rid of these goddam sinuses, I'm converting to something alternative."

"Are you afraid of it at all, the surgery?"

"No, actually I'm not."

In the few days before her surgery, Molly was indeed both busy and cheerful rather than apprehensive. In a literal way she was getting her house in order. She had had so very little energy in the preceding months there was a lot that needed to be done. Now, though still feeling considerably less than well, she did quite a lot. She went through her closets and pulled out clothes to be given away, and packed them in boxes; she packed up some books (misguided presents, many of them, or duplicates from her library or Paul's) for the Friends of the Library. She answered some letters.

In the balmy drought-season fall weather, her mood was high—although her health sagged; her nose and her head felt weighted. But soon this would all be over, she thought. No more of this heaviness in her brain, these headaches, her intolerably runny nose. And she felt the freedom of no more Dave in her life. Quite soon, she thought, there would be no more doctors at all whom she had to see.

She went to Dr. Stinger's office for what she had thought was a preoperative examination and consultation with him; he was to explain the coming procedure. But instead she found, again, the two very polite Chinese residents. And in a jovial way, still feeling her elated sense that her trouble was almost over, Molly asked them, "Polyps still there?"

"Oh yes," they assured her, as though that were good news.

"Well, let's hope the surgery takes care of them. Next time I see you, I'll be all well."

They smiled at her, encouraging, very polite.

"You'll see Dr. Stinger in the OR," said his nurse, with a smile that added: Lucky you to see him at all.

"I wonder why Dr. Stinger didn't find the polyps on the MRI," Molly later mused to someone. Or maybe only to herself, for no one answered.

"We didn't like what we found up there," said Dr. Douglas Macklin, at Molly's bedside, after the operation, in the Recovery Room. He took her hand.

How nice and kind of him, was what Molly thought. She felt warmed and comforted—for what she did not quite yet know. She was still very, very groggy, half-anesthetized. But pleasantly so. Nothing seemed very serious or important. Nothing hurt, or was even uncomfortable, and it was very nice just lying there, her hand firmly clasped in Dr. Macklin's hand.

In an idle, conversational way, and partly just to prolong their nice new connection, she asked him, "What did you find?"

"Quite a large tumor. Unfortunately. A really big one." He paused, and then came the words that Molly was to hear so often, repeated to her over and over and over, in the days and months to come, in tones of amazement and disbelief: "A tumor the size of a golf ball."

Why then and later did Molly envision this alleged golf ball, miraculously produced by herself, as green? She could never decide. Surely she had never in life seen a green golf ball.

She asked Macklin then what seemed to her the obvious question. "Why didn't he just take it out?" It had been clear from his voice that the golf ball was still there—and as things turned out there was no clear answer to her question.

"Well, you see, it was, uh, not benign. And so there is some question of the appropriate procedure."

"Oh, not benign? You mean malignant?" Molly was still conversational, and somewhat distant. Most of her mind still peacefully floated somewhere else.

"Uh, yes. Possibly radiation first, to shrink it. We just aren't sure yet. Dr. Stinger isn't sure . . ."

Molly's later reflections included thoughts on the extreme reluctance of doctors to use the word "cancer," often referring to it, when they must refer to it at all, as simply "CA," which in

California is doubly confusing. But she only thought of all that later. For the moment she was only thinking, Oh, not benign. Malignant.

They stayed in that pleasant posture, Macklin holding her hand, for quite some time. How nice of him, is what Molly was mostly thinking.

It is possible that she even drifted back to sleep, for in her next interval of consciousness Dr. Macklin was gone, and it was Dr. Stinger who stood beside her bed. He was frowning and not, of course, holding her hand. He would never hold a patient's hand, she knew, and maybe no one else's hand either. Short, dark, handsome, and cross, he stared down at her.

He addressed her, "Mrs. Bonner?" As though to say, Will you ever, ever wake up?

Forced, or so she felt it, to make conversation, Molly responded, "Oh, hello." And then, "You found a golf ball inside my nose?"

No smile. "It's not a nice tumor."

"Some are nicer than others?"

There was the smallest twitch at the corners of his mouth. "You could put it that way."

They were getting nowhere at all. Obviously, she thought, Molly had to take charge of the conversation—if that is what they were having.

She asked him, "In that case, what are my chances?"

For the first time he spoke up clearly. "About twenty-five percent, I'd say."

"You mean, a seventy-five-percent chance that I'll die?"

He hesitated for the tiniest moment before he repeated himself. "Yes. You could put it that way."

"Oh."

Curiously, Molly was not especially upset by this news. It was not that she was depressed; in no sense did she long for death, as perhaps a very old or a very ill person might. It was simply a peaceful acceptance of what she was told was coming next, by these authorities, the doctors. She even thought, Well, in that case I won't even have to think about getting a job. And she also thought, It's too bad I'm not religious, I could look forward to seeing Paul in an afterlife, really telling him off, at last. But alas, she was not, and so she could not. But there did seem a sort of logic in it: Paul dead and then her too.

Still, she felt very peaceful.

She must have dozed off then, again, with peaceful thoughts, for when she opened her eyes again Dr. Stinger was gone and standing by her bed there was, of all people, Dave Jacobs.

And that is what she said as she felt herself smile: "Well, of all people."

He was very serious. Dead serious. "I think it's good that I'm here."

He looked strong and wise. Slightly angry, even, and so Molly said to him, "I guess so."

Even more seriously, frowning, he said, "I saw Stinger."

"Oh."

He said, "I'll be by to take you home tomorrow morning." He added, "Your friend Felicia was here but I told her to come to your place in a couple of days."

"Oh. Okay."

Never mind that she would very much have liked to see Felicia right then. At that point Molly felt herself given over to the care of doctors, and Dave was a doctor. He was one of them.

NINE

For the next three weeks, a period that Molly later saw simply as the time between surgeries, she became another person, a woman hitherto unknown to herself or to anyone who knew her: she was quiet and passive, docile, mildly depressed. She did not suffer the acute panic, the dread that might reasonably be expected with a golf-ball-sized tumor, a cancer, behind her nose. She was in truth somewhat numb, not fully conscious. At night she took heavy sleeping pills; in the long afternoons, when they did not have appointments with doctors, she read long trashy books that dulled and preoccupied her mind.

"They" of course meant Molly and Dave. Dave made the appointments with doctors, and together they trundled around to a wide variety, with various specialties. More ENT people, radiologists, surgeons, internists, cardiologists, even a dentist. "But I already have a dentist," Molly feebly argued.

"This man has a specialty in radiology."

"Oh." So much for Dr. Gold, who was only a dentist, with no fancy specialty.

"It's a wonder he didn't drum up a new shrink for you" was Felicia's comment—or one of her comments.

"You know he doesn't hold with that. He's got endless anti-shrink stories."

"So does Sandy. *Did* Sandy. So boring."

"I think they don't like people smarter than they are."

"Sandy would never admit that anyone else was smarter."

"Neither would Dave, actually. And certainly not *my* shrink. And Shapiro is smarter."

But that conversation took place considerably later; at the time, even behind Dave's back, Molly was not rebellious. She was quiet, and grateful, and not quite all there.

Dave, by contrast, seemed more himself than ever. His large eyes were brighter, his step more quick and lively, even his voice was deeper and more firm. In between doctors, when he was not explaining what had been said (there were rather few explanations, since Molly was felt not to understand much, medically speaking), he joked and laughed a lot. Molly came to see that he was having a very good time; he was truly in his element.

Molly was in a sort of protective cocoon of blurred half-consciousness for most of the time. Not quite all the time, though: occasionally she would emerge, her old intelligent, somewhat fearful, questioning self.

One day she asked Dave, "If this tumor's the size of a golf ball—you doctors keep saying that—how come Dr. Stinger didn't see it on the MRI?"

They had not been back to see Dr. Stinger since Molly's operation—a curious fact, if one gave it any thought, which Molly had so far not done.

Dave scowled. "That's a good question. Frankly, I wonder if he even saw it. The MRI."

"What? He didn't see it?"

The scowl deepened to heavy lines of Dave's high bald-domed brow. "Ask your pal Macklin. He admits that he didn't see it. He just talked to the radiologist about it."

"But—"

"You're right. This may be a malpractice issue. I'm honestly trying to decide what you should do."

"But I didn't—" Molly had not meant that she even thought of suing; being a relatively reasonable, non-litigious person, she had simply asked what seemed to her an obvious question: How come the tumor was not seen on the MRI? Golf-ball-sized. (Green.)

However, even if she had had no intention of suing, should not this decision be up to her—and perhaps a competent lawyer?

But she went back into her cocoon; it was safer there.

At another time, she came out to ask, "How come all the doctors we see are men?"

"It just happens that way. Believe me, we're seeing the best in town. None of them so far have happened to be women. But that could happen. I certainly have nothing against competent women doctors, nothing whatsoever."

"Oh."

Different, widely differing (male) doctors were visited, but the format was much the same. First, a long wait in the doctor's waiting room, followed by a nurse's summons to an examining room. At last, the doctor's entrance, followed closely by Dave, who somehow managed always to be present. An examination, and then Molly was sent back to the waiting room, while Dave and the doctor talked. *Consulted.* This last was by far the longest phase of the visit.

One day, during a more than usually lengthy session between Dave and the visited doctor, Molly became aware of her old (former) habitual intense impatience. The nurse was occupied on the phone, and so Molly got up and walked over to the door, left half-open, of the doctor's private office.

". . . interesting, very common in Japan," she heard the doctor say to Dave. "Statistically—"

And then they both looked up at Molly, who had timidly tapped on the door.

Dave frowned, but mildly, before standing up to shake hands with the other doctor. "Well, this has been very interesting."

"Very interesting," the other one echoed.

In the elevator: "It was interesting," Molly complained. "Why couldn't I have been there? They have these tumors in Japan all the time?"

"Not all the time, but statistically—oh, you don't understand. And I have to confer with these doctors. It's essential. Essential for you, I mean. You'll just have to learn some patience."

And Molly, rebuked, absorbed the familiar admonition, and returned, more depressed, to her semiconscious retreat.

At night they drank quite a lot. Dave was a two-martini man, and so that is what they had, plus a bottle of wine with dinner. Dave liked steak and potatoes, and they had a lot of both. Sometimes chicken. Not very hungry, Molly nibbled as Dave scolded: "You've got to keep your strength up. You're bound to lose some weight with surgery, and probably radiation, so the more you go in with . . ."

But I don't much like steak, Molly did not say.

All the wine made her sleepy, and if she woke in the night she took a pill. She had no dreams.

Respecting what he referred to as her "illness"—he did not say "cancer," ever, nor even "CA"—Dave did not touch her much in bed. A blurry good night kiss, some vague reachings in the direction of her breasts, hands from which Molly groggily moved away.

One morning at breakfast Dave told her, "Today you get your wish. We're going to a woman doctor. A radiologist. And not only a woman, she's Japanese. Now, is that politically correct enough for you?"

PC or not, the Japanese woman doctor was very pretty, small and daintily featured, with short feathered black hair and large sexy eyes.

More alert than was usual for her these days, Molly understood that the issue was whether to radiate and possibly shrink her tumor, her golf ball, her CA before or after surgery. An interesting issue, obviously.

".. . of course a great deal would depend on the wishes and opinion of Dr. Stinger" was what Dr. Tanamini at last murmured to Dave, in her very soft voice.

After a pause, "We are no longer connected with Dr. Stinger," said Dave, in his loud stiff voice.

"But I—I most highly respect—" began Dr. Tanamini, with what sounded like real alarm.

"I understand your respect," Dave told her firmly, as though giving an order, and then he did give an order, to Molly. "Molly, I'll meet you in the waiting room."

The next conversation, between Dave and Dr. Tanamini, seemed to take even longer than most of Dave's conferences did, and Molly gathered from his face and his tone when at last he joined her in the waiting room that it had not gone very well.

"She's terrified of Stinger," Dave muttered, out in the corridor. "So annoying—she's probably the best in the business."

"She learned a lot about these tumors in Japan?"

"What?" Dave gave her an are-you-crazy? look, familiar to Molly from somewhere—and then she remembered Henry Starck, who thought most of her ideas were crazy.

She was about to remind Dave about the tumor statistics when he seemed to remember on his own.

"Oh, Japan," he said, dismissing Japan. "No, she's just generally good on rare tumors of the head and neck. But she's totally intimidated by Stinger. Won't make a move."

"Maybe they're lovers."

"Oh, Molly, for God's sake—"

"But they could be—doctors too—"

"Molly, please. This is serious. Anyway, so much for her. Tomorrow we see Bill Donovan, at Mount Watson. You remember?"

During this strange interim period of Molly's life, her friend Felicia was mostly in Seattle—with her new friend, her lover, the professor. She was also between jobs, and, more important, keeping away from Dr. Raleigh Sanderson. "It may sound silly but I'm really scared of him. Doctors can go just as ballistic as anyone—after all, you don't have to be a dope like O.J. He was saying wild things, like I'd ruined his life.

"But Seattle is really the greatest—you'd love it. Maybe you should think about moving up here? Or maybe I should?" Felicia laughed, her old rich careless sexy laugh. "I don't know, you see more water there. Somehow in San Francisco there's water all around, you don't see it as much. Of course his apartment is right up above the waterfront, and near the market, so wonderful, the most voluptuous fish, and vegetables—every night I make something wonderful. But dear Molly, how are you? Is Dave a help or just a bully? Of course at this point I'm so anti-doctor—"

"So am I, and he's both," Molly told her. "I long to get rid of him but I can't right now. I just want to be well, and never see a doctor again. He makes me feel guilty and ungrateful."

"Like a parent."

"Exactly," Molly told her.

"There's a wonderful sort of garden here built up above the freeways. The plants absorb all the noise and the smells, so it's really peaceful, it seems magic, enchanted."

"I think you're in love with Seattle. And the professor?" asked Molly. "You like him too?"

Felicia laughed again—at herself, from the sound of it. "It's all so hard to sort out, you know? Relief at his not being Sandy, plus my feelings about this city. Plus he's a very nice man. And at least I know I'm not madly in love this time—that's probably the best sign of all. Listen, do you want me to come down when you have this surgery? Honestly, just say so and I'll be there in a flash."

"Oh no, it's still so goddam uncertain. When and where, and who's the lucky doctor who gets to do it. Who gets the green-golf-ball prize."

"So lucky I could get this appointment." Dave said this many more times than twice when they drove south, down the Peninsula toward Mt. Watson Hospital, and the famous, marvelous Dr. William Donovan. Molly, repeating those words back to herself, became interested in their order, which clearly put the emphasis on "I could get." On "I." Dave was to be the hero of this episode in her life, Molly clearly saw, and in a blurry way she wondered just what her own role was to be; she felt that if Dave was to be heroic she was not. At best she could be the rescued maiden, a markedly non-heroic part. At worst, she supposed, she would die of surgery, some strange unprecedented slip of the knife, or just a bad reaction to being anesthetized. Curiously the idea did not bother her a great deal. I won't feel a thing, she thought, and she further thought, That might teach all these medical hotshots a thing or two.

The facts of how she felt, and had felt for these past several weeks, had seemed to be lost in the shuffle. No one asked, and Dave, the obvious target for complaints, seemed to regard her remarks on that topic as just that—complaints. Also, even if anyone had wanted to hear her symptoms, Molly would have had some trouble articulating just what was wrong. How to describe a generalized malaise, a weakness, a heaviness everywhere, but especially in her head (could the golf ball weigh a lot?), and intense fatigue. She could not, and had given up trying.

In the late afternoon, in the year of drought—the last drought before the floods of the following year—sunlight mantled the hills south of San Francisco, golden and benign. To their left the huge flat bay shimmered, gold, and giant silver planes rose noisily, ceremoniously, from the overcrowded airport. And everywhere, on every side, new and expensive subdivisions: tomorrow's slums.

"It's hard not to enjoy a drought," Molly contributed, breaking a silence.

Dave frowned. "You won't when water's rationed."

And Molly thought, not for the first time: How badly, really, we get on. We can't even discuss the weather. Which led her to the further, the truly depressing thought: I can't get out of this just now. This goddam tumor, this fucking "CA" has anchored me.

Hallowed Mt. Watson Hospital was Spanish in design, acres of red-tiled roofs and stone arched corridors. Alien, and to Molly intimidating. In perfectly tended gardens, on this bright fall late afternoon, giant chrysanthemums of burnished gold stood steadfast among their oversized and unreal green-gray leaves. Endless gardens. Endless corridors. She could easily be lost in them, Molly thought, or confined, and never get out. She could end up caring for chrysanthemums, cautiously, carefully. Alone.

With some little trouble they came at last to the specified office, down many halls and turns.

Since she had been prepared as though for an audience with the Pope, Molly was a little surprised by the relative simplicity of the great Dr. Bill Donovan's office, which could have been any doctor's. There was the requisite giant glass-topped desk with its large and clearly very recent photo of what must be a second, trophy wife, a tousled, toothy young blonde with twin blonde babies. The framed diplomas and certificates.

Dr. Donovan too was blond, a large bluff man with the aggressively swaying walk of a football player—or a surgeon. Shaking hands heartily with both of them, saying to them collectively, "Call me Bill." And then to Molly he said, as every doctor before him had said to her, in almost identical tones that mingled intelligent concern with condescension, "Well, young lady, what seems to be the trouble?"

As if they didn't know. Had not been forewarned about the Great Green Golf Ball.

Dave, on the long drive home, was elated. "So *lucky,*" he said many times, as he had on the drive down to Mt. Watson, but now with even more emphasis. "So lucky, he's just about to go off on a trip to Bermuda but he agreed to do it. I'm so glad I argued and wouldn't just take the man he recommended. He may be very competent but Donovan's done this same operation twenty-three times."

Molly thought, Now he's going to say that there's no substitute for experience, and Dave did say just that—as her attention wandered off, and she looked out the window at the glistening dark reservoir, which reminded her of lakes in Maine, or New Hampshire.

The wonderful lucky news, on which Molly was feebly trying but wholly failing to focus, was that wonderful Dr. Donovan, "Bill," was going to perform the requisite surgery on her head the following Monday. Molly knew that she should feel strongly in some way about this event—she should probably at least feel fear—but she did not. So far she had only reacted to the news that she, that *they,* would have to get up very early to get to the hospital by eight, to be prepped and ready for surgery. No breakfast and no dinner the night before.

Looking over and misinterpreting whatever expression Molly wore at that moment, Dave told her, "You mustn't be frightened." He reached to pat her nearest knee. "You're really a brave good girl."

Molly saw no point in arguing. And indeed how could she possibly explain to him that she might as well have already been anesthetized? She was drugged, she was out of it.

Given what she had been told by Dr. Stinger, that her

chances for survival were one in four, it is odd (she much later thought) that she did not, before surgery, contemplate Death. But she did not, she *could* not; sheer inability, not avoidance, and not "denial," made that thought—made all such thoughts— quite impossible. She could no more have contemplated death than she could have imagined the universe, or the Milky Way. Or God.

At no time did she clearly think, I might die. Or: What would it be like if I did?

TEN

Unlike Molly herself, Felicia was aware of a sudden, unreasoning dread as she approached her house, in the airport taxi. This was two days before Molly's surgery, and Felicia thought, I'm frightened for Molly—suppose it doesn't go well?

But then, in part because she could not bear another answer, she told herself that of course it would go well. Molly has the best possible care, and she is a healthy and relatively young woman.

But she, Felicia, in the early fall hazy twilight, was even afraid of her house. Afraid to get out of the cab and go in. To propitiate whatever was so scaring, she overtipped the driver—who did not seem to notice. A surly, dirty-blond curly-haired boy, he barely thanked her, and drove off, leaving Felicia to face her house alone. Standing there out in front, with her Seattle bags.

Still frightened, she thought that perhaps in her absence someone had broken in; it happened so often these days that it barely made the papers anymore, so you didn't even know how often.

Telling herself that she was being ridiculous, and noting that at least she had progressed from serious preoperative concerns about Molly to the considerably less serious housebreak worries, she opened her front door. And saw that the house was exactly as she had left it: the same minor mess, a clutter of newspapers piled on her breakfast table, the empty coffee cup that she did not have time to wash out before the plane to Seattle. The slight, faint layer of house dust that an absence, an emptiness, brings. She walked through the house, seeing nothing amiss, and opened the back door that led out to the garden.

No changes there, and she stood for several minutes savoring the November smells of loamy earth and the slight bitterness of chrysanthemums, the sweet rot of fallen apples. The neighbor's cat, who always looked more like a fox, with her wild brilliant eyes, flicked her beautiful brush of a tail in Felicia's direction, before scurrying under a wall of ivy.

So much for the marvelous powers of intuition on which she had always prided herself, Felicia thought. And she thought again, At least my fear was not about Molly. I know she'll be okay.

She turned back to the house, the hall, and she opened the door to her bedroom—in which, on the bedside table, there was an enormous vase, one of hers that she kept in the kitchen closet. And a giant sheaf—three dozen? four?—of yellow roses.

At which Felicia's heart jolted, and her breath momentarily stopped in sheer panic. She thought, Sandy, and in that petrified instant she imagined him entering the house like an owner or a most intimate friend, with his own key. Going into the kitchen, the closet, and finding the vase that he knew was there. Taking it to the sink and turning on water, so domestic, and probably remembering what she had told him, that warm was best for roses. She could perfectly visualize his carrying the vase, quite heavy now, from the kitchen to her bedroom, the confident swagger of his walk somewhat thrown off by the weight. Smiling to himself, recalling her fondness for yellow roses. Even thinking, Now everything will be all right. Will be just as it was.

The fool! The jerk!

No card. Just her knowing that he knew she liked these roses best—and proving that he could still walk into her house.

She would have the locks changed tomorrow, and how very stupid not to have done that before! But there was still the night to get through.

An hour later, though, with a glass of wine and a bowl of good vegetable soup from her freezer, Felicia was able to think, How nuts, to be terrorized by some flowers. Or even by Sandy, who could be a little irrational, certainly, but who was after all a respected, respectable doctor, who might scare her a little on purpose, but who would surely not do anything really crazy. Surely not do anything that would get him into public trouble.

While heating the soup and taking a first sip of wine, she had put in a call to Molly, who sounded okay. "No, Im not scared at all," Molly said. "Actually I hardly think about it. It's odd, but it seems so unreal. Surgery on my head? It makes me feel like Humpty-Dumpty. Listen, I have to go. Steak is being announced." She lowered her voice to a whisper. "Jesus, I really hate steak. No wonder I'm getting so thin."

They both laughed, and hung up, as Felicia thought, Poor Molly, with so much of Dave.

She reflected too that it was odd, out of character though for Molly not to have asked, And how was Seattle? Will? And odd that she herself had not said: This sort of creepy thing just happened here. There were these flowers in my bedroom . . .

"The cabin" is how Will had referred to the house he owned north of Seattle, high up on a bluff above the sound, with a magnificent view of surf and rocks and a beach, which the house seemed designed to ignore. The only windows were small and very high up, the roof steep and sharply ridged.

Heedlessly, Felicia reacted; she said, "Good *Lord,* Will, such a fortress." But as she was about to try to cover what instantly seemed tactless, she noticed that he looked pleased at her observation.

"The architect managed to do pretty much what I told him to do. And he agreed that you really can't tell what's out there in the woods these days." Saying this, Will looked grim, very military, so that Felicia was sure he did not mean wild animals—and sure too that she would do better not to hear about whatever he did mean.

In fact, Will's bearing was always military, though at first Felicia had simply seen him as very erect, with the perfect posture no doubt demanded by some school, some parent. Even in bed. Waking early in the morning, he sat upright as though in response to a bugle call.

Inside, this house was opulently dark. Dark leather chairs and sofas, wine-colored velvet draperies, dark walnut panelling hung with what had to be family portraits, ancient and somber, very rich people from at least a century ago.

Those ancestors and their implications were the first (and lesser, actually) surprise in terms of Will that Felicia observed in the course of that visit. Like most people who have always lived with a comfortable amount of money, Felicia assumed the same to be true of her friends, and she was always embarrassed and upset when it turned out that someone had grown up less than comfortably, in that way. In the course of things, except in her shelter work, she did not meet the genuinely poor. Curiously, the closest she had come was Raleigh Sanderson, who had angrily told her more than once, after more than enough martinis, "You're so young! Your parents have really made it, you don't even remember the Depression. I tell you, we were really scratching around back then."

But Will, she recognized as they toured his "cabin," was genuinely rich, and had been so for many generations. No doubt that was how he could afford to be a professor.

In Seattle she had not got this whiff of what her mother

would have called *real* money—or, in Felicia's view, worse—*old* money. "But no money is really real, and none of it's very old," Felicia had argued. "Oh, darling, you know what I mean." And Felicia did know. Will's apartment on the lake was pleasant enough, but spectacular only in its setting; it did not contain wonderful "things," just a lot of books and shabby-comfortable chairs—what Felicia assumed to be standard-issue professorial gear.

She had also noticed a rather large number of much-enlarged news photos of military actions, including some bloodily bandaged Civil War soldiers—but she assumed that this had to do with history, what he taught, rather than with specifically military tastes. But in the cabin, she was ushered into what Will had said was his study—and there was a room (four walls, no windows) entirely lined with what at first she took to be replicas of guns, big toys, but she quickly understood that they were real, real guns in a variety of shapes and sizes, in walnut and silver and plain dark heavy metal, from very small, just a couple of inches long, to enormous. And all upright, erect in their green plush cases.

Ready for action.

"These aren't loaded, are they?" she could not help asking.

"Of course not." But he seemed curiously pleased at the question. "There's only one loaded gun in the house, and I keep that hidden."

That's one too many, Felicia thought, and just managed not to say. "These are just for fun?" she asked.

"You could put it that way. I like to have them. To me they're very beautiful." His tone was a little defensive.

" . . . arsenal . . . " she could not help murmuring.

He snorted, unamused. "Some people would certainly call it that."

"I think anyone would," she said rather quietly. Anyone outside the NRA, was her further thought.

At dinner, though, fueled by a couple of glasses of wine, she asked him, "You don't actually belong to the NRA, do you?"

He smiled somewhat condescendingly. "Yes, *actually* I do. You see, as a historian, I happen to take the Second Amendment seriously."

"Oh Jesus, Will . . ."

That night, in bed, after love, he whispered to her insistently, "This is what's important. Love is. We may disagree on a lot of superficial issues . . ."

But guns are not superficial, Felicia was too sleepy to say. And she was less sure about love.

Unhappily, on the plane going back to San Francisco, as they flew over rich dark-green beautiful mountains, Felicia read in the morning paper about another shooting: a ten-year-old boy with his father's supposedly unloaded gun shot his sister in the head, not killing her though "damaging" (wrecking) her brain. Not exactly the fault of the NRA, or certainly not Will, although in a sense Felicia felt that it was.

And so, although restored to her own house, her bedroom, from which she had removed the ominous, beautiful roses, Felicia did not fall easily to sleep. In her mind she was writing to Will: "I'm sorry, this may sound silly, but I am so turned off by guns. I really hate them, everything about them. It really comes to this, I just can't have a relationship with someone in the N.R.A."

And she was writing to Sandy: "Please, no more flowers." No point in telling him about the changed locks. "The roses are beautiful, but—"

She must have eventually slept, for at some point in the dark of early morning she awoke to the sound of someone walking around in her garden. First the creak of her gate, and then the crunch of cautious steps on the gravel path. A faint tiny trickle of water: Christ, could someone be peeing there?

Panic froze her; she could neither move nor think. She imagined the person outside looking at her house; was that the point of his presence, to see her? Might it be someone who had watched the house and thought she was still away? Might he try to break in? Or if it was Sandy (her blood and pulses knew this to be the case), would he come in, with his key? How could he *pee* out there?

Cold in her warm, familiar bed, she lay there, until she realized that for a long time there had been no sound at all. That whoever (Sandy) had gone, and the sky was lightening.

After breakfast, in her sunny fall garden, there was no sign at all that anyone had been there—and so maybe no one had? But Felicia was sure that it had not been imaginary. She had clearly heard someone. Who *peed.*

"I know there's no connection, Will and Sandy couldn't be more different, really," Felicia said to Molly, over lunchtime bowls of soup, at Molly's. "It's just that both of them have scared me lately, and I'm not a frightened person. But Sandy was so angry when he hit me, and then doing creepy things like sneaking in flowers. And Will with all those guns."

"Anyway, you got your locks changed?"

"Early this morning. You'd be amazed at how quickly they come and do it all. I guess they're used to much worse emergencies than mine. It's not a good sign."

Molly did not seem to be drinking her soup, which must have cooled off by now. Every now and then, she brought a spoonful to her mouth, took a small listless sip, and returned it to the bowl. Her visible lack of appetite was painful to watch, especially for greedy Felicia. In fact Molly was visibly, painfully not herself; she was literally not all there, although from time to time she spoke, sounding more or less like herself. Now she said, as though considering, "I'm not afraid of Dave, I just can't stand him, he's suffocating, and he's so unpleasant. But I don't seem to get rid of him, so maybe I am afraid."

"I don't think you're afraid. Jesus, Mol, you don't feel well."

"That's certainly true—and having Dave around all the time—I really can't wait for it all to be over. You know, Dave too."

Although Molly was obviously thinner, she moved more heavily than before, as though her thin arms and legs were weighted in cement. At first Felicia had thought that Dave might have her on some cheer-up-don't-feel drug, but then she decided that Molly was simply drugged with her own entire discomfort, which of course included Dave.

"It's so complicated," Molly went on. "He naturally thinks he's being wonderful, and I guess in a way he is, which makes me feel very guilty. Along with everything else. He's exactly like a parent. Like both parents. And he really hates the cats."

"Yes." Felicia wanted to say, Look, just get rid of him, and I'll do everything. I'll bring you home from the hospital and move in here with you and make nice meals. Later on, she decided that she should have said exactly that, and not only said it but put it into effect—forced it, if necessary. But at the time she was too intimidated, less by Dave himself than by the fact of his being a doctor; she was unable not to think that maybe Molly should be with a doctor now, and how lucky in a way that Dave should be one. That he should be so nuts about Molly. "We both have to get away from doctors," she told Molly, laughing a little.

"Yes, at this point I can't even stand my dentist. I had to see him yesterday—something about radiation."

"You're having radiation? You know that?"

"Well, I guess so. It seems definite to everyone. All the doctors."

But Felicia felt that to Molly nothing really seemed definite. She was blurred, her eyes not quite focused, her voice hesitant and vague. If I were having surgery on my head for cancer, and then radiation, I would be in bed screaming or at the very least in tears, Felicia thought. Probably I would do something really infantile like move back home. And then she understood that possibly staying with Dave was Molly's version of screaming, and that instead of crying she had willed herself into a passive semiconsciousness.

"You'll never guess who called me," Molly was saying. "Matthew, out of the blue. Of all times."

"Matthew?"

"Paul's brother. His twin, but they're totally different. Matthew's in insurance. The only interesting thing he does is deep-sea diving." She added, "So odd he'd pick just now to want to see me. But then his timing's always been strange."

"You don't want to see him?" Knowing what the answer would be, Felicia at the same time was thinking: Jesus, that's what Molly really needs right now. Paul's twin.

She herself had not really liked Paul much, for somewhat complicated reasons. She thought she had recognized in Paul some of her own worst (she thought) qualities; like her, he was a little vain, and he was a flirt. And she blamed him for allowing himself to get killed like that! He didn't have to do that to Molly. It was as though he had left her twice.

"No," Molly was saying in a definite way. "No, I don't."

"Well, you don't have to. Right now you don't have to do anything you don't want to do."

"Except for this goddam operation."

"Well yes, you do have to do that."

For no reason they both began to laugh, a little hysterically.

ELEVEN

With tubes in her nose and down her throat and in both arms, Molly lay on her hard white hospital bed, in the evil half-light of nighttime. She heard discordant TV sounds, and jarring, incomprehensible human voices speaking strange languages. She thought, If only I could make them turn off the TV, but there was no way for her to speak, to make any sound, with the tube in her throat.

She knew that she was in Intensive Care, but did not know how she knew that.

The operation was over, it had been a success, she thought; she could remember doctors smiling, self-congratulatory. Donovan. Dave. But now she could not speak, and both large clocks on the wall in front of her said 3:15. Next to the TV screen, a small nurse stood talking to a man of about her size—an orderly, maybe. Sometimes they both talked to the other two women in the room, in Intensive Care. But there was no way for Molly to get their attention, and in a distant way she thought, This is the worst night of my life. Not pain, but the purest, most total discomfort.

One of the other women in the room was Spanish, maybe Mexican, South American, and sometimes friends or relatives spoke to her in that language, very softly, soothingly. But at times the small nurse addressed her loudly, in English. "Rosa, do you know where you are? Did you just have a baby, Rosa?" Did they think she was crazy? Was she crazy, poor Rosa, and if she had a baby where was it? Molly hoped the baby would not come into their room, but of course it might.

Her legs were all right, Molly found, no tubes or binding, and so she began to thrash them about, kicking up and down, hoping to attract someone's attention. And after a while the small nurse came over, and, in her loud voice (did she think Molly was crazy, too, or deaf?), asked if something was wrong.

With her fingers Molly spelled out "TV"—at the same time shaking her head emphatically, as strongly as the tubes allowed.

"Oh, you want turn off TV?"

Molly nodded. Yes, PLEASE. Yes.

With a slight frown, the nurse went over and turned it off, first giving an explanatory whisper to the orderly.

Molly was grateful; the room was a little quieter, but this did not help as much as she had thought or hoped it would. There was still so much light, and voices from everywhere, from the two other beds and from out in the hall.

"Rosa, are you in the hospital? Do you know where you are?"

The other woman, who seemed to be very old, only moaned and sobbed occasionally. And Rosa never spoke, but was only spoken to in those harsh, intrusive voices—voices that also interrogated one of the people who came to see Rosa.

"Are you married, or only boyfriend?"

"Married. Husband."

The old woman sobbed.

This is a chapter of hell, Molly put it to herself, and then she thought, No, hell is not even near here. Hell is homelessness and AIDS and sick children and cold and out of food—sometimes all of those. Hell is not an expensive suburban hospital, with state-of-the-art cutting-edge doctors and machines. And heat, and light. This is only extremely uncomfortable. It seemed important at that moment to know the difference.

A tall woman in white who must have been a new nurse, new shift, turned the TV on again, though not very loudly. Molly could not quite see the screen; although it was there she could not quite focus on it. Both clocks now said 5:35, or was there only one clock? Was she going blind?

"I'm going to take the tube out of your throat," said the nurse, and as suddenly as she had spoken she reached and yanked. Excruciating pain. "That's the only way to do it," said the nurse.

But at least the tube was out.

"How many clocks do you see up there on the wall?" was one of the first questions a new young doctor asked Molly, a few hours later—a doctor new to her, that is; God knows where he came from.

Timidly she answered, "One," having figured out that that was the desired response. And sometimes there was only one, but why should there ever be two? She was being visited by a cluster of doctors—far be it from her to try to count them.

"Sometimes," a doctor began to explain to her, "after such a major major trauma to the head, vision is blurred for a time. But almost always this condition is temporary."

Almost always? What about the times it is not temporary, but permanent? Double vision for life? Molly thought, How perfect that I should have married a twin. But maybe I've always had double vision, and there was really only Paul. This perfect senselessness made her smile.

Misreading her smile, the doctor responded. "I'm glad to see you smile! No problem there, your parotid came through fine, and the facial nerve. Our Bill here is really a genius, you're a lucky young woman."

And you're a very dumb young man, saying everything twice to a woman with double vision, Molly thought but did not say.

"Well, I don't know about any genius," Dr. Donovan came

forth modestly to say. "Eight hours of damned hard work by all of us, and I have to say we had some luck. All of us did. But the tumor came out pretty clean, for such a big one."

"You mean you got it all?"

"Uh, yes. We think so. But of course you'll have some radiation, and that should take care of, uh, any other possibility."

It was extremely rude to go to sleep when people were talking to you, were trying to explain something difficult. Molly knew that, but she was so terrifically tired, exhausted. She closed her eyes, and she must have slept for at least a little while for when she opened them only one doctor (clearly one) was standing at her bedside. Dave.

". . . shoved your brains aside," he was saying.

"What?"

He grinned, white teeth enormously gleaming. "They had to. But those guys know what they're doing, believe me."

Shoved your brains aside. The words reverberated chillingly. Molly closed her eyes, hoping that Dave would go away—that everyone, everything would go.

" . . . guess you don't feel much like talking."

"No, I don't."

A nurse came, and in slow motion pulled out the tube from Molly's nose. As with the throat tube, there was a very harsh strong pain, so that she cried out, "Oh Christ!"

"Sorry, but that's the only way I can do it. As quick as I can, but you'll feel better now."

It was not the nurse's fault, Molly knew that. The nurses did not mean to hurt her. But surely there was some other way to remove a tube? Maybe under a general anesthetic?

In some later interval of consciousness Molly mused, and wondered: Did the process that seemed to make most (nearly all) doctors so insensitive, so gross in their perceptions and their speech ("shoved your brains aside"), did that process or training apply also to nurses? Or was only a certain very definite personality type drawn to medicine in the first place? An imponderable, but in her current state almost any issue was imponderable.

There was only one other woman in her room, Molly at some point realized: a very young South American woman who had just had a baby (who was up in the nursery, "doing very well"), and who was visited by a lot of Spanish-speaking relatives, including a very young husband. A woman who was somewhat disoriented, but getting better. But how could she, Molly, have imagined two women? From what dark part of her own imagination did the very old woman appear?

Perhaps her brains were shoved aside for good. However, at least it was clear to her now that there was only one large clock on the wall in front of her bed.

"You'll feel much better in another room," said a later nurse. "Your own room." This seemed unlikely: She would not feel any better anywhere, was Molly's thought; she could not move, or be moved. But it turned out to be true. Her bed with its surround of tubes and machines took up almost the whole space of her tiny new room, but there she was, alone. More privacy. Less noise.

Where was Felicia? Dimly, not urgently but often, Molly wondered. It was unlike Felicia not to appear with baskets of food and flowers. Or certainly to call. But no one came to see Molly except delegations of doctors, or nurses or technicians wanting blood. Or Dave, by himself. And no one phoned her but Dave. Darkly she wondered, Had Sandy Sanderson at last done something terrible to Felicia?

She remarked to Dave, "It's odd about Felicia. So unlike her not to show up, or at least to phone."

He grinned. "I called her and told her not to. And I told her you weren't taking any calls. Except from me."

"But, Dave—"

"Look, you've been through a major major trauma. I don't want anything to go wrong."

"But—"

In a sense he was right, Molly knew that. She knew that she was not up to even the smallest social effort. But still, Felicia in any form would have been a comfort.

Instead of Felicia, Raleigh Sanderson came to see her. She had been half-asleep, half-lost in one of the murky, uneasy private fogs in which she now seemed to spend most of her time. Not quite knowing him at first, she did remember that he was a doctor, and at first she thought, Oh God, one more, then recognized the familiar snowy white flag of hair, and the arrogant surgeon's walk.

"Well," he began—and proceeded to tell her about the brilliance of the surgery she had undergone. "Major major . . ." They all seemed to like that phrase, Molly noted. "And you did very well," he added, implying that her performance was not exactly up to that of Bill Donovan, but that given her limitations as a patient, a woman and a non-doctor, she had done quite well.

Molly did not think Raleigh Sanderson had come all the way down to Mt. Watson to check on her condition—and she was right.

"I'm really worried about our friend Felicia," he began—as Molly could almost have predicted.

"You are?" she asked. "Really, why?" She hoped it would not take him long to tell her; she could feel herself beginning to fade out, her shoved-aside brains to blur.

". . . trip to Seattle—irresponsible—"

Molly heard all this somewhat indistinctly, but she tried to answer as clearly as she could, hoping to cut short their conversation. "I think she wanted to see Seattle. Everyone says it's so great." And then she must have blanked out entirely. She woke up to find no one there in the room with her, and only the dimmest memory of a visit from Raleigh Sanderson. From Sandy. Was that possibly another thing made up entirely by her—like the second woman, the old and very feeble Spanish lady in Intensive Care?

Molly was not allowed out of bed so far, and thus was forced to ring for nurses or aides, whatever, for bedpans. She did not get used to this; it became only faintly less embarrassing as the days and nights wore on.

However, very late one night, at some unreal post-midnight hour, in answer to her summons, from the eerily bright outer corridor a mysteriously beautiful man appeared, white-haired but young, with smooth cream-coffee skin and large deep dark eyes.

Unable at first to speak to him, Molly stared.

But he seemed to know. He said, "Oh, you need—" and he went back out, not saying the humiliating word for what he was to bring.

After all that was accomplished—wordlessly (both embarrassed, they avoided each other's eyes)—he came back into the room. "Is there something I could do to make you more comfortable?" he asked.

He was the first person in the hospital to use that word to her, Molly reflected: "comfortable." Her grateful heart went out to him. She said, "It's kind of you to ask, but I can't really think of anything."

"If you sit up for an instant, I could help with the pillows. There, that's not too bad?"

"Oh no, that's really better." As if by magic, in that one instant he had improved the comfort of her bed. Gratefully, Molly lay back. "You're a nurse?" she asked him.

He smiled. "No, nothing so elevated. I am basically what they call orderly."

Molly smiled back, wanting to say to him, I too am orderly, an orderly person, I can't help it. But he might not think that was particularly funny. And she really wanted to say, Please stay with me. And so she only smiled.

"In a general way, you are feeling better now?" he asked her.

"Yes, I really am, I think." How nice of him to ask, Molly thought again.

"It was I who brought you to this room from the Intensive Care," he told her. "But you could not remember."

"Well no, I don't. I couldn't see very well then, everything doubled."

"You kept your eyes closed, and I worried that you must be frightened."

She said, "I was," so touched by his concern that she could have cried.

"Now I will let you sleep," he said. "And I will hope that you feel much better tomorrow."

Thinking of him, her mysterious visitor, Molly lay awake for a while, but happily so. The fact that this kind and beautiful and exotic man was around, was somewhere near, was cheering to her. She could even ring her buzzer, and maybe he would appear to her again. She wondered about his life: Was he married, or living alone, was he possibly gay? And then she thought, How terrible, as though these days only gay men are kind and sensitive. She somehow thought that this man was not gay, not married, but a sort of loner. Her response to him was not sexual, despite his beauty; she rather felt a human, deep response to his kindness, his concern.

Dr. Bill Donovan appeared periodically, always surrounded by his group of acolytes. Or, more frequently, the acolytes came by themselves. They always seemed extremely happy to see her—not for any personal reasons, Molly was sure, but because she was regarded as a triumph, living proof of their consummate skill. In a self-congratulatory way they spoke among themselves: "Beautiful nose, no scars. You can barely see that line across her forehead. Her hair growing back already. Great job!"

She looked great—they all said that. No one asked how she felt, and when she thought of it, Molly recognized that she did not feel too terrible, she guessed. Just miserable, for no reason.

"When do you think I'll be able to go swimming?" she asked Dr. Donovan during one of his increasingly rare visits; she had been thinking about going home, things to do to get back in shape. (How to get rid of Dave.)

Donovan smiled widely, with his perfect small teeth and happy eyes. "Oh, probably next week." He seemed to rethink this, and added, "You might have to wear one of those nose things."

Was he kidding, was this a dark black joke? Swim next week?

Months or even a year later, Molly, still not swimming, pondered his advice, which remained opaque: no one could seriously believe that Molly could go in swimming the following week—or, for that matter, next month—when she was flattened by radiation. Did he simply not care at all what she did, once his surgery was accomplished?

Dave came to see her, very pleased with himself, with the hospital, the doctors, even with her. Much much later, when Molly was finally well and had parted from Dave, she said to Felicia, "I feel so guilty toward him—in his way he did help a lot." Felicia told her, "Listen, don't you feel guilty. The whole experience of your illness surpassed his wildest dreams of happiness—he'd never had it so good. And just remember, he didn't do a thing that all your friends wouldn't have done, if he'd let us."

In any case, Dave clearly loved it there in the hospital. He took every possible chance to talk to doctors and nurses—even, to Molly's horror, asking about her BMs in her presence.

"Good Christ, Dave, how could you?"

"You're so squeamish about all the wrong things. People talking or even writing about sex doesn't bother you at all, but an innocent bowel movement—"

"Dave! Please!"

"You see? You're hopeless."

"I'm having a lot of trouble sleeping," Molly confided to the nurse who seemed most approachable. "The noise and all." She felt that she should not complain about so relatively trivial a problem, but felt too that unless she slept soon she would die—which at this point seemed almost desirable, a long, long sleep.

The nurse, a large and handsome middle-aged black woman, was sympathetic. "The noise, you're right, it's pretty terrible. I don't know how anyone can sleep. All this trundling up and down corridors."

"You must be glad when you go home."

"Oh really, I really am." The nurse smiled, and then spoke in a serious way. "But you need to get some sleep, I don't think you'll be going home for a week or so. So, I'm going to give you a real knockout drop," and she handed Molly a small brown pill. "You take this early, about seven-thirty or eight, and I can guarantee you'll sleep."

"Wonderful."

Molly was still dubious, but she appreciated what had felt like sympathy.

And she took the pill at eight, convinced that it would not work.

It did. Almost right away her mind began to float outward, as though she was lying back against pillows, so comfortably, in an unmoored boat on a lake in Maine. Sometimes she opened her eyes to sky, to shifting clouds; at other times she looked back to observe the shoreline, the sandy beach, big gray rocks, and birches, bent down from the bank, that rose up from the sand steeply to some woods of pine and hemlock, and more birches.

Or she was not in a boat at all but right there, in her hospital room, and she wondered sleepily, now almost awake, Where is Felicia? Why hasn't she come to see me? But then she floated out again, in Maine, on the lake.

A rap on the door brought her back, but only partially. Vaguely she thought of the beautiful dark and mysterious person, the orderly, and she smiled, anticipating him. Would he possibly kiss her good night?

The door pushed open, and Molly knew then that she was still asleep—or perhaps she had died in her sleep.

It was Paul who kissed her, passionately.

TWELVE

"It was Matthew, of course. But I never quite woke up, and I thought I was kissing Paul. He must have been startled."

Home at last, Molly lay in her own wide sunny bed. At the moment, she was being visited by Felicia, who had brought a great bunch of roses, the last from her garden. "How'd he get in?" she asked Molly, speaking of Matthew, whom she had never met; Paul was enough, she thought. She said, "It must have been late."

"Easy." Molly laughed. "He said he was a doctor. But it's more of a Paul kind of caper, actually. Matthew's always been very law-abiding."

"Maybe now he's inherited Paul's character. Don't twins sometimes do that, shift back and forth?"

"That's what their mother said, but then when Matthew called the next morning he was more like himself. Pretty stiff. But very proud of his out-of-character exploit. He said all you need to prove you're a doctor is an expensive suit and a pushy manner."

"Sounds right. Sandy pays two thousand for London suits— can you believe it? Is Matthew living here now?"

"Oh no. Or I don't really know where he's living. I seem not to be getting things straight."

"Me neither," Felicia told her. And then she said, "I'm really getting scared about Sandy. I keep seeing him, or else I'm hallucinating."

"Maybe he's stalking you."

"I suppose, but could he be, really? A famous doctor and all that?"

"O.J. was famous."

"If Sandy is stalking, you'd think he'd be better at it. I mean, do it so I wouldn't see him."

"But isn't part of the point to scare the woman?—let her know you're stalking?"

"Of course. You're right," Felicia conceded. "He's probably terrific at stalking. In control, as usual." She added, "I'm going to start looking for another job. I think that would help." And then she said, "I could swear I heard him in my garden last night. I think he was, uh, peeing. *Again.*"

"Why do you think it was Sandy? He pees in some special way?"

"I thought I got a glimpse of his hair in the streetlight."

"What an odd thing to do, though. To pee in your garden."

"He has a problem with his prostate. And it would be a way of saying he's not afraid. And claiming territory, like a dog."

Molly smiled; she felt grateful to Felicia for making this a funny story as well as a scary one. Somewhere in the story, though, there were threads that she was too tired to follow. And some clue that she had forgotten. In fact, for some weeks she did not remember that Sandy had come to see her in the hospital.

Molly had been talked into leaving the hospital before she wanted to. Before she felt that she was ready to go. "Forced out," is how she thought of it, but that was possibly too strong— and unfair to Dr. Bill Donovan, who had come to her one morning, with his proud and happy entourage of residents, and announced, "Well, young lady, you'll be ready to go home tomorrow. Just can't keep you around anymore, as much as I'd like to. You've done so well."

"But I'm not—I really don't think—" Molly weakly attempted to argue. What she meant was that she could not yet take care of herself, as she was used to doing. Even if she hired someone to come in and cook and do errands, she could not quite tell Dave to go away, please to leave her.

As Dave full well knew. "You've got to listen to Bill, and do what he says. He's had years of experience with this."

"But he's the one who said I could go swimming next week."

Dave paused, but only for a moment. "You may have misunderstood him. He probably meant next month, whatever he said."

"But I didn't misunderstand—he said next week." Too tired to argue, though, Molly let it go. In fact, once she got home, she was too tired to do anything except to lie back against the pillows of her bed, to watch the birds that plummeted from the eaves of her house to the tops of trees, clustering there in ceremonious droves, big black-feathered birds with their tiny curious heads and lively beaks. Raising her eyes to the statelier, grander view of the Golden Gate Bridge, the magnificent, lordly hills of Marin County, would have taken too much of an effort. She was not strong enough for such grandeur, not now.

Dave was taking care of her.

"I could just have Lupe come more often," she had told him wistfully, her first day home.

"Lupe's hopeless, you know that. You just like her, some female-sympathy thing. I told her to take a little time off, and in the meantime Pat said she could give you some hours. She'll get everything done in no time."

All true. Lupe, whom Felicia had come upon in the shelter (she had shifted from Open Hand) and who needed work, was indeed quite hopeless at cleaning, and she tended to break almost any machine. She dusted around things and was too small to reach most shelves. But she was also sweet and eager to please, and her great dark-brown eyes were full of precocious sorrow. (God knows what the generals in Guatemala had done to her family.) Whereas Pat, a large grandmotherly type from Texas, was a perfectly functioning, perfectly quiet machine herself, whose hard white expressionless face was terrifying to Molly.

"But I'd have trouble telling Pat what to do," Molly told Dave. "Or asking for anything."

"That's your problem, not hers. Just force yourself. She'll do anything you say." He added, "Besides, you won't see her much. We'll be down at Mount Watson getting your radiation." He grinned very happily.

The half-shaven front of Molly's head was still quite stubbly; she supposed it was growing back, but it seemed to grow far more slowly than even grass grew, or a man's scratchy beard. She tried adjusting scarves, but the effect was all wrong: she looked exactly like what she felt herself to be, a woman with something to hide. A woman ashamed.

"I guess I'm not good with scarves," she told Felicia, on the phone. "You know—some are, some aren't."

"I have an idea. I'll be right over," Felicia told her.

Felicia brought over two nice big wool berets, one bright red, the other black.

In which Molly felt—not exactly herself, but someone very stylish, and quite disguised.

At Mt. Watson, in all those terrible broad bright high-tech corridors, many people in wheelchairs or just walking around wore some sort of covering on their heads. Seeing no other berets, Molly tried to pretend—to believe—that she had worn hers on purpose, so to speak. She had chosen this bright-red beret, so jauntily positioned, and she was not in a wheelchair or a hospital gown. She was standing up straight, and walking as fast as she could.

In the waiting room (she seemed to spend most of that day in various waiting rooms, or just waiting somewhere), she observed an elderly man in a wheelchair. A patrician head with fine thin hair, a broad lined brow, and wide pale eyes. But dressed in the awful greenish hospital garb, and some terrible slippers. And there he was, in his wheelchair. Those old eyes avoided Molly's eyes as though from shame at his situation, certainly not of his choosing. His reduction—to this.

In all the time that she spent, hours and hours in those corridors, Molly saw that same look again and again, a look of embarrassment, of wondering, What terrible thing have I done to be brought so low, to this place of punishment and pain?

In another waiting room, this time for X-ray, there were two young men, both husky-looking construction workers, who seemed to have become friends in this place, waiting together. One with a transplanted heart, the other for a bone marrow transplant. The bone marrow man had a pretty wife and a lively very small daughter along, and he picked up the little girl and held her high as she squealed with pleasure.

Dave had listened intently to all this exchange, and explained it, more or less, to Molly—but undoubtedly getting the illnesses straight. "You see?" he said. "Things aren't necessarily so bad for you."

"I know that. But I still don't see why everyone has to wait so long. Everywhere."

"Everyone is busy."

"Yes, but the patients are sick."

"Oh, sick," he muttered, as though "sick" were nothing to "busy." And Molly would not even view herself as sick, and so was left with her guilt, guilt for not being the exuberant good sport that the men were, with far more life-threatening, terrifying illnesses.

The longest wait, the longest process, was about the making of a mask.

"A mask?" she asked Dave.

"For radiation. You'll put it on every time you come down so they can aim right, hit precisely the right spot. So you won't lose all your teeth or go blind." He chuckled.

"Dave, can you possibly think that's funny?"

"You might as well inject a little humor into it all, don't you think?" He chuckled again; for him, this was a wonderfully satisfying day, his total happiness was impenetrable.

The making of the mask involved breathing through straws—and was suffocating. This is insane for a person with sinus-breathing problems, was Molly's thought. *Insane,* she nearly screamed. *Very* nearly.

"What about side effects?" Feeling remarkably controlled, at the near-end of that long hospital waiting day, Molly asked this question of Dr. Donovan and Dr. Duveneck, the chief radiologist, and a bevy of lesser medical men, whose names she either confused or quite possibly was not told.

"Probably no effects whatsoever," said Bill Donovan.

"Sort of like coming down with the flu," said Dr. Duveneck.

Though they had spoken almost in unison, both those sentences came through quite clearly to Molly, firm and contradictory.

But the two doctors smiled at each other as though they had perfectly agreed.

"Almost nothing. Negligible," said Duveneck.

"The mildest flu." Donovan smiled.

And the younger doctors smiled too, agreeing with everything.

"But don't they know what they're doing?" Molly fumed. "How can they do anything so drastic as radiation to a person's head if they don't know what the effects will be?"

"They do know the effects. Very precisely," Dave assured her. "It's *side* effects you wanted to know about."

"But that's important too. I mean, does your hair fall out, do you throw up a lot?"

"I think you're confusing chemo and radiation."

"Maybe. But I still would think they'd know more. There's a big difference between 'nothing at all' and flu."

Dave conceded. "That's true. But it may vary a lot among patients."

"And doctors have never had it themselves, right? Christ, don't they ever ask patients how they feel, and listen to what they say?"

"You are the most irrational girl—woman! Lord! laypeople—"

"You're the one who said I'd go blind or lose my teeth if they got it wrong!"

"They're not going to get it wrong. You're getting the best possible, state-of-the-art medical care. I've seen to that. You don't appreciate—"

Dave never finished that sentence, at that time or later, ever; he never actually said, You don't appreciate me. But that was a continual subtext, and of course he was right; Molly did not appreciate him, nor what he had done for her. From whatever motives—and whose are ever pure? He had gone and he continued to go to enormous trouble for her. He had taken her to the surgeon who had managed to "get it all," very likely had saved her life. Could another surgeon have done the same? This of course was something that Molly would never know. And she tended to focus on the impurity of Dave's motives rather than the results of what he had actually done. She concentrated on his needs to control her, and to *be* with her, as well as his busy joy in a medical setting—and she thought much less of the fact that she was *okay.* She was well, or she would be well, once she got over the effects of radiation—whatever those effects were to be.

She would not even sleep with him. "You keep me awake," she accused. "And I don't feel great yet—I really need to sleep." She added, "I need all my strength for this fucking radiation."

"Your language!" He scowled, but could not deny the logic of what she said, and so he slept on the studio couch in her study-guest room.

Molly dreamed of Paul, in this strange post-op, pre-radiation period, as she had not done since his death, when she used to wish that even in a dream she could see him again. But these were not good dreams; the Paul in these dreams was cruelly reckless, unkind, and aloof—a man whom, although she recognized him as Paul (he could be like that), she had not remembered until he showed up in her dreams.

She thought of the night when he had come to her in the hospital, and she had kissed him, so passionately, but then he turned out to be not Paul at all; he was Matthew, the boring twin.

THIRTEEN

"Really, though, why did we ever marry doctors—don't you wonder?" Jane Stinger, wife of Dr. Mark, asked this not rhetorical question of Connie (Knowles) Sanderson, wife of Raleigh, over lunch at a health food restaurant out on Clement Street, in San Francisco. Both recovering alcoholics, the two women first met in a Sausalito AA meeting. The fact that both were married to doctors seemed one more linking coincidence. Also, it turned out that the same reasoning had led them both to this Sausalito meeting, rather than one in San Francisco: as prominent doctors' wives—or, rather, wives of prominent doctors—they did not want to run into people they knew. Who knew them. They had not met each other before, although they might have done so at doctors' cocktail parties, or some volunteer wives' group. But both Connie and Jane had more or less dropped themselves out of all that. Too, since Jane and Mark were some fifteen or so years younger than the Sandersons, their circles did not quite coincide. Mark's being Jewish would also have made a difference, *still,* in those doctor groups.

But in AA circles the two women had become strong friends; as they themselves would have said, they were supportive and caring of and for each other. And, having begun with the intense and intimate revelations that were encouraged, the "sharing" at meetings, they had continued in that vein, on that level. Marriages, sexuality, children, drugs, politics, money—all that had at one time or another been viewed, and reviewed. And often laughed at; maybe the best of all was that each woman found the other reliably amusing. The very Bostonian Connie and Irish (from Queens) Jane McBride Stinger.

Certainly they could not have looked less alike, but perhaps that very dissimilarity formed another bond, as did the fact that each had basically disliked her own looks, her "type." Jane was small and dark, pretty and voluptuous. Years back, on Mark's insistence, she had had her nose "done." She now felt that it had been overdone; it was very small and turned up, piquant. "My mother says I look like a typical mick—her phrase—and for once she's right. But Mark said early on that since noses were right up there, up front, and his specialty, he couldn't be married to one like mine. Big joke. He also said why did he have to marry a mick with a big Jewish nose? Well, that's his problem. And now with more self-esteem I'd like my old nose back! It was more me. Well, of course it was."

Connie was tall and straight and now, without booze, almost thin again. Her hair was vague, flimsy. Gray-blond. Her eyes large and dark gray-blue. Dry-skinned, tending to lines, but her skin too had improved from no drinks. Her nose (unfixed, though Raleigh too had made that suggestion) was long and finely modeled, somewhat overshadowing her small but sexy, plumpish mouth.

Although this was familiar ground, Why doctors? she answered Jane's question anyway, more or less. "For one thing it was something we did, back then," she said. "Marrying interns from Mass. General." By "we" she meant Boston girls who came out the same year she did, or thereabouts. Interns had been very popular at those forties and fifties deb parties, the first lavish "real" big parties since the war. And though some of those interns came from what the girls' mothers would have termed "no background," to the younger women they seemed genuinely more exciting and more adult than the Boston-Milton-Harvard boys they already knew. And medicine seemed a much more interesting direction than banking or manufacturing or Boston real estate. Just as, to the doctors from no background, the debs with their family houses on Chestnut Street or Brattle, in Cambridge, their summer places in Beverly or Ipswich—those girls, with their long blond hair and good white teeth and sailing tans looked both glamorous (though many were very flat-chested, but you can't have everything, reasoned the doctors) and substantial. Perfect raw material for doctors' wives, for mothers of doctors' children (and a bunch of children might help in the breast department, they thought).

Since Jane was not from Boston, there was no point in Connie's explaining all that, for the moment. Instead she said, in her confessional, sharing voice, "I thought Sandy was so terrifically sexy. You might say I married for sex."

Jane laughed. "Me too, in a way. I thought Mark was so good-looking. Funny, it's supposed to be men who marry for sex and good looks."

"Oh, but they don't really, do they?" asked Connie. Then, responding to her own question: "Or young men don't. Certainly not ambitious young doctors."

"Right. Those trophy wives must be for second or third tries, probably. First they get success, then sex."

"Actually, Sandy married me for all the things I was trying to shake off," said Connie. "My parents, all those big lavish lonely houses. The heavy silver." She sighed.

"Is this just doctors or most men, do you think?" Jane mused.

"What I think is," Connie pronounced, "doctors *are* most men, only worse. Well, that's not fair, and it sounds awful," she corrected. "I only mean they're more focused than most men are. Eyes ahead. Not much peripheral vision."

Jane agreed, "They sure are focused. Mark, honestly, he used to make these lists, this stuff for me to do. God, I gave up nursing for that? And then he'd check things off. He didn't like it a lot when I'd gone out for lunch instead. And got plastered. He didn't even know about the other stuff."

By "other stuff" Jane meant a lot of dope, and many, many lines of coke. Not to mention some LSD. And occasionally sex with various men who were doing those things too. She had "shared" all that recent history at meetings, so that by now she was able to allude to "stuff." At the meeting she was encouraged to go and have some tests, which she did, and she came out all right, HIV negative, and no other bad signs. Her sponsor urged her to confess everything to Mark, to confront him with it, but Jane was able to argue reasonably, "Look, I'm probably going to dump him—I'm really working on that with my therapist too. I can't afford to give him any more ammunition. Let him just think of me as a simple alcoholic. His mother was right about what happened if he married an Irish shiksa."

Those were Jane's vices, drink and drugs and fairly promiscuous sex, all of which she had now stopped doing. Mark's vice, or one of them, was gossiping to Jane, things he should not have told her—names, illnesses, everything. This had begun fairly innocently when Jane was one of the nurses who knew those cases too. But he had gone on talking—boasting, sometimes. Thus, Jane knew all about his patient Molly Bonner, the friend of Felicia Flood, whom good old Sandy was in love with, or fucking—however one wanted to put it. So far, Jane had not told her friend Connie of this interesting gossip, and not telling was beginning to make Jane uncomfortable; it seemed a form of deceit. Although Connie pretty much knew about Felicia—good old Raleigh had seen to that.

At the moment, Connie was continuing her doctor theories, a topic she often attacked with gusto, like a long-hungry person at breakfast. "And in a way doctors are our earliest experience of sex," she went on. "Examining you in all those forbidden places. I remember I had a big childhood crush on Dr. Wainwright, my pediatrician. He was Jewish, but he'd been at Harvard with my father. No final clubs of course. He was what they horribly called a 'white Jew.' Can you imagine?"

"Too easily," said Jane. "Mark was probably a white Jew too."

"I should have married a Jewish doctor," Connie mused. "There was one I really liked. Bob Weinberger. But I wouldn't have dared. Someone from Cedar Falls, Iowa, was bad enough."

In Cedar Falls, on their last trip there, as she looked into their room in the Bed and Breakfast that had been enthusiastically chosen by Raleigh's mother (Belle Sanderson, from Raleigh, North Carolina), what Connie thought was, Damn him, he's told his mother that we're in trouble, marriage-wise, and she's trying to fix things up with this horrible room.

For the room was indeed described as The Anniversary Waltz Suite. A pink-and-white room, with occasional touches of gold. White wicker chairs, settee, lamp stands, and magazine rack (Connie had to guess at some of these functions), and white wicker headboard for the giant-sized bed. Which was overlaid with a rose-and-gold counterpane. And above that fancy headboard, an even fancier arrangement of white net that was coyly held in place by some life-sized or larger plaster doves. (White plaster doves, thought Connie.) The windows were treated with more white net, and white lace, and rose-colored draperies.

In a large alcove, framed by yet more swatches of white lace, again held in place by white plaster doves, an oversized, round bathtub took up all the space. A Jacuzzi, actually; there were directions for controlling its flow. A Jacuzzi for two.

"Holy shit," was what Raleigh-Sandy said, on viewing this stage set. "Where's the phone?"

"Over there." Connie had spotted a white princess (of course a white princess) telephone in a nest of pink roses.

"Do you think it works?"

"I certainly hope so." For once, on this particular weekend, Connie was as concerned with a functioning phone as Raleigh was; she was expecting news of her (well, *their*) new grandchild. While he only wanted to hear from some nurse, or maybe that fat blonde secretary, Felicia Flood, whom he should be tiring of about now, although he did not seem to do so.

Raleigh strode over and pulled the instrument from its bed of roses, picked up the receiver. "Doesn't make a fucking sound. Fucking thing's dead."

"Maybe that's why it's buried in roses." Connie forced a laugh.

"Very funny. Just because you don't need the phone—"

"Actually I do. Katie's very pregnant, remember?"

"As if I could—oh, fuck. I'm going downstairs to check it out."

He stalked out. She could hear him heavily on the stair, and then his voice, not words by the angry sound. When Raleigh was angriest he spoke most slowly, pretending patience and control. But at any moment he might give in and shout.

In the meantime Connie unpacked for them both.

In addition to the Jacuzzi there was a perfectly straightforward bathroom, Connie noted with relief. A shower (single), a double basin, and toiletry shelves. She was tidily arranging things, his shaving equipment, her pale-green Clinique jars, when Raleigh with all his noise returned.

"You're not going to believe this, Jesus Christ! She thought we might want a private line—now there's good thinking—but it can't be installed until tomorrow. In the meantime, in effect, we have no phone."

He stared at Connie as though she had had some part in this outrage.

Intending helpfulness, she asked him, "Couldn't you call in to your office, on her phone?"

"How brilliant of you. Yes, I plan to, in an hour." He looked at his watch. "God in heaven. I told her that I'm a doctor, which she must have known—Mom wouldn't pass up that chance—but I meant that I had to have a phone. But, she told me all about her daughter's ulcerative colitis! Holy shit! Colitis. No wonder I left home. How does old Durham stand it here, that's what I want to know."

It was a trip that began by being bad, and got worse. The men who came from the phone company to connect the phone were unable to do so. When Connie at last reached Katie, their daughter, from the manager's phone, Katie said that her doctor had said it might be another week. Raleigh fumed, and went out to make phone calls. And it rained, a mean bleak cold rain, with angry spurts of wind—as Connie trudged along unfamiliar streets, in search of the local AA meeting.

She was thinking bitterly of the romantic echoes set off in her silly young mind by the name Cedar Falls when Raleigh had first pronounced it. She was thinking too, No wonder he's sometimes mean, his native weather is vicious.

Even from some distance she could see that a large note, a message, was tacked to the church's downstairs door. And she knew more or less what it would say: No meeting here today. Sorry.

Connie's soul shrank, like something left out in the rain and cold overnight. She felt herself shrivel as her mind contracted into one single thought: I will have to have a drink. Just one perfect martini—well, maybe a double, in a nice clean sparkling glass. One perfectly chilled double martini, in a dim-lit, warm, and welcoming morning bar (there used to be many such bars in Boston, if you went out to the right neighborhoods; Connie acquired a special wardrobe for those bar days, cheap, friendly, inconspicuous clothes, in which she looked like a nice old middle-class drunk, who was running to fat). She could see herself now in such a place, rescued from the awful cold and rain, shrugging off her Burberry, and taking that magic first sip.

She headed fast from the church over to the tacky, two-story main street, where she passed no bars, nor for that matter any bookstores—none at all. She walked and walked and walked, until suddenly before her was the B and B where they were staying, and then, cold and dazed, she was back in the white dove suite, feeling more defeated than triumphant; after all, she had not exactly decided not to have a drink, she just had not found one, and she was not quite able to believe that any Higher Power had prevented her from coming upon a bar.

Raleigh's mother was sick that weekend, too sick to see anyone but her son the doctor. "I just feel so terrible, and then there's all this rain, and you all came all the way out here to see me," said Belle (Bates) Sanderson, formerly of Raleigh, North Carolina.

But then the next day the skies all cleared, and the sun shone, brilliant if not warm, and Connie walked, and walked, and walked all over the semi-familiar ugly little town. Its shabby, general charmlessness was occasionally broken by a graceful, broad-porched Victorian, with spreading roofs and low-branched leafy trees. The people that Connie passed, those also out walking, seemed fatter and unhappier than most people—than people in California, certainly. She felt a wave of compassion, then, for poor Raleigh, growing up in this stunted town. No wonder he was dazzled by Boston, even by her.

"I think Raleigh and I were exotic to each other," Connie told Jane Stinger, continuing her theme. "It's funny, but we were. I was actually the most boring, conventional Boston girl you could imagine, but he'd never met one before. And all that stuff that bored me silly, the deb things, the teas and dances and breakfast parties, turned him on. I think he thought the Ritz Bar was really glamorous, and the Napoleon Club, and Lafayette—all those tired old places. And he certainly turned me on, he was really sexy, and not afraid of girls like those ultra-nice Boston boys from St. Paul's or St. Mark's. Maybe all Midwestern high school boys are like that, but I didn't know any."

Jane sighed. "Mark certainly wasn't afraid of girls. He was sort of contemptuous, actually. There was always this underlying attitude: it's only a body, what's such a big deal about touching it?" She sighed again. "Sometimes I think I just liked him because he's bossy and mean. Like Dad. Like I was used to. I was addicted to mean."

"Oh, me too."

"Plus the class thing about doctors. I know it's a joke—my son the doctor, all that—but it's really strong. Our mothers really wanted doctors for sons, and sons-in-law."

"How about girls?" asked Connie. "They're encouraged to go to med school?"

Jane hesitated. "I don't know, I'm really not sure about that. In my day we weren't especially."

"God knows we weren't in mine." And then quite suddenly Connie laughed. "The other day I thought of something funny. Years ago when the children were in kindergarten and I was driving a car pool, there were two little boys who drove me absolutely crazy with bathroom jokes. You know, all that poopoo-doodoo stuff. Every day, on and on. Gary Solomon and Eric Winston. And those are the two boys out of that car pool who went to med school—by now they're doctors. Interesting, don't you think?"

"Very. I've always thought doctors were sort of hung up that way. Honestly, some of the jokes they think are really funny. They might as well be four-year-olds."

A pause, while both women munched on vegetables, sampled the bread, agreeing that it was good, all very good. And then Connie asked the question that had been in her mind for some time, as they went back and forth on this general topic of doctors. "Are you really going to do it?" she asked. "Do you think? Leave Mark?"

Jane hesitated. Then, "Yes," she told her friend. "But it may take longer than I thought. I don't think things are going too well with him right now. A doctor he really respects—Douglas Macklin, do you know him?"

"A little."

"Anyway, Macklin is really ticked off. He thought Mark goofed badly over a case, someone he'd referred. They've been arguing over the phone at night. Macklin says Mark should have paid more attention to an MRI, and of course he could be right. Mark sounds very defensive about it. This woman whose sinusitis turned out to be an ugly tumor. Malignant." Jane paused, then looked directly at Connie. "Actually, it was that Molly—"

"Oh, the friend of Felicia."

"Right."

There was a pause, during which both women pondered the bad luck of Molly, whom neither of them knew; they had only heard of her as the friend of Felicia Flood, whom they did not actually know either.

"And there's something bad with a Dr. Tanamini," Jane continued. "This Japanese woman Mark really likes. He really respects her, he says. He means as a doctor but someone else told me she's beautiful. But she seems to be mad at him too."

"I think there's something bad with Felicia and Raleigh too," Connie contributed. "He's acting so crazy. Angry. He just stares around, in this furious way. And at night he sometimes goes out and then he comes back in a very short time. I mean half an hour or so. Not like the old days when he had all these so-called emergencies at the hospital—of course some of them actually were. I guess. But these days he could hardly do more than drive around the block a couple of times."

FOURTEEN

Alta Linda. Gradually all Molly's doctors, including Dave, began to mention this name, in a hushed and reverential way. A hospital and treatment center where a rare and special, cutting-edge form of radiation was available. "Particle therapy." Much stronger and more accurate than radiation. Alta Linda was somewhere in Southern California, not far from L.A.; this treatment was available there, and in only two other centers in the whole country, one in Boston, the other in Minnesota.

At first all this talk seemed to Molly simply part of the background noise of doctors' conversations; they liked to exchange news of breakthrough treatments. But then very slowly she began to understand that what was actually being discussed was the possibility of *her* going there. For treatment. Particle therapy. Two weeks at Alta Linda.

"No," she said, having finally grasped what they meant. *"No.* I hate Southern California."

"But—"

"And how can I need any more radiation? After six weeks here."

"How can you take a chance on something so important?" Dave countered.

"But there's at least a chance I didn't need it at all. If Donovan really got it all."

"You did have to have radiation." Dave spoke with more force than logic, Molly felt: everyone had radiation after cancer surgery, and so she must have it too. Just in case some tiny grain—or rather, cell—of the great green golf ball lingered on.

He added, "And particle therapy—these machines they have—do you know they cost fifty million dollars? Fifty million. At this point it's mostly used for prostate cancers."

"Oh, of course. A fifty-million-dollar machine? Prostates, of course. Not breasts."

"Is that supposed to be some feminist joke?"

"Not particularly."

Actually, the very contemplation of a fifty-million-dollar machine exhausted Molly, and she was sure that she did not deserve, or require, such treatment.

But: " . . . fewer side effects—doesn't penetrate the brain stem," Dave was saying.

"I'd rather go to Boston."

"That's too far, I couldn't commute to Boston." He added, "We'll have to go down one day early so they can measure you for a mask."

"No. I can't do that again."

"You don't know how lucky you are," Dave muttered. He could have added, "to have me," but he did not.

In a thick gray wet winter fog, they drove down Highway 5, California's central artery, the direct and efficient north–south route, for the most part straight and flat, undifferentiated, without the distraction of "scenery" or views or, for that matter, of population, houses, towns. "You see?" remarked Dave. "How fast it is? And this is not exactly weather for the coast."

"I guess not," Molly murmured weakly. She had put up a feeble fight for the coastal route, and now she (still) thought that even in the fog it would somehow be beautiful, there would still be something to see. Besides, why hurry to Alta Linda? She saw no cause to rush. The small amount of packing required by this trip had taken all her strength. In the car, as Dave drove fast and relentlessly, she lay back against the seat, her eyes closed. Dave was right: she could not have seen the view, even had there been one. The fog seemed to exist inside her head, as well as all over the landscape.

Six weeks of radiation at Mt. Watson, or something, had left her with no strength. The basic problem was nausea, not the sort of nausea that makes you actively ill (such a relief if she could be, Molly thought; if it were a question of throwing up, it might be over with sometime), but rather a steady low-grade dizziness in her stomach, so that eating or just drinking soup, or milk, or even water had become nearly impossible tasks. This condition seemed to have settled in; she could not remember a former or imagine a future self who liked to eat. Just getting out of bed had become a terrific chore; packing, thinking of what to take and putting it into a suitcase had been a terrible strain. She had not been able to concentrate, and now, as they drove, she could not remember putting in her toothbrush—any toothbrushes. Of all things to have forgotten.

That day of blank gray driving seemed to last forever—until Dave announced that they were almost there. As things turned out, they were not: there was another hour or so of a highway, off the freeway, an endless area of used-car lots, garages, cheap motels.

They were to stay in the hotel advertised as being closest to the hospital, a Hilton, which, after some confusion back and forth on this highway from hell, Dave managed to find.

Twin beds (a welcome surprise). Molly fell onto one of them, the one closest to the window. "I forgot my toothbrush," she said just before falling asleep.

"I'll get you another."

"Get two! Please."

"I'm going over to the hospital. Don't worry if I'm not back right away."

Molly woke from a small unhelpful nap, happy to find herself still alone. For a moment she crazily thought, If I just moved to another room, and used another name, could Dave still find me? I don't need any more radiation.

Instead, she dialed Felicia, who asked her, "What's it like there?"

Molly considered, looking around. "Well, just outside my window there're some palms, sort of scruffy, and there's a big black sign that says SUNDAY CHAMPAGNE BRUNCH, ALL YOU CAN EAT $18.95."

"Oh. What an odd number."

"Isn't it."

But then Dave's key turned in the lock, and there he was. "I don't know why they gave us twin beds," he said. "I told them—"

"I'll call you later," Molly said to Felicia.

The hospital was a huge spread of arched and ivy-covered bright new stone, invitingly disguised as a motel. There was even a tall thin black man with a top hat out in front, greeting people, directing traffic. But once inside, in those greenish antiseptic-smelling corridors, anyone could tell that this could only be what it was—a hospital, and mostly for the severely ill.

There seemed a great many middle- to late-middle-aged men in hospital robes, in wheelchairs, or dressed in street clothes and asking directions at some desk, or standing in line. "Prostate patients," Dave whispered too loudly. "I hope that's something I can escape. The statistics on impotence—"

The main business of this hospital, the radiation-particle-proton therapy (all romantically subsumed under IMAGING), went on in the lower floor. In the basement, underground. Appropriately, Molly thought: a medical hell. Dangerous machines that cost fifty million dollars.

But before they went down to all that: "First I want to show you some of the rooms," Dave told her, pushing UP. "They're really nice."

"Why? I don't have to stay here."

What Dave found nice was the fact that the rooms were all two-person suites. "That way all patients get better care," he chattered. "Less work for the nurses, see? Nice big shared bathrooms."

" 'Shared,' how horrible."

"Jesus, Molly."

"Shouldn't we go down for my appointment?"

"You're right, it's just time."

As they whooshed down in the elevator, Molly thought as she had before that Dave was much less compulsive than she about times of appointments, as though in some sense he felt himself in charge. Which God knows she did not.

The treatment room was larger and brighter than those for radiation at Mt. Watson, otherwise very similar: a white gurney-table, below the bright and infinitely complex machinery. Several technicians, low-key, friendly, and helpful.

And the treatment took the same amount of time. *Flick.* A fraction of a second.

"I don't feel any different," Molly told Dave, back in their Hilton room.

"You're not supposed to."

"Neither of us ever knows when the other one is kidding, do we. That's not a good sign."

"Oh Molly, for God's sake, let up."

If anything, she felt slightly worse in Alta Linda. A more pervasive nausea, an inability to eat that was almost absolute. Bathing, she regarded her naked white body, which seemed to jut sharp bones.

.   .   .

Dave's elderly, invalid mother lived in Long Beach, with one of her daughters, Dave's sister; Molly gathered that they did not get on and that Dave worried about this household. He felt that he should go to see them. "But I don't see how I can leave you like this," he said to Molly. "You're not really trying to eat."

"Yes I am. And I'll eat just as much if you're in Long Beach. Or as little."

"I doubt that."

"Please. You're just adding guilt to my other problems."

"Maybe a feeding tube," he mused.

"NO."

"If you can't eat we'll have to do something."

The something that eventually was done was to put Molly into the Alta Linda Hospital, into one of those two-person suites, with bathroom, that Dave had so admired (had he even then been making this plan? Molly later suspected that he had). At the time she even agreed; she was so weakened, so demoralized by weakness, that she had no choice, she felt. And, somewhere in her enfeebled consciousness she had a dim sense that getting Dave away to Long Beach—getting herself away from Dave—would be an improvement. A step.

But that was not immediately true. The doctor in whose charge she had been left, Dr. Shepherd, was almost never there, and his brief appearances seemed hurried; he sounded harassed. He asked her, "How long have you had this anorexia?"

"I don't have anorexia—it's from radiation. Nausea."

"Well—" His tone implied that one eating disorder was the same as any other. "Dr. Jacobs suggested a feeding tube," he told her. "We could put it in right there—" He gestured at her stomach.

"NO."

Startled—such a weak woman and so defiant, still—he hurried out.

"My mother isn't doing very well," Dave told her, on the

phone. "And Rachel, they just don't get on. It's pretty much of a mess—it may take me a couple of days to sort it out. You'll be okay."

"Sure. I'm really much better," Molly lied.

"Great. I talked to Shepherd—he thought you were doing really well."

He never looks at me, Molly did not say. He must have me confused with some other patient, some recovering anorexic.

"This is the worst place I've ever been," she whispered to Felicia, over the phone. "You wouldn't believe. Last night I rang for a sleeping pill, I really needed one, and I got it three hours later. I had a roommate, this very old Filipino lady, but they took her somewhere else. Or maybe she died. My doctor would like to get rid of me. If I'd just eat a couple of meals and go away, he thinks. This place reminds me of a women's prison in some movie from the thirties."

Nurses, or maids, orderlies—someone kept turning the TV on, so that despite herself Molly watched wars, bombings, artillery attacks, tanks in deserts, and natural attacks of ferocious weather, floodings and tornadoes, freezings, earthquakes and fires. At some point a doctor muttered in her direction, "Sometimes I think I hate Arabs."

She whispered back, "Sometimes I hate doctors."

Dave called and she told him, "I really think I'd be better off in the hotel. This hospital food, and the television—I can't sleep." She knew that she must not say, I hate it here, it's horrible.

"How would you get back to the hospital for your treatments?"

"Taxis! They're all over!" Molly had not in fact seen a taxi in the area, but at this point there was no lie that she would not have told.

"I'll talk to Shepherd."

Then suddenly, in a bursting open of her doors, the next afternoon, good fortune arrived in the person of Felicia, windblown and tanned, with her ravishing smile, fair hair a beautiful tangle. She was laughing, out of breath. "God, you're right! What a terrible place! I had to ask all these directions and everyone tried to lose me." She laughed again. "Even the hills down here are hideous! Southern California!"

They stared at each other, and then Molly laughed too. "You've come to rescue me!—or at least take me back to the horrible Hilton."

"Sure! And I'll do it in style! I've got my father's new Lexus, they're in Jamaica."

Dave had in fact called Dr. Shepherd, who, with more alacrity than Molly had so far seen, signed her out. "Lucky for you your friend showed up to take you," he remarked. "There are no cabs. But maybe you noticed."

"No, I didn't."

Half an hour later, standing in the middle of Molly's hotel room, Felicia stated, "This is one of the most depressing rooms I ever saw. Even the view. Such ugly hills, and that billboard." And then she asked, "Don't you want to sort of unpack?"

After a moment, and to her own surprise, Molly answered, "No," and she began to smile—which felt unfamiliar, as though she had not used just those facial muscles in weeks. She said, "You know, there's really no reason to stay here? I could just check out, and you could take me home?"

"But—" But Felicia was smiling too, not really making an objection. "But why not!" she then said. "Great!"

"Could we possibly drive up the coast, do you think?"

"Sure. Highway Five is really deadly."

"I *know.*"

At the coast the fog had lifted, and there, below the furrowed, dangerous cliffs was the roiling, fierce bright sea, all brilliant greens and blues—wild free water. Molly, dozing since they had left the hotel, since Alta Linda, came wide awake, exhilarated, and very slightly afraid.

She said, "Of course there's no reason for me to have any more radiation." She knew that she was talking to herself; metaphorically, she was whistling. "After all, I had six weeks of it at Mount Watson, and another week here."

"Seems like a lot. I wonder if we'll see any whales—this is the season for them."

"It's so beautiful," Molly breathed. And then, "Dave will be totally furious."

"Let him be furious. He's an angry person. And he left you alone in that ghastly place. Really, was seeing his mother all that important?"

"Well, it was, but it's also been going on like that for years." Molly suddenly laughed. "He's probably back in the hotel by now. Big surprise." (It turned out later that this was exactly the case: Dave came back earlier than he had said he would: "I left my *mother,* just to take care of *you.*")

"Big surprise for him."

They both giggled like high school girls, there in the fresh clean salt air, sun-streaked, smelling of sea.

But in addition to the childishness, that foolish triumph, even more strongly Molly felt a clear and adult certainty: she had taken charge of her own life, she had listened to her own clear inner voice. She had freed herself, at least temporarily, from the ruling tyrants, from Dave, from doctors.

From hell.

FIFTEEN

"Childish! Irresponsible! I don't see how a woman of your age and general intelligence could be so—" Dave's tirade went on and on—with occasional lulls, small pauses for meals and other necessary business—for several days.

According to him, Molly had greatly inconvenienced, and *alarmed,* everyone at Alta Linda Hospital, and almost everyone at the Alta Linda Hilton, never mind that she had checked out, given credit cards, all that. She had not said exactly where she was going. She had, as he said, alarmed the hospital and the hotel—*not to mention* what she had done to Dave himself, and his mother, who was much too old for such shocking surprises. And his sister. Also old.

Although Molly was not feeling very well, she made what seemed to her quite logical responses: only for one night had anyone not known her whereabouts, the night when on the way home (driving up the gorgeous, glorious coast!), she and Felicia had stopped off at the Mission Inn, in Carmel. Which was hardly hiding out. Both the hotel and the hospital had her home address; why did they need to know where she was the next day? Why did Dave's mother need to know anything at all, or his sister?

She might as well not have spoken. Dave, never a good listener, on this occasion chose not to hear or to acknowledge a word she had said. Were all or most or many doctors poor listeners? Molly and Felicia had discussed this question, and had only, fairly, decided that both Dave and Sandy listened poorly, if at all. However, the same could even be said of nice Dr. Macklin, and certainly of Dr. Gold, the dentist. Dr. Shapiro listened, but then that is what he did: shrinks listened.

". . . as well as danger to yourself. Possible recurrence . . . best possible medical opinion . . . fifty-million-dollar machine, perfectly aimed and accurate . . . take advantage . . . never expected any thanks . . . danger to the brain stem . . . don't know how lucky you are . . ." Even his strong teeth looked menacing, and his shining head.

But I only left a few days early, I'd already had a lot of their perfect radiation. Molly did not even bother to say this—again. Nor did she really listen to whatever he was saying. Perhaps from him she had learned (in which case she should indeed be grateful) to tune him out, so that his words had no meaning, and the sound of his angry voice as he paced her bedroom barely grazed her tired consciousness. She stroked the sleek purring black cat by her side and she wondered, How could anyone possibly not like cats? Caesar, Napoleon, Hitler—Dave. Well, it figures, she thought.

At other times, though, she felt that he was probably right, and that she was in fact irresponsible, a causer of trouble. Ungrateful, as her parents had more than once pointed out. And in church, the General Confession: ". . . done those things which we ought not to have done, and left undone those things which we ought to have done, and there is no health in us." The Confession resounded in her mind, especially that last: no health in us. For, as though in punishment for her flight, her misdeeds, she felt worse and worse. Barely sustained by vitamin pills and chicken soup (Felicia's, homemade), she was not getting appreciably stronger, or better, so far. She lay weakly in bed. She slept fitfully, poorly, plagued by bad dreams.

"My mother's worse," Dave told her. "My sister. You can't live here alone. I wish you'd put that goddam cat down—he's probably feeding you germs."

But Dave's voice was beginning to fade out, even as he said, quite clearly: ". . . move in here? You don't have good sense. You have to be taken care of . . . get married?"

At this Molly came out of her fog to say very distinctly, "But we don't even like each other."

"Oh, don't be silly."

But sometimes, and for increasing lengths of time, she felt all right. She could bathe and dress and walk around in her living room, admiring that bright spectacular view, the bay and the melodramatic bridge, all that water—or from her bedroom she could look out onto her deck and think of more flowers. Of going to a nursery, planning and choosing, even working a little in all that potted soil.

She was all right being up for a while, but then she had to get back into bed, or at least to lie down there. She felt that she was magnetized by her bed, in love with it; going to bed was her true and only aim in life these days.

Felicia said, "Sandy must be stalking me, I know it. I couldn't just happen to see him as much as I do. But who could I complain to? He'd deny it, and as he knows, he's perfectly safe. I'd sound such a fool if I went to the cops about Dr. Raleigh Sanderson. They probably even know who he is. Oh, this is interesting: I also saw Connie the other day. Remember Connie, the fat Boston drunken wife?—the perfect excuse for Sandy, and for me? Well, I knew who she was, somehow, but so thin, I couldn't believe it. I have to say, she really looks good. A lot better than he does, actually."

"Where'd you see her?"

"At the Cal-Mart, down an aisle, so we weren't exactly confronted with each other. But I'm sure she recognized me too. Anyway, she looks great. Do you have to be an alcoholic to join AA? I thought I might try."

Molly laughed. "I don't know—you could give it a whirl."

"Connie just looks like a very nice, not very happy woman. When I think how I used to bad-mouth her, so terrible. I guess I was just excusing myself. With a lot of loud talk, so I wouldn't hear any inner guilty voices. Well, I'd never do that again. Not that that's going to do poor Connie any good. Though I'm hardly the only one."

They were sitting in Molly's bedroom, Molly in bed, Felicia in the bedside chair. And Felicia's warm presence was cheering to Molly, no matter what she was talking about. Molly felt a little stronger, and the soup that Felicia had brought, this time a fish broth, was especially good. Molly actually was able to sip it with no effort—and for dessert there was a little pot of baked custard.

"And this really weird thing's been happening *again,*" Felicia continued, and she frowned in a concentrating way. "I told you: Someone comes into my garden at night, not always at the same time but every night—God, I've got to get a new gate put up back there, one that locks. Anyway, he comes in and he walks around a little, and then, then he takes a leak, he *pees*—honestly, that's what he must be doing. I can hear it. Sometimes I think it's sort of funny, but then I don't, and I'm scared."

"Sandy, do you still think?" But even as she said this it sounded unimaginable to Molly: Sandy, Dr. Raleigh Sanderson, performing such a personal, private act as urination out in the open air of someone's garden, late at night?

"Well, of course at first I thought it's got to be Sandy. But now I'm not so sure. It just doesn't seem like his kind of gesture. He's too much of a snob, if you see what I mean. He wouldn't do something so ordinary. So lowly."

They both laughed, and Molly choked a little on her soup.

"Just eat," Felicia told her. "Don't try to talk, just listen, and finish your soup."

"Yes'm."

"Sometimes I think it's some poor homeless person, and I should leave some food out for him. You know, some battered old guy who's made my garden part of his nightly rounds."

"Felicia, you'll end up feeding the world. One of those women who adopt about thirty children, and God knows how many dogs and cats."

"I'd like that. It'd be a lot better than getting married, I think."

"You could do both, you know. Get married *and* have children. People do."

They laughed as Felicia said, "Oh, you're so conventional. Anyway, with the men I seem to pick I'd better not. Will would probably teach them to shoot their way through kindergarten."

"Felicia, this is the best baked custard I ever had. Honestly. Beats my mother's all hollow."

"It's so great to see you eating. Honestly."

Somewhat later, after Felicia had gone, Molly's phone rang, and she answered. "Hello?"

"Hello. Molly? Molly, this is, uh, Henry Starck."

"Henry! Henry, how amazing. Where are you?"

"Well, I'm here. I mean I'm in San Francisco, at the, uh, Mark Hopkins." A tiny pause. "I hope you don't mind my calling?"

"Of course not! I'm so glad—"

Their somewhat perfunctory conversation took longer than one would think, and then Molly remembered that they had always brought out in each other this tendency toward an over-elaborate politeness; it was something they had in common. So that almost any exchange between them took forever, and got nowhere, really. This time it inevitably took quite a while for

Molly to explain with the delicacy they both required that she was more or less indisposed (how lucky, she thought, that she did not have some grossly indelicate illness—although any cancer, come to think of it, was fairly gross), and that she was more or less housebound. Recovering. And it took more time for them to agree that Henry would come to see her. That afternoon.

The first surprise with Henry was how very well he looked. Molly remembered him as pale and worried, a too-thin, old-young man. Only ten years older than she, he had looked and seemed much older ("a very good candidate for a father fix," Molly had told Dr. Shapiro, describing Henry and that marriage). But now—he had somehow dropped off years. He was heavier, almost sleek, with a healthy tan and filled-out cheeks. A more confident, weightier walk, and clearer eyes.

"Actually," he explained, in response to her more than polite exclamations of pleasure: how nice to see him looking so well, and so young! "Actually, I too am recovering. Things got a little hairy, in terms of booze—did anyone tell you I'd married again, and that didn't work out at all? Basically she was an alcoholic too." (The word had great emphasis: his alcoholism had never been stated between them before.) "But when things fell apart I was the one who went to AA, which turned out to be the best move I'd ever made. I'd been to a lot of doctors but they were no help at all."

Henry talked for quite a while about how much better he was, even recovering from so much anger at his parents, and come to think of it at everyone, including her, Molly, his former wife. Molly was aware that her attention wandered.

Her mind drifted here and there, quite idly. She wondered if she and Henry could marry again, now that he was so well, and she was almost well; would he like to get in bed with her right there and then, possibly? Not for sex, she knew that she was not up to anything so strenuous, just for lying there and touching. But maybe not. She wondered if she would ever see Dave again, and then she remembered that he had called that very morning and said that he might drop in later, just to see how she was doing, "even though I'm no longer on your case," he had added, with heavy irony. He had spoken to Dr. Shepherd—and others—at Alta Linda, had tried to explain her actions. How surprised Dave would be if she remarried Henry Starck.

Possibly to stop all this random drift, to bring herself back to Henry, there but distant in his visitor's bedside chair, Molly began to tell him what she had done—or to try to. "I ran out on some very special treatments," she told Henry. "Proton therapy? The machines down there at Alta Linda—a totally ghastly place, by the way—these machines cost fifty million dollars. Can you imagine? But I just couldn't stand it there, I really couldn't. I was getting sicker and sicker and they were talking about a feeding tube. 'Intubation'—isn't that a horrible word?"

"But you really just ran away from there?" Henry was smiling, and Molly remembered how pleased she used to be when she could amuse him.

"Well, a friend of mine, Felicia—you must meet her—she came to see me, and I drove back here with her. By the coast, so beautiful, absolutely ravishing—"

"Are you sure you didn't need to have those treatments, though?" Henry was now frowning slightly, a more familiar expression. His lawyer look.

"What I really think is that I never needed any of them," said Molly earnestly. "I'm quite sure terrible Dr. Donovan got it all. I don't know why, I'm just absolutely sure that he did. The whole goddam green golf ball—did I explain about that?"

"No, I don't think you did."

"Well—Henry dear, I keep falling asleep. Would you mind—could you come back?"

Instantly on his feet, "Very easily, in fact," said Henry. "What I didn't quite get around to telling you is that I'm moving out here." And with the lightest irony he added, "At last."

Once Henry was gone, for no imaginable reason Molly felt

much better, not sleepy at all, so much better that she thought, Why on earth am I lying here in bed? I'll never get well like this.

And so by the time Dave arrived—having dropped in, just as he threatened—Molly was up, freshly showered and dressed, and making a cup of tea for herself in the kitchen. She offered him some.

"I'll make it. Shouldn't you be in bed?" He was scowling.

"No, I'm spending too much time in bed, it can't be good for me. I was thinking I'd take a walk."

Dave's frown deepened. "I really don't think you're quite strong enough. Unless—let me go with you."

"Well, maybe I won't go. Probably you're right, I'm really not quite ready." She said, "So amazing, Henry—my first husband—came to see me." She added, "He says he's moving out here."

"Just to be near you? How nice."

"Oh, Dave, really."

Was Dave a little crazy? Molly wondered this as he scowled again, but then she thought, No, not crazy, just more than a little hostile, and especially to me. Is this only because I don't love him? Suppose I were wildly in love with him, would he hate me less, or more? She sighed, and wondered how Dave had actually felt about Martha, his wife, or—for that matter—about his mother or his sister.

After he had finally gone, she was indeed too exhausted for a walk.

Late that night, after Molly had been sound asleep for a while, her downstairs buzzer sounded, waking her up. Her watch said 2:22. No one would come to see her at that hour, of course not. Unless: Henry, seized with a longing for her? But he would not; he was not an impulsive person. More likely some passing drunk—and Molly thought then of whoever, whatever homeless person came nightly to Felicia's garden. Sandy? And could Sandy have rung at her door? At the sheer unlikeliness of this she tried to smile. But she was frightened, lying there alone in the dark, half waiting for her buzzer to sound again. It was a long time before she could go to sleep.

SIXTEEN

"... and nothing happened to me. I mean, there I was, lying next to this *blonde,* this bodacious babe, and very nice too. I could tell she was intelligent, and she was squirming around, she really liked me, she was ready, wanted to do it, but on my side, nothing. Limp as a dead mouse, and just about as interesting. The spirit was willing—willing hell, in my head I was raring to go, but nothing, Doctor, nothing. Not one stir. Tell me, Doctor, is it going to stay like this? Because if it is, I'm telling you, I'm heading right off the bridge, I mean it. So tell me, Dr. Sanderson."

"Well, as you know, the prostate's a little out of my line. I'm not at all an expert there—"

"Come on, you know more than I do about that stuff."

"Well, the prognosis is usually pretty good, especially these days. I don't have exact figures at hand. But since there was no malignancy—"

"Just tell me what usually happens. I mean, I expected some trouble with my wife, we've been pretty much out of the loop for a lot of years now, but when I met Licia I thought—"

"Licia? What an interesting name." Short for Felicia? Jesus Christ, would she? Fucking bitch.

"Short for Alicia, some silly Italian family nickname. But she's such a great girl. And she was so nice, you know, helpful, touching me there, and even with her mouth—"

"But aside from this problem, you're feeling generally okay? No chest pains, or dizziness?" Jesus Christ, the things patients expect you to listen to! Why did he have to hear about this man's goddam prostate? WHY? Just because this dumb jerk was originally his patient, came in for his annual checkup, and dumped all this prostate garbage right out on Sandy. As though he didn't have certain problems of his own. As though he didn't have, in fact, his own prostate to worry about.

"I feel fine," said the patient, Mr. Blank. "I just can't get it up."

It is like a bad joke: a doctor who has a known medical condition but who will not go to the appropriate specialist, a urologist, to have it checked out. Who is in fact afraid of possible surgery. Very funny. How Felicia would laugh if she knew. How Connie would laugh. (Although it is not true that either woman would laugh; they are both too kind. A woman will kill you with kindness, if you let her.)

"I can't get it up, and my life isn't worth living like this," said the patient, the bald stupid jerk, who should have been satisfied with his functioning mitral valve.

"Come on, man, of course it is. Sex isn't all that important," said Dr. Sanderson authoritatively as he stood to end the interview, and ran a self-assuaging finger through his own thick virile hair. He had just remembered that he had to go to a party that night with Connie. For AIDS, or some damn thing. He said, "I'll see you next year."

"Right. And thank you, Doctor, thank you very much."

For what? Sandy smiled, his large friendly farewell smile, and gave a parting wave. Asshole—who cares if he's impotent?

. . .

"What a handsome couple, you two! So handsome, looking so young, both of you, really fit. You've heard the old saw about couples getting to look alike? *Well.* What a handsome couple!" Sandy felt as though he had been hearing those words all night, an infernal chorus in this party from hell—or, rather, in hell—hell being a nine-million-dollar mansion on Pacific, full of doctors, his colleagues, and their wives. No visible or identifiable girlfriends, though of course these days some of the women were doctors too. Black tie and tickets at a thousand per, and word was out from the Medical Society that they had all better show their faces, and their dollars. And their wives. "Handsome couple": that is what all these people said to Sandy and Connie—meaning no evil, probably.

There were some guests who were not doctors, of course; not many doctors were willing to shell out a grand for a benefit, these days. And the first people Sandy saw—Sandy and Connie, that is—the first to say, "What a handsome couple," were (wouldn't you know?) a really handsome, younger couple, Josh and Susie Flood, parents of Felicia. Looking good themselves (but why shouldn't they?), looking very very good. Susie looked very young, in a way that such small fair women can; at a distance she looked about the age of Felicia. And very unlike Felicia, thank God—except that as she smiled just then, Sandy saw a shadow of Felicia's smile, some similar aligning of facial muscles around the mouth and at the corners of her eyes. He had no idea what if anything Susie knew about him—whether, that is, she had the least idea about him and her daughter. Felicia had never mentioned confiding in her mother or, for that matter, talking very much to Susie at all.

He watched as Susie and Connie greeted each other with those ridiculous social female air kisses. So hard to tell how women really feel about each other, what they think, what they know. Josh Flood was big and good-looking, in good shape but hair getting a little thin on top (something Sandy always noticed). His face a little too pink—blood pressure? He could be a candidate all right.

"You two look so terrific—handsome couple!" chorused Susie and Josh, with their big white smiles.

Twenty years ago, when open heart was still large news, greetings at such big parties were different—greetings to Sandy, that is. In those days it was you, you, singular you. *Sandy,* looking terrific. None of this "handsome couple" stuff. But back then, of course, Connie was fat and usually sloshed, standing erect but barely so, with a visible effort. Whereas Sandy himself was—well, what was he, actually, what that he is not now? He was trim and lively (still is!), a first-rate surgeon, and more than competent in the sack. The trouble was, these days there are too many guys around of whom the same things exactly could be said, too many young studs (let's face it, younger than he was), and God knows too many doctors. As bad as lawyers, almost, Sandy believes, although still a shade more honest. All doing open heart as a routine procedure, and transplants too. Nothing remarkable about a skillful surgeon now.

It's the world that has changed, Sandy concluded; he has not, and he glared around at the rich, familiar, but suddenly inimical party, the myriad smooth, well-tended, self-satisfied, intelligent (but rarely brilliant) faces. The snobbish, judgmental eyes, and careful mouths. He had then a moment of truly hating all those doctors, and their expensive wives.

If he had not been a doctor, he would have been a carpenter, something that Sandy has never told anyone, but it is the truth. For a year there, back in Cedar Falls, everything was going very badly for him. He was worried, terrifically worried, obsessed over acne and masturbation (surely linked?), chemistry and baseball. At that time he had one and only one comforting friend—God knows not his parents, or his shitheel older brother, Durham (Durham! his mother was nuts), now a successful broker in Davenport. Sandy's friend was an old retired guy named Alton Smith, who lived on a shack on the river, near the falls, and who used to be a carpenter. He still had a great set of tools; in fact, that was all he had. Alton's wife had died, and his house was wiped out when the river flooded, but he still had his tools, his saws and hammers and lathes, and all sorts of nails, many thousands of nails. And he had a lot of lumber scraps lying around, lengths of boards and pilings, some dragged in from the river, driftwood, nice colors. He would let Sandy knock stuff together, and talk about ideas for building things. Sandy made drawings of houses, but he never wanted to be an architect, as Alton suggested; he liked doing things with his hands, and that was what he did well.

Alton was short and fat, red-faced from booze and blood pressure, probably, and he wore outrageous clothes. Sandy never wanted to run into him in town, to be seen with Alton. (However had they met? Sandy could not remember.) But out there in the woods, by the river, Sandy had a wonderful time; he loved all Alton's stories of houses he'd built, his descriptions of special kinds of wood and how he'd come by them. Alton never mentioned his wife or anything about his personal life, and that was fine too. The last thing Sandy wanted was intimate revelation—which is still pretty much how he feels, come to think of it.

In a very quick but fully realized fantasy, then, Sandy imagined a whole other life for himself, the one he might have had if he'd stayed at home in Cedar Falls, and gone to school there and learned from Alton to be a master carpenter. In this life, he builds a big house for himself, for himself and his family, a broad spreading house along the riverbank, with flaring wings and graceful porches under the eaves. And his wife is large and blonde and generous, with ravishing jewel-blue eyes and an endless appetite for sex—with him. And some round blonde sexy-bottomed baby daughters, who all look like their mother—who is, of course, Felicia.

What actually happened was that after a year or so of knowing Alton, going to see him, Sandy's acne cleared up, he masturbated more and worried less. And he also began to have girls. A pretty new teacher gave him an A in chemistry, and he started playing tennis, instead of baseball. All of which led eventually to Harvard Med, and to Connie. And San Francisco, and a big house that Joe Esherick designed, on Green Street. And kids with big drug habits and little black children, living in Oakland. (How many kids does Genevieve have by now? Katie? He should know, and he doesn't dare ask Connie.)

At just that moment, as though to remind him, and as though he needed reminding, a black waiter with a tray of champagne glasses brushed past, as handsome as O.J., and as masked, almost no expression. Hey, *boy,* Sandy would like to say. Not so fast there, keep that up and you'll still fry.

Instead, he simply tapped the waiter's arm and very coldly, very politely took a glass of champagne from the tray.

He was drinking too much. Feeling the too-familiar pressure on his bladder, Sandy wondered, Has it been half an hour? Forty-five minutes? Oh, at least an hour, *please.* A perfectly normal interval between pisses, for a man of his age.

Emerging from the bathroom, Sandy saw a woman whom he thought he knew approaching, but no name came: small and dark, pretty, sort of sexy. Jewish? No, Irish. Some young doctor's wife, of course. Mt. Zion, probably. What in hell was her name? They'd talked at a party once, even flirted a little.

"Oh hello, you look wonderful, great to see you—see you later, don't let me keep you!" Smiling and laughing, they said these things to each other. And five minutes later Sandy remembered her name: Jane Stinger, she was married to that smart little ENT man, who was Jewish. Mark Stinger. Patients didn't like him, nurses either, Sandy had heard. He himself had never exactly taken to Stinger, Sandy realized; like most short men, Stinger was pushy, not very polite. You could say he didn't know his place. Sandy smiled to himself as he thought this—a forbidden thought, certainly not PC. He could not have said it to Connie—or Felicia, come to think of it.

And there he was, Mark Stinger himself, standing frowning and alone, no doubt waiting for his wife.

Sandy witnessed then a somewhat curious vignette.

Mark Stinger seemed to recognize someone, some friend, whom he was both glad and a little alarmed to see, and too surprised for the moment to hide either of those emotions. Next, Dr. Tanamini, Tara Tanamini, the beautiful Japanese radiologist, approached Stinger, who smiled quickly but seemed at the same time to motion her away. Tara Tanamini's yellowish skin in an instant went dark red, and it occurred to Sandy that he had never seen an Oriental person blush before. And Dr. Tanamini, her small nose uplifted, walked on, as though Stinger had not been there, after all.

In another minute Jane Stinger came out of the bathroom and walked toward her husband.

It all seemed oddly familiar to Sandy; too clearly he remembered the Stinger (male) role for himself: parties at which he had had to warn someone off from a too-warm greeting. Connie, though usually too drunk in those old days, would soon be along, from wherever. Including the night at a Black and White Ball soon after he had started up with Felicia, who was crazy about him then, and who, out of character for her, had drunk too much champagne and who was, as Connie later remarked, all over him when Connie came back from the can.

"That was just some secretary, a new one," he had said. "Miss Flood. She must think that's the way to get ahead. I guess she drinks too much."

"Well, isn't it, with you?"

"Jesus, Con—"

"You won't like it when I join AA."

"What on earth do you mean by that?"

"You just won't, and I'm going to. I'm sick of feeling like this." Sandy had not taken her seriously at the time, but actually as things turned out she had started going to all those meetings just about then—and what she had said was prescient: he didn't like it, it made her an unfamiliar person, no longer predictable. Although of course, as a physician, he had to admit that no drink was better for her.

". . . there's Jane, how great! I didn't know they'd be coming," Connie was saying as she headed over toward the Stingers.

"Have you seen?" was Jane's greeting. "The loveliest juice bar. Cranberry and tomato and everything." She frowned. "In addition to the booze."

Knowing that what he said would not go over well, Sandy was nevertheless compelled to say it: "I'm loyal to the grape myself. And this stuff is first-rate." He reached to a passing tray for more. "Join me, Mark?"

"Guess not. I'm going the Calistoga route these days."

Insufferable prig of a prick. Not to mention pussy-whipped. Sandy gulped at his champagne.

An hour or so later, after several more glasses of champagne and several more trips to the bathroom (a few of them urgent but finally unproductive), Sandy believed that he was not exactly drunk, but that something was monstrously wrong.

Wrong with his whole life. In that gold and marble room, all hung with yellow silk and green brocade, and stuffed with roses, roses, everywhere you looked, cramming the air with their heavy, heavy fragrance—in that room, in that here and now, Sandy was faced with the total failure of his life. The final unmasking, the puncture of his once-successful imposture as a worthwhile person. He was old and his plumbing was failing; he soon would be rendered impotent, probably. His wife had changed, unrecognizable, and he had lost the love of his life, the loveliest most generous Felicia, by his own stupid violent hand.

Doctors. He looked malevolently around the room, at all their faces, all swollen with self-importance and self-deception. They actually believed the old doctor myths, the brilliant science and saving of lives. Whereas, at best, they were all more or less like him, like Dr. Raleigh Sanderson, a very skillful mechanic, with very good instant (mechanical) judgment. He might have been a good carpenter too, although he was probably not creative enough to be the really terrific carpenter-contractor-architect that Alton Smith was.

In the bathroom, despite great feelings of pressure, nothing came. No drop.

SEVENTEEN

"I feel better than I think I should, if you see what I mean." Molly had not known this to be true until she said it to Dr. Shapiro.

"You think you should have been punished for running out on Alta Linda," he supplied, with his smile.

"Exactly. And in a way running out on Dave. I think especially Dave. I'll probably never hear from Alta Linda, but of course I'm hearing a lot from Dave. He's so punitive! But why can't I just tell him please to go away for good? Do you think I'm afraid of him, in a way? I guess I must be. He keeps using that horrible word, *recurrence,* and I guess I think that will be the form of my punishment. The great green golf ball will return."

Dr. Shapiro's smile had, again, the effect of making her darkest, most terrible fears seem implausible, farfetched.

Another good thing about talking to Shapiro, perhaps to any good shrink, was the fact that you didn't have to make sense; in fact, you were not even supposed to; a thing that Molly had to fight was a native, perhaps inborn tendency to want to be lucid, as well as entertaining, amusing, interesting. "I am not here for the enjoyment of Edgar Shapiro," she had frequently to remind herself early on in therapy. In the bad old days when she went in

and came out still weeping, lamenting the double loss of Paul—
his defection from the marriage, and then his death.

And so now with no explanatory transition she could illogi-
cally continue: "So odd, the better I feel the more I miss Paul.
Again."

"Maybe you think that he should be around to enjoy it with
you. Your improved health."

"Oh, I do think that. He should. God knows he wouldn't
have liked me sick—he couldn't stand any illness. But now that
I'm well—" To her astonishment, embarrassment, and extreme
annoyance, tears filled Molly's eyes, and choked off her voice.
"Oh shit, I'm so tired of crying. I'm tired of missing Paul, and
being sick, and I don't want to have this fucking golf ball in my
head anymore."

"The chances are very good that you don't have it anymore."

"Really? You think that? Dave of course doesn't."

Dr. Shapiro paused, considering; his opinions were never
rash nor impulsive. Also, Molly had a secret suspicion that he
found strictly medical issues a welcome change from his usual
nebulous run of problems. He said, "Yes, I do. You had a lot of
radiation at Mount Watson, and more at Alta Linda. Of course
it could happen, a recurrence. But I repeat, I think the chances
that it won't are very, very good." He smiled briefly. "And I
don't think you need more punishment. For anything."

"I always forget you're a doctor." Molly said this gratefully,
meaning: You're kind and intelligent and tactful—unlike most
of them. She had never explicitly stated these thoughts, but she
believed that he caught the affectionate drift.

The bookcase closest to the leather chair in which Molly sat
held fiction, alphabetically arranged. Nearest was F: Fitzgerald,
Flaubert, Max Frisch. Not many I's, and then J, mostly Henry
James. A lot of James, and then Joyce, those huge thick books.
Had Shapiro bought and read all those books, or was his wife
"the literary one"? It was the sort of question that there was no
good way to ask. Sometimes Molly admired the classic taste in-

volved in this collection of the great; at others it made her feel querulous: where are all the more personal, idiosyncratic choices? she wondered. The small private favorite books to which one returns, and returns? However, on closer inspection, as her attention meandered on to G, there were Mary Gaitskill, Mavis Gallant, Mrs. Gaspell, and Mary Gordon—all, as it happened, favorites of Molly's. But she chose not to mention that either.

She often thought that it was fortunate that this was not an orthodox analysis, in which the rules compelled her (at least theoretically) to tell him everything that crossed her mind—all stray and sometimes rude, often sexual and occasionally hostile thoughts that she had about him, about Dr. Edgar Shapiro, with whom she was confronted—and much better this way. Molly had also thought that she did not like the idea of an invisible doctor sitting in judgment near her head.

They had agreed to call what they were doing "psychotherapy by an analyst," and so, as Molly sat there and considered the possible size and shape and energy of his sexual member, she did not have to mention it, she thought. Nor for that matter did she have to tell him how beautiful Paul's cock was, the lovely skin on it, and veins. How she loved the feel and taste of it.

She only said, "I do miss Paul," as tears filled her eyes (again!) and she added, "I guess I'm not all that much better."

"I think you're doing very well," he said, in his quiet way.

She had thought a great deal too about his face, in the course of these visits. The sad, slightly slant brown eyes, long bony nose, and wide, very mobile mouth—on whose every flick of expression she concentrated, passionate to read. What did he think?

Now, not wanting to talk about Shapiro's face (nor anyone's genitals), Molly hurried along. She said, "There're times when I think my whole head is just permanently messed up. When I feel dizzy and nauseated. *Still.* And tired. And it's still hard to eat. If it weren't for Felicia I'd probably starve. You know, I think she should come to see you. Or someone, as a patient. That crazy Sandy, Dr. Sanderson, is stalking her, I know he is. She looks up and there he is, and she thinks he comes into her garden at night. Honestly. And Felicia isn't crazy, it's not the kind of thing she'd make up. She's not at all paranoid. Of course the person who really should come to you is Sanderson, but fat chance."

Her eyes strayed then back to the bookcase, and some of her attention went there too. Because of the length of the shelves, G was just below S, and there in S Molly saw a book that she had never seen or certainly not noticed before: *The Med School Murders,* by E. Shapiro. It was so placed that the jacket was exposed, a gaudy scene of men in white, all splattered with red, presumably blood. It was an old-looking book; it must have been published a while ago.

Involuntarily she exclaimed, "You're not that E. Shapiro?" Pointing.

He was startled. More than anything she had ever said, or asked, this had truly caught him off guard. "What's that doing there?" he demanded (as though, Molly thought, she were his wife, or the maid). "I mean, I didn't know it was there, it wasn't—new secretary—" He was groping to recover. And then in his old controlled voice he told her, "Actually yes, I did write that one. Alas. When I was in med school at Columbia I was pretty broke and I owed a lot of money, and I thought this would be an easy way." He smiled, not happily. "I was wrong all around. It wasn't easy and I didn't earn a lot."

"Should I read it?"

"I don't think you'd find it very edifying." This was said quite stiffly and without, Molly noticed, any offer of a loan of the book; she had borrowed other books from him, once or twice.

"You stopped with that one?" Even as she asked this, Molly felt that she should not have, but she was unable not to ask (also, that prohibiting voice was the one she had tried to learn to ignore).

"Uh—no." By their rules, most of them unspoken, if he answered her at all he was compelled to be truthful. "There were a few more." He grinned, very humanly. "I got into it, I couldn't stop. My escape, and addiction."

This conversational vein was new, and Molly was uneasy in it, dimly apprehensive. She asked, "It's sort of fun?"

"Mostly it's a change from what I do." Very resolutely he told her, "I never took it seriously at all."

That afternoon, in her branch public library, Molly moved along the shelf of S to Shapiro, E., embossed on the old library-linen covers of three books: *Dead White, Dire Emergencies,* and *Death Comes to the O.R.* Aware of guilty, spying feelings, she checked out all three.

On the other hand, Molly told herself as she walked the few blocks back to her house, he had published those books, and had chosen to do so under his own name; they were there for anyone to read—why shouldn't she? Although she knew perfectly well that her trip to the library had been a special one (she had barely left the house before), she had gone quite purposefully to the shelf of S, in the Mystery Section. And she almost never read mysteries, and then only those writers she especially admired, like Ruth Rendell, or Carl Hiaasen.

Back at home, back in bed, she began to read.

Dead White seemed to be about a serial killer of nurses. Many nurses turned up dead, and it gradually emerged (not too gradually, the book had a certain pace) that two of them had been having affairs with the same (married) doctor. The affairs were steamily described, with much emphasis on breasts, mostly (of course) very big ones. At first, small-breasted Molly experienced some of her old inadequacy feelings, until, more maturely, she thought, How dumb of him, how obvious.

She flipped to the front of the book to the publication date: 1948. He must have been very young then, still in his twenties, probably; she put Dr. Shapiro's current age as somewhere in his

sixties. Was he still in med school? The other two books came
out in 1946 and 1950, respectively. Like a well-planned family.
Diligently procreated.

Molly skimmed them all, quickly, voyeuristically. Guiltily.
There were more large breasts and even some bated breath. Perspiring foreheads, racing blood, and churning stomachs. Molly's
thought was, This stuff is awful, how could he do it? And (a
worse thought), How can I tell him what I think?

How have I managed to read them all? For that is what she
had done, she realized a few hours later. She had flicked through
all three, skimming along like a hungry bird, avid for garbage.
She had paid almost no attention to what was going on; she supposed that all those novels had plots, some story must have carried along all that freight, but she could not have said what really
went on in any of the three. Sexual encounters, quite a lot of
that: fucking that was breathy and perspiring (racing, churning)
but at the same time rather vague, romantic. Rather forties,
Molly supposed.

But, in herself, what was this enthusiastic, even obsessive
pursuit of the youthful sexual fantasies of E. Shapiro? For she
had to admit, she had galloped along, propelled by God knows
what unmentionable lust of her own. Her transference? Is this
what was meant, an unseemly sexual interest in one's shrink?
The substitute for one's hopelessly loved dad, in her case a dif-
fident, indifferent, and frequently depressed alcoholic, more
feared than lusted-after.

In any case she dreaded what she imagined as the necessary
conversation about these books, her admission that she had not
only read them, but judged them bad. Terrible—in fact, real
trash.

Surprisingly, Dr. Shapiro spared her. He seemed quite un-
shocked at what she had done, her deliberately going to the
library after his books. He even laughed. "And there you were

stuck with them, poor girl. You probably thought you had to read them, too." He said, "I know they're junk. It's just a trick I learned to do. Which proves I'm not a writer. A real writer could never turn out such garbage, I'm sure. Gore Vidal wrote some early mysteries for money but his were good, actually. You see? He's a writer. And he had the wit to make up a name. Edgar Box, I believe. I wish I had. But the money got me through med school. The only problem is, as you discovered, the damn things are still out there, with my name on them."

"Do many patients read them?"

He became vague. "Oh, every now and then. But, once again, you seem to expect some punishment for what you've done. You even seem to think it's deserved." This last was said in his usual tone of kind and intelligent concern, and Molly responded as she often did, with feelings of gratitude and a sort of pleased surprise: "Oh, you mean I don't have to feel like that?"

They did not (thank God) get to her (theoretical) sexual interest in him.

Nor did they during the next scheduled hour talk much about Molly's emotional attachment to her father. "Dave at worst reminds me of my father." Molly had said this before— God knows she had—but she had at last learned not to worry about repeating herself in this situation. "Both such bullies, I mean. But of course Dave doesn't drink—that's one of his pluses, for me. You know that was one of the first things I liked about Paul. His not drinking. That made me think he wasn't dangerous, I wouldn't get hurt. Well, I only was hurt when he got out of the marriage and then got himself killed. But we think he didn't mean to do that, don't we?" She gave Shapiro a small ironic smile; they had been over this point a great deal and actually had been unable to reach conclusions. "What I didn't think about much with Paul, and maybe I should have given it some thought, was all the bad stuff he did when he was drinking. Really bad. He and his first important girlfriend had fights, and I think he really beat her up. That's awful. I mean a lot of people, even alcoholics, never hit anybody, even if they're drunk."

"That's quite true."

"So maybe on some level I was a little afraid. He always might revert to type, so to speak. It's interesting. Matthew, his brother, drinks a little but not much. I thought it was supposed to run in families."

"Not necessarily. Your father was an alcoholic, and your mother, and you're not."

"So far." She laughed. "I really must be getting better, don't you think?"

"Yes, I do."

No thanks to your lousy novels, she did not say.

EIGHTEEN

"The point is," Matthew told Molly with the small half-smile that had been Paul's smile, or one of Paul's smiles, "you'll have roughly twice the income that you do now. Sorry to be the bearer of bad news." And he laughed, Paul's laugh. (Although, the more she saw of Matthew the less he resembled Paul, she began to notice.)

"But I've got plenty of money now. If I hadn't had all this medical stuff, I'd be really rich."

"Well, now you may be anyway. Think of it that way. Compensation, in spite of yourself," and he laughed again.

"I don't especially want to be rich. I don't even like rich people."

"I knew you'd say that."

Molly smiled, acknowledging predictability, but isn't everyone? she thought. More or less predictable? And anyway, how did Matthew know all that much about her opinions? She tried, and failed, to imagine a Paul-Matthew conversation concerning her character. They simply did not have such intimate, personal conversations. (It was Molly's belief that most men did not, but how could she know for sure?) Paul and Matthew went back to Montana together, where they had both grown up, for trout fishing, sometimes cross-country skiing in the winter. In August they liked to hike along rivers, the east fork of the Bitterroot; they made camp and cooked, and they drank, back in Paul's drinking days. "But what do you talk about, in all that time?" Molly had once or twice asked Paul. "We talk about the trout, they're very absorbing. And of course I tell him all about you, every single tiny most personal detail," he teased. "I told him you were oversexed." "Oh Paul, honestly, I'll tell him you are too."

Molly involuntarily smiled, remembering silly times with Paul, but then she wondered, Just what *had* he said, if anything? Molly's the original knee-jerk bleeding-heart left-winger? She hates the rich, even the ones who don't vote. Could Paul have said all that? It was not even true. Not quite.

Nor was it entirely true that she hated money, of course not. When she gained a little weight it would be fun to buy some great new clothes, and in the meantime she could order some from catalogues. Size 4—a terrific size on paper, but she was actually skinny, all bones, she knew that.

And she could at least double the money she sent to good places, Food-Not-Bombs, Open Hand, New Start, St. Anthony's. She and Felicia could even start their own food and shelter operation, which they had discussed from time to time.

And when she felt well she could travel again; all those trips with Paul had whetted her appetite. All she had to do was to get well. To eat.

Partly to get away from this unwelcome drift in her thoughts—eating problems, which often seemed hopeless—she asked Matthew, "How on earth did you do this, double my money?"

"Mostly luck. There was a company I knew about, and so. Mergers—bonds—corporate earnings—" Seeming to notice then that Molly's attention had wandered off, he stopped. "You don't really want to know."

"Maybe I don't. I find that stuff so hard to understand."

"And basically not interesting, right?"

"Well, I guess not. But it is interesting to you?"

"Unfortunately it's become all I know anything about, really. Joanne always tried to educate me in the law, but that didn't work out too well."

Why was he speaking of Joanne in the past tense?

Matthew answered this obvious but unasked question. "I guess we're splitting up this time," he said. "I mean, for real. Never divorce a lawyer, it's murder."

"I already did. Henry Starck."

"Oh, that's right, I forgot."

"Actually, he's very nice. He *is* very nice," Molly felt compelled to add.

Some ancient Hebraic law, she believed that she had heard somewhere, dictated that a widow should marry her husband's brother, and she thought, I'm glad I don't have to do that. In some ways Matthew is almost as ungiving, conversationally, as Henry was. Besides, she further thought, Paul and I weren't entirely married anymore.

She had to go down to Mt. Watson for a follow-up visit.

Dave had called, seemingly in a spirit of forgiveness, to say that it must be time for her to see Bill Donovan, and that he thought he could make time to take her down. He was trying for a tone of general disapproval, Molly could tell, but his voice was still enthusiastic, eager: he wanted to go back to Mt. Watson.

Molly felt a little mean, depriving him of this pleasure, as she told him, "Thanks, but Felicia said she would."

This was not true, but how would he find out? Though he must have caught something in her voice, for he said, "Are you sure? I don't think you ought to drive that far alone. Not yet." He sounded disappointed.

In fact driving down alone was exactly what Molly intended.

Felicia, quite out of character, was sick. Besides which Molly wanted to make the trip alone.

And she liked it very much, driving down in the clear bright unusually warm February weather—though almost all weather was unusual these days, Molly had noted: droughts and floods, heat waves in December, and snow and freezing days in June, in California. All as random as cancer seemed to be, and as extreme, and often as unwelcome. But the day was beautiful. Molly admired the New England look of the reservoir, with its slope of evergreens down to the shore, and even some of the houses on those expensively subdivided lots (one acre each) looked pleasant. She thought, I could live down here? But with all that money I could actually live anywhere, in Barcelona or Venice, in Paris, Prague, or Trieste.

Once back in the halls of Mt. Watson, though, and more specifically in the waiting room, Molly no longer felt romantic or adventurous, or even very rich. She was just a patient, as guilty and anxiety-burdened, as close to panic, the longer she waited, as all the rest.

After about half an hour, during which she thumbed through some old *Time*s and *Newsweek*s, the nurse announced that Dr. Donovan could see her now.

"Dr. Jacobs isn't with you?" was Donovan's greeting, along with his big bluff smile. Molly thought that if she were a nicer person she would later tell Dave that she had been asked that question; being missed by eminent doctors would surely please him.

"No, he isn't" was all she said; no explanation seemed necessary, or actually possible. She had no idea what they had made of that relationship, hers with Dave.

Once she was in the examining room, in that chair, interns and residents swarmed around Dr. Donovan as he again, for his audience, recounted his feats inside her head. "When we'd opened her up and some of those brains moved over—"

Had he really said that? Yes, he had. Molly could not have made it up, but she could stop listening to anything further that was said along those lines, and she did. How handy it would sometimes be, she thought, to be able to faint at will. Except that in this present instance, here and now, if she fainted they would probably clap her right back in the hospital.

"How do you feel about the shape of your nose?" Bill Donovan asked.

Knowing this to be perfunctory, that she was supposed to say, Oh, it's better than ever, I always wanted a small nose, Molly more truthfully told him, "It's all right. I think I liked it better before."

"If you ever want to fix it—"

"Look, the last thing in the world I want is another operation."

Everyone smiled at that sentiment; it was apparently understandable even to them, the doctors, although Bill looked not wholly pleased.

He next said, conversationally, "I hear you escaped like a little bird from Alta Linda. Can't say as I blame you. Depressing place. But if you were my wife I think I'd turn you right over my knee."

"How lucky for both of us that I'm not."

After a startled moment Bill managed to laugh, a gruff semi-guffaw. And Molly was as startled as he that she had actually said that. It was the sort of thing she usually thought of later, and wished to have said. How brave of me, she thought. How out of character.

On the drive home, though, she fell back into a more familiar self-critical mode. She should have asked more questions. She should have complained about not feeling well, about her nausea. And she should have asked in a general way about effects of radiation: how long did they continue, usually? Even if it would have been hard to break into that web of doctors' conversation, she should have tried; she should have questioned and complained. It was all very well to have these conversations with Felicia about the general insensitivity of doctors, but some of it was really her own fault. You get what you ask for, has often been said, and you don't get what you don't. That is perhaps an unreliable rule (surely she had not asked for the green golf ball), but in this case, talking to doctors, it seemed to apply.

Felicia stayed sick. "Nothing real," she said to Molly, on the phone, "just lousy feelings in my head. It could be the weather. Some allergy."

"Or it could be a nice green tumor. You too can have a golf ball."

"You won't laugh if I actually do."

"That's absolutely true, I won't."

For her dinner alone, Molly made her favorite single-person meal: a large bowl of pasta, angel-hair, with butter and garlic and scallions. Parmesan. A small green salad, a glass of white wine. A little bread, nice and fresh and chewy.

She was chewing on the good bread, looking out to the peaceful vista of gardens behind her house, and thinking that since she would have all that money, what she most would like was a leisurely trip to Paris, so reliably beautiful, fantastic food, and the art, the river, and the trees. As she happily imagined all that, something suddenly went wrong within her mouth. She bit on something hard; at first she thought it was a little stone in the bread—how amazing. But then she spit it out and saw, small and white, a tooth. Her own, and her tongue discovered the gap: a lower front tooth.

In the mirror she saw that she could fit it back in, but of course there was no way to affix it. And without it she looked comic, a Halloween pumpkin instead of Humpty-Dumpty. Or, when not grinning, she looked sad and terrible.

Dr. Gold, the dentist ("the sententious dentist," Molly had sometimes called him to Felicia), rubber-gloved hand in her mouth, began by saying, "Doesn't look too good. Lot of tissue damage that I can see right off. Radiation, bad stuff for your teeth and gums. You must have had quite a lot of it." He replaced his hand with a clamp that was rather like a horse's bit.

He said, "The wife and I are just back from Baja, and the prices there are not great, I tell you. Every night, a twenty-dollar cab ride from our hotel to some restaurant? Those guys have caught on quick, believe me. Of course you can't blame them, but still we'd counted on some bargain to make up for Paris last fall. But the restaurants too, Stateside prices. Of course we were going to the recommended ones, probably pretty fancy for your average Mexican, and actually not too many Mexicans there, just the help. And tourists. Germans and French, not so many Japanese as you see most places. I'm going to have them make you something they call a flipper, nice new tooth on a little piece of plastic, fits right into your mouth. Later we can talk about a bridge. Of course the problem is that some more of those teeth could go. I just don't like the look of those gums."

Dr. Macklin, who was very fond of lawyer jokes, told Molly two new ones—new to him, that is—and since she liked him she laughed appreciatively, and she said, "Those are good but I still like the lab rat one the best."

"Oh yes, that's a classic. But tell me how you're feeling. Really," and he frowned slightly, in his kind, concerned way.

"Well actually not too great. I guess it has to do with physical weakness but I just feel mildly depressed a lot of the time. I wonder what really happened to my head when they were doing all that. I sleep all right but I have terrible dreams that I can't quite remember—they slide away like fish when I try. I don't feel the kind of desperate unhappiness I did when Paul was killed, just sort of low-grade despair, like flu." As she said all this, it occurred to Molly that she should be saying it to Dr. Shapiro, and she thought, How like me to tell my symptoms to the wrong doctor. I used to tell Dr. Shapiro about my sinus problems.

Dr. Macklin's frown had increased. "You know you're pretty much describing how I felt about a year ago," he said. "My separation. We're still working it out."

This was the first time Molly had heard of a separation, but she smiled sympathetically.

"What helped me a lot, though you may not like the idea of this," he said, "was Paxil. It seems to work for some people who have no luck with Prozac, which I'd tried. I could give you just the very smallest dose, if you wanted to see how it goes."

"Uh, should I ask Dr. Shapiro? Too?"

"Of course. Talk to him, and then give me a call."

Macklin divorced—would he remarry? Molly had really never thought of him in that way, but now she did, and she thought, He's quite attractive, really, and very nice, for a doctor. On the other hand, responsible doctors, which he certainly is, do not involve themselves with patients, so I can just forget it.

"Paxil might be worth a try," said Dr. Shapiro. "Take it for a few weeks, see how you feel. Though you know that in a general way I don't like those drugs."

Almost as soon as she started it, the Paxil made Molly's nightmares disappear. All gone—in fact no more dreams at all.

But, curiously, without dreams she slept considerably less well; her sleep was thin and ragged, unsatisfying, unrestful. She also experienced a slight increase in nausea, and eating problems— conditions that she did not immediately connect with Paxil.

"I just read where it says 'Possible Side Effects,' " Molly told Dr. Shapiro. "And it mentions nausea. Isn't that an odd pill to give someone who's already nauseated? And insomnia, it mentions that too. Don't doctors read the small print?"

"You're quite right, it certainly may not have been a good idea," he agreed. "It did seem worth a small try. Macklin meant well, and I did too. But I'm very glad you decided to give it up."

She asked him, "Do you know if Dr. Macklin is really divorced? I had this wild idea that I could introduce him to Felicia."

He smiled—knowing and amused and affectionate. "I'm sorry, I don't keep up with doctors' marital status."

"I really don't understand how doctors' minds work," Molly told Matthew, a few days later. "To give a nauseated person a pill with that as a possible side effect? Sometimes I think they don't think."

"They don't think in the way that other people do" was Matthew's considered view. "They seem more narrow in focus."

"Exactly," Molly said. "Remember, in *Howards End,* 'only connect'? They don't put things together. Doctors don't. Don't see a whole picture. I think that's what sometimes gets them into trouble."

"One of the things." And then Matthew added, in his sober, conservative way (at those moments very unlike Paul, who was rash), "I'm not sure that you want to hear this, but you're looking really good. I was thinking, maybe we could go for a hike sometime? Would you be up for that?"

"Sure," Molly told him, with what she feared was evident lack of enthusiasm. She felt well enough, she thought, but she didn't want to spend quite that much time with Matthew—alone, she thought.

NINETEEN

Felicia was so sick, and sick for so long, that her mother, not given to visits, came to see her. Susie, in perky new pink polka-dots, bearing an enormous bunch of bright-pink roses, which perfectly matched her dress, and saying to her daughter, "Oh *dear,* how can I always forget that you have your own roses? A whole garden full of them!"

They both knew why it was that Susie did not remember; they knew that Susie's prime concern with gifts of flowers was that they should go well with whatever she was wearing—she could hardly think about the contents of a recipient's garden. And too, as she herself would have quickly pointed out, she was so rarely at Felicia's house that for all she knew Felicia could have converted to total zucchini by now.

"They're so beautiful," Felicia told her mother. "And they just match your dress. Maybe you could put them in something in the kitchen?"

While her mother was in the kitchen Felicia dozed off, just long enough to dream that Susie was not there—she was alone, and so it was with a little surprise that she woke to see her mother carrying in a bunch of roses in a vase. Somewhat sleepily she said, "Oh how pretty. They just match your dress."

"Darling, you said that before." Susie frowned. "Do you think you're really all right?"

"Well, I'm not, not really. This goddam flu."

"Sweetie, you must see a doctor. I'll get Harry DeGroot, if I have to bring him here myself."

"Mother, please don't call Harry DeGroot—you know how I feel about those socialite doctors."

"Well! And Raleigh Sanderson, such a great friend of yours for a while, wasn't he? What's ever happened to him, by the way?"

"Oh Mother, I honestly don't know." This was more or less true. Felicia still was hearing strange unpredictable sounds in her garden at night, at varying intervals, about which she still hesitated to call the police. But she was never entirely sure that it was Sandy, although in a way she was sure, it had to be Sandy. She also did not really know her mother's true view of her own alleged friendship with Sandy. She had wondered: Did other women really talk more to their mothers? Would some other woman say, We had this terrific affair, but then he hit me? Molly had never talked much to her mother, Felicia knew, but then Molly's mother was an alcoholic. And her own mother was a very silly woman, a silly woman with moments of insight, even of stray humor.

All that Susie ostensibly "knew" about Sandy and Felicia was that Felicia had worked for him for a time, and had liked him very much. Sandy and Connie were close to but not precisely *in* Susie's social set, Susie and Josh's group being just a little younger, a little more stylish—God knows they were stylish.

Felicia's immediate problem, not unconnected to the larger problem of Sandy, was that, lacking him, she had in effect no doctor to call. "You're a healthy young woman," he always said. "I think these yearly checkups with so-called internists are highly overrated. If something goes wrong I'll find a real specialist for you. In the meantime, if you feel a cold coming on, just call me. I'll know what to do, I promise. And in your case I make house calls."

So that now, with what seemed a very bad and persistent case of flu, so much aching, such entire fatigue—she had no one to call.

Molly had several times said that Felicia should call her doctor, Douglas Macklin, and Felicia herself was not at all sure why she resisted this suggestion. Very likely through some really irrational association, like linking Dr. Macklin with poor Molly's dreadful tumor, the cancer about which she persisted in making her black (and some not very funny) jokes.

And so, resolutely, Felicia now said to her mother, "I think I'll call Molly's doctor. Macklin, Douglas Macklin."

"What a nice name. But I've never heard of him."

Well, that's a good sign, thought Felicia, and she closed her eyes, and went halfway back to sleep.

"I'm really glad you're not working for that Raleigh Sanderson anymore," her mother said as Felicia half-asleep thought, She does know. "Very bad news, that man. I've seen him operate at parties. Of course I don't mean really operate, you know? But I never thought about it that way, actually. Most doctors *are* operators, you know?" And Susie giggled with pleasure, amused by herself, as usual.

Or had her mother really said anything at all? Quite possibly Felicia had only dreamed it, for when she opened her eyes her mother had gone, and the room was full of the scent of her bright-pink overblown roses.

One of the many things that Felicia would never tell her mother, nor even Molly, was the *strangeness,* the extreme oddity of her feelings as she lay there at night sometimes and heard the faint sound of those footsteps in her garden. She was not frightened, though perhaps should she have been? To herself she excused this possibly irrational fearlessness on the grounds that so far Sandy had done nothing dangerous, and if he meant to harm her, then what was he waiting for? Far stranger, though, than her lack of fear was the fact that she was truly turned on—no other clear way to describe it. She lay there aware of gathering blood, of heat, in her groin. Of moisture, even.

So crazy, she was obviously feverish. Or, she wondered, is this how battered women respond to men who beat them? Does this explain why sometimes they stick around for more? More likely, she thought, they are just too scared to move, and a really frightened woman would not be turned on. This is part of my fever, she thought.

In any case, she was more than a little aroused, and she lay there in the scent of all those roses remembering—not Sandy furious, hitting her, bruising her face, but Sandy the incredibly sexy man with whom she had spent all those long amazing hours, those hours and hours, having extraordinary sex. Doing it over and over, in different ways, in this very bed. She remembered how with him she came, and came again, and again. His cry of triumph when after all that he came too, deep inside her.

Felicia even smiled. No wonder she was turned on, and not really frightened, remembering.

Douglas Macklin was very nice, Felicia thought, and sort of sexy—though not at all her type, thank God. And, though he did not as a rule make house calls, he had come there to see her; very probably Molly had twisted his arm, somehow, exaggerated the gravity of Felicia's flu. Maybe he and Molly would eventually get together? Molly had said that he was recently divorced.

Lately, Molly had mentioned Matthew Bonner, Paul's brother, somewhat too often, Felicia thought. She thought: If Molly tells me that she's really in love with Matthew or even just sort of involved, I can't stand it, I really can't. Paul was bad enough, and this one could easily be worse, this supposedly boring brother. He probably only pretends to be dull, and underneath is as mean and dangerous as Paul had been—or as Felicia thought he had been. Anyone that attractive had to be mean, in her experience.

"I guess flu is the best diagnosis I can come up with," said Dr. Macklin, with his pleasant, cheerful smile. He had examined her discreetly; Felicia felt a mutual awareness of the sexiness of their situation, or she thought she did—alone in her house, she in a semi-sheer nightgown.

He said, "It has gone on a long time, and you have had a lot of fever, but I think it's on the way out. No real point in starting you on antibiotics now."

"Oh no, taking them makes me feel awful. Unless I eat a lot of yogurt. Would you like some tea or something?"

"Actually I'd love a glass of water. Can I get you anything?"

"A glass of Clamato? It's my new addiction, there's some in the fridge."

"In that case I'll join you."

He came back with the two glasses, and sociably they sipped at the cold tomato juice.

He said, "You must be happy to see Molly looking so well."

"Oh, really! I think she looks great. Still sort of thin but of course I envy that," and she smiled as she thought, He'd be very *nice* in bed, very thorough. Caring and kind—and how come no one like that really turns me on?

"We were all very worried," said Dr. Macklin, frowning, and perhaps with more feeling than he had intended. And then, as though to change the subject, with much less interest he said, "Nice place you have here. It's okay for you, living alone?"

"Yes, usually I love it. But lately this very odd thing's been happening." And she told him about the late night prowler in her garden. "Usually, he, uh, urinates," she finished.

"Some poor old guy with a prostate problem," said Dr. Macklin. "Honestly, though, you should let the cops know."

"I guess I should." Giving him her most honest, wide-blue-eyed look, "I will," Felicia said, knowing perfectly that she would not. It was Sandy, out there prowling. Checking on her. How embarrassing if cops came and found him there! And he couldn't get into her house without tripping the alarm, as he knew. "But I always turn on the burglar alarm," she told Dr. Macklin piously.

He said, "Molly's place must be quite nearby."

"Well actually it is, it's just up the hill." As she gestured, Felicia noted that the doctor's glance followed in the direction, as though Molly's house and perhaps she herself were visible.

As Felicia thought, Oh.

She asked him, "You don't like living alone?"

His smile twisted to one side as he said, "I'm getting used to it. You know, I was married a long time, and now I'm not. I'm getting into Progresso soup—all that."

"You can use Progresso for a pasta sauce," Felicia told him, and she explained just how.

Polite but totally uninterested, Dr. Macklin thanked her, and their conversation languished. He got up to go.

She thanked him for coming, and he told her that he hoped she'd feel much better soon; he was sure she would.

She asked, "And from now on, Molly will be okay?"

Looking a little grim, he promised, "Yes, she will."

"Isn't he really nice?" Molly asked. "Did you like him?"

"Yes, very nice. And so good of him to come over. I think I'm much better."

"You don't sound very interested."

"In Dr. Macklin? Molly, I'm not. I've had it with doctors, remember?"

"Honestly, Felicia, you make these rules."

"Besides, I got an idea he was more interested in you."

"Douglas Macklin? Oh, really not. Or only as a patient."

. . .

That night, as she lay in bed, still feeling some ache of flu, though diminished—she really was better, Felicia thought—she began to hear the by now familiar pad of footsteps on her garden path, and she smiled to herself as she thought, Dumb Sandy, he must know that I know who it is out there, what a silly game. Can he possibly imagine I'll come to the door and ask him in?

Felicia had a sudden bad thought then: What if it isn't Sandy after all, but someone who seriously wishes me harm?—someone more truly, more seriously deranged than Sandy?

At that thought she experienced fear like a large cold cave within her chest, a dark hollow space, and she shivered as, at that moment, a heavy blow sounded on her front door.

Not Sandy. He wouldn't do that, would he? Rigid, cold with panic, Felicia listened to the totally silent night—even no cars passed at just that moment.

Should she call 911? Suppose they took an hour or so getting there, as she had heard that they sometimes did. Something that women in the shelter talked about: whether or not calling 911 was worth it, the waiting and the hassle.

At that moment it was not much help for Felicia to tell herself that in such a "good" neighborhood the police would probably come right away, and that probably the person she feared was a famous doctor who would not really hurt her. Probably.

In the morning she found that someone had thrown a large hunk of broken concrete, as from some street repair, against her door. She called the alarm system to see why this had not set off her alarm, and then waited for the promised inspector to arrive.

TWENTY

On a narrow ridge high above the bright Pacific, on a brilliantly blue January day, two tall thin people, a man and a woman, both obviously strong though not young, together battled a ferocious, chilling wind. They looked somewhat alike, those two, both with silky gray-blond hair, blue eyes, fine fair skin, now flushed with the blood of cold and exertion. They were not brother and sister—that was somehow obvious—but possibly distant cousins. They wore sturdy, good old hiker clothes, neither new nor Californian but rather New England in their look, as were their wearers. Who were, in fact, Connie Sanderson, wife of Raleigh, and Henry Starck, former husband of Molly Bonner; they had met at several AA meetings and felt some affinity, even beyond that of a joint recovery from addiction. They bonded as friends. An enthusiasm for hiking was the acted-out part of the bond—they had not yet discovered their indirect but highly personal connection, the Sandy-Felicia-Molly relationship.

Below them the ocean roiled and crashed, a bright green streaked with blue, with wide white lines of foam. More immediately, leading down from their path, was the steep crevassed slope of wind-battered green-gray furze, and off to their right, dark towering majestic trees, redwoods and smaller cypresses and firs, and leafless winter brambles, thick with thorns. Impossible to speak below a shout in the heavy wind, but from time to time the two exchanged a small and mutually shy smile, acknowledging the beauty of the day, which was extreme—an extraordinary day—and also the commendable exertion that this hike required of them. Recovery was great, as they did not have to say.

But despite the exceptional beauty all around, the gift of amazing weather—January, even in California?—Connie was finding herself a prey to far-too-familiar bad thoughts. Feminist but unhelpful. The sequence began with Felicia, of whom she was all too aware. Of course she had seen Felicia, it seemed a great many times; she felt that she knew every tiniest patch of Felicia's perfect, poreless skin. The sequence of thoughts went like this, with just a few variations: That girl is a good thirty years younger than Raleigh is, and they both think—and very likely everyone else thinks—that is perfectly all right. Whereas if I, a good ten years younger than Raleigh and in what one would call good shape—if I took an interest in a younger man, everyone, including the man himself, would view it as obscene, pathetic, quite out of the question. Even if the difference was only, say, ten years, as with this Henry Starck. But to whom, thank God, I am not at all attracted in that way. Nice as he is.

Just last week at a meeting, a woman's "share" had been about exactly such an experience: "It was so terrible," this woman said. "Really it was why I stopped drinking. And these days I never think about it, I never see *him,* thank God, but sometimes it just surfaces in my mind, and I have to deal with it all over again." A pretty woman, in her early forties, probably. But not feeling pretty: she hunched over heavy breasts, and her beautiful large black Latin eyes were both mournful and accusatory. She said, "I was having some drinks after work in this bar down on Union Street—Perry's? Everyone knows it's for pickups but I was really okay by myself, and then this young guy came over asking if he could join me. Not all that young, maybe ten years younger than me, and he said he was a doctor. At Children's. Very cute and blond, and did he know it. I think at a distance I look younger than I am, or something, because right off, when he sat down, I felt like he was kind of disappointed. But I didn't let that idea register, really. And disappointed or not he kept right on ordering these drinks. You might say he had a little problem too? God, do doctors drink?" (*Do* they, Connie had thought. Some of them can put an ordinary lay-alkie right under the table.) "Anyway, we had lots, and he kept getting cuter and cuter, though I can't say we had a lot to talk about—I mean, why would a doctor be interested in my dumb life? I'm a social worker. Well, the truth is, as he got cuter and I got drunker I also got hornier and hornier, you know? Anyone else get like that? So at last I just thought, What the hell? Why are we both here anyway—to get laid, right? So I just flat out said to him that luckily my place was around the corner, on Greenwich? And he looked really shocked—God, I'll never forget that look—and he said, he really said this, he said, 'Sorry, I think you're a year or so out of my age range, and besides I like legs, not tits.' Can you imagine? Was he really a doctor? Could a real doctor be that mean?"

Damn right he could, and meaner, Connie had thought; of course he was a doctor. But she thought too, How utterly terrible, how could anyone, even a doctor, be so cruel? She felt it as though it had happened, really, to her, and she had to lecture herself severely: Come on, being empathetic is one thing but this is sick—you've never made a pass at anyone in your life, even drunk, and you probably won't, certainly not now that you're not drinking. You're in recovery, remember?

She said to this nice Henry Starck, shouting above the wind, "Remember when picnics used to mean a gallon of wine and some cheese?"

He grinned and shouted back, "I think I've done a little better than that. Food-wise."

"I'm sure."

For he had insisted on bringing the lunch. "In my new life I'm a cook," he had said. "You won't mind?"

"Of course not." And maybe in my new life young men bring home-cooked picnics to me, Connie had thought.

Perhaps a half-mile ahead of them was the tip of the headlands, and much farther away, in distant waves, a small boat battled forward, up and down, like a child's rocking horse. Closer to hand were rocks and beaten-down grasses, and a wind that was almost visible, so fierce and strong and capricious in its direction.

They had stopped their forward stride and simply stood there, craning ahead, until Connie said, more loudly than she would have chosen to speak, "We don't have to go out to the end now, do we?"

"No, actually no one will know if we don't." Neither could hear the other's laugh, but they smiled relief to each other and turned in silent agreement toward the sheltering trees and a cleared patch of ground. A little sunlit space, with a log for a possible backrest, or maybe a table. Or both.

They sat, and Henry began to bring out food from his knapsack as Connie thought, Well, such a nice young man, I can't imagine Raleigh bringing a picnic, but of course with Felicia he doesn't have to. She had heard of Felicia's exceptional cooking skills, along with the fabled blue eyes and the famous skin. Catching herself in such thoughts—so *passé*, so *vieux jeux,* she should be far past all that—she asked Henry Starck, because he was handy, was there, "Tell me, do you ever have any bad thoughts, still, about your former wife?"

"Odd you ask that." Henry's mouth moved rather little as he smiled. "My first, former wife lives out here now, and we're just in a way at last getting to be friends. She lost her husband, and then she had some unusual, awful cancer, but now she seems to be all right." He smiled again. "I'm trying to get sort of used to her again. She's called Molly Bonner. I always liked her name, never even wanted her to change it—"

"Really? She's Molly Bonner?"

"Yes, why? Do you know her?"

"Well, not exactly." And as best she could, Connie explained the connection. She finished by saying, "It's almost scary, isn't it, the people you know a lot about when you don't actually know them. As though in some way everyone were famous."

He did not quite see what she meant, Connie could tell. Also, like most men, he was made nervous by personal conversations.

He said, "Molly did mention such a friend. A Felicia. Who'd taken care of her, she said."

"Probably. I've heard she's a famous cook, and probably terribly nice. But you can see that my view would be a little biased."

"Of course."

Henry's sandwiches had a rather sweetly old-fashioned quality to them, Connie felt—at least in terms of intention. There were cucumber and cream cheese, egg salad and watercress and pâté, but he seemed not to have grasped the principle of thin bread, nor, with the cucumbers, cutting off crusts. Even as she praised them Connie struggled with heavy bites of sandwich.

She said, when she could, "It's sort of like a picnic in Maine, don't you think?"

"Oh, absolutely. In fact I was just thinking that. Also thinking how provincial I am, in this beautiful spot to refer things back to Maine."

"I always do. But where did you go in Maine?"

"A place called Bailey Island, it's up off the coast—"

"Oh, but I know Bailey Island. My cousins had a house . . ."

This all led to a complicated but enthusiastic conversation: Henry (of course) knew Connie's cousins, the Forbeses; he was a very distant relation, and so it could be said that Connie and

Henry *were* related very distantly. Which would not have come as a surprise to anyone observing the two of them.

Sitting there out of the wind, among sheltering trees, they were very warm in the full sunlight of early afternoon. Having eaten all she could, and possibly exhausted their conversation, Connie felt that they should leave now; on the other hand, why? She was happier than she could remember being for quite some time—and she was thinking, I'll have to bring Katie and the grandchildren here, they'd love it—when out of the blue, so to speak, Henry Starck did something quite remarkable, and crazy: he leaned over and kissed her, very warmly, firmly, and lingeringly, on her mouth, and then he said, "I hope you don't mind, I've been wanting to do that all day."

Connie smiled, quite unable to say anything at all—though various things occurred to her, sentences tumbling against each other in her mind: You're beautifully handsome, shall we go back to my house right now? Did you know I have three black grandchildren? Should we move in and live together? I think I love you—is that all right?

As though in answer to all those questions, he kissed her again, more briefly but still sweetly, warmly. He said, "This isn't like me at all, I don't know—" And he laughed. He said, "What an amazing day!"

At that exact moment of their looking at each other, surprised and smiling in the sunlight, something extraordinary happened: from the mass of brambles and scrubby pines a small pointed gray-brown face peered out, curious and frightened feral eyes, dark gold, a black nose, and, as it instantly turned to run back and away from them, a long high bushy tail.

Connie breathlessly whispered, "Was that a feral cat—out here?"

Henry laughed quietly. "No, it was a fox. We have them in Maine."

"So beautiful."

"Wasn't it?"

After the fox they were silent for a time. Connie leaned back against their log, in the gentle, sedative sunlight. She was thinking how she would tell the grandchildren about the fox. Ethan, Adam, and Laurel, six, five, and three, respectively, a little young for hiking, Connie thought—and she also thought, for the thousandth time, What a jerk Raleigh is, how can he refuse to see Kate, the mother of these children, our *daughter?* Ostensibly because Kate never married either of their fathers, but really because both of those men were "gentlemen of color," as Raleigh with his high heavy irony would put it. Black. It was true that Kate was not the most responsible woman alive; she never got along especially well in jobs, but she loved her children, had fun with them, and was fiercely protective—more than you could say for Raleigh, Connie thought.

She had an impulse to tell this nice young man, this Henry Starck, about Kate and her children, but she did not. After all, these days just being kissed did not mean all that much; Henry Starck did not necessarily want to hear about her grandchildren. Besides, at just that moment she did not feel grandmotherly.

She hardly knew him; how could she expect him to care about her family?

Besides, he'll probably remarry Molly Bonner. This sudden intuition hit Connie broadside, with the binding force of truth.

Should she tell him, though, that Raleigh this week is off at a conference in Aspen? Heart surgeons all skiing together, in some terrifically expensive resort. All free, and undoubtedly charged to their patients in some way.

But what does it matter what she tells him, if he's going to remarry Molly Bonner?

Henry asked her, "Did you have any special plans for tonight? I mean, if you're free by any chance, I thought we might—"

"Well yes, as a matter of fact—"

TWENTY-ONE

Since he had removed the family photographs, those glamorous wife-and-children-at-Christmas shots that all doctors seemed to have, Dr. Macklin's walls were somewhat bare; this must have been true for some time now but Molly had just noticed, and noticed too some minor attempts at redecoration: two Piranesi prints, and, on the mantel, in place of the red-haired actress wife, was what looked to be a small gold baseball trophy. And so she asked him, "You were a baseball star?"

"Only mildly, as an undergraduate. Before my serious premed days. I really wasn't so great. Just tall."

"But you got this trophy."

He grinned. "They had to give it to someone. Every year. Now tell me, how've you been feeling?"

"Okay, I guess. On the whole. But not entirely right, you know? Eating's still sort of a problem, and I don't have a lot of strength."

He frowned a little, then got up and went over to his mantel, where he first removed, then replaced the baseball trophy. As always, Molly was surprised by his height, he must be at least six three or four, and still thin. And now that she knew, she thought he moved like an athlete: he was lithe and quick, purposeful. He was an attractive man, he really was; why hadn't Felicia felt it?

". . . takes a while," he was saying. "I'll bet you've heard that one a couple of thousand times. But I've been thinking, there's a doctor just out from Mass. General, a young guy, but he's supposed to be really good. Just starting out in internal medicine here. I think, uh, I think I'd like you to see him." For some reason he didn't quite look at Molly as he said this.

Irrationally appalled, she first thought, Oh! he's abandoning me, I must be hopeless, I must be even sicker than I feel if I have to go to this new doctor, and she wailed, "But why? I don't want a new doctor, I've been to so many already, and I really like you—"

His acute discomfort was obvious, and he then began to backtrack. "Well of course you don't have to," he told her. "God knows you have seen a lot of us." And then, visibly pulling himself together, he said, "The problem is really mine. It's just that I, uh, I thought I'd like to ask you out to dinner, or something, and if you weren't my patient—"

Horribly, childishly, Molly began to cry. She said, "I need a doctor, not—" Not a new lover, she had almost said, but there it was, unsaid and heavily between them. Because of course that was what she meant.

"Come on now," he said, to her tears. "Just forget I said that. Of course you need a doctor, and I am your doctor." He smiled, and touched her shoulder in a friendly way.

No longer crying, she managed to smile; she asked him, as though joking, "You mean I get to choose?"

"Of *course.*" He said, "Let's just forget all about that other, okay?" He grinned. "I can if you can."

"Sure," she told him—quite sure that neither of them would forget. Sure that their connection had, if imperceptibly, changed.

· · ·

"This is a very hypothetical question," Molly said to Dr. Shapiro. "But if you, uh, found yourself attracted to a patient, what if anything would you do about it?"

He made an odd and, to Molly, unreadable gesture involving both hands, but she gathered that he intended a total dismissal of her question. And he said, "That just wouldn't happen."

Oh, are we all that unattractive? She did not ask this, but she did ask him, "How can you be so sure?"

He laughed. "You have to be sure of a few things in this life." Then he conceded, somewhat: "I suppose you're right, it could, I could. But my safeguards seem to me entirely trustworthy."

Molly let him pause, and only looked her question.

"Okay," he said. "Two main safeguards. One, the nature of my relation to my wife, and, two, my own analysis. I think I would see any flicker of attraction as some momentary revival of an old neurosis."

"The nature of my relation to my wife": that was a long phrase to which Molly both at the time and later on gave considerable thought. Did he mean that he was so sexually drugged, bemused, besotted by his wife that he could not have the lightest, most passing impulse toward any other woman? Or did he mean that his rational control of himself was so total that, to any flicker of outside interest, a voice would instantly chide, Come on, it wouldn't be worth it?

At the moment he was smiling, in his shielded way. "Do you want to say why you ask?" His classic question.

Oh Christ, thought Molly, he is somehow thinking of me, of himself and me; he is wondering if I could possibly think him drawn to me. And so, as quickly as she could, she told him what had happened with Dr. Macklin.

"Well," he said, seeming truly surprised. "That's certainly one way to handle it."

"And you get the noncommittal prize one more time," to her own surprise Molly broke out. "Of *course* it's one way to handle it. Raping the patient would be another. One way to handle it— Jesus!"

A pause. "What concerns me is less Dr. Macklin's behavior than your reaction to it."

Calming down, she drew in a breath. "Okay. I was hurt. Pretty crazy, no? I felt like he was abandoning me. Whereas he was really being what you might call super-kosher."

"Indeed you might. Or scrupulous, if you were a Catholic. Anyway, a super-honorable man. If just slightly confused."

"We both were, and I didn't handle it very well."

"No, you were okay. And I don't think your feeling abandoned was all that crazy. You still don't feel terrific—you still need help from your doctors, you think."

Molly smiled, acknowledging kindness; he really was a kind person, she often thought.

Why then did she suddenly hit out at him, though gently? Later she thought she might have been getting back at him for the statement about his wife (but why?). She laughed, not kindly, as she said, "Actually what you would do if you were attracted to a patient is write some salacious novel about it, wouldn't you?"

He smiled. "You're probably right."

Molly went to her gynecologist for an annual checkup, but she did not ask him about possible attraction to patients. For one thing, the very idea was too horrible: lanky, hopelessly ugly Dr. Summers, with his carroty hair and cranberry drinker's nose.

For another, she did not have a chance. Dr. Summers had decided to become a novelist, and having somehow got the impression that Molly read a lot, liked books, he wanted to talk about this marvelous new project. "It's so easy," he announced. "I just plug in the old computer and let those fantasies go. Eight, nine pages a night, it's really fun. And I've got this program for plots. It must be a lot like psychoanalysis, all this stuff comes out. My wife would be really surprised, so would anyone who knows me, I guess. Of course a lot of it isn't mine but things patients have told me over the years. I just change their names and there it all is. I hope no one recognizes themselves—herself, I guess I should say. This may feel a little cold," he said—unnecessarily; the speculum was already in place, and very cold.

"I have to admit, I think about doing talk shows, all that writer stuff. On the other hand, maybe I should just do it anonymously? The fact of what I do, being an ob-gyn doctor, might prejudice people one way or another. I could just make up a name for myself, along with all the characters, and put it in another city. Although a lot of it would be a lot of fun, I think, signing books and all that. And it's all so easy, I really don't see why more people don't write novels."

"A lot of them do, it seems to me," Molly told him.

"Well, I guess you're right. But I think most people have never even tried. Does that hurt?"

Molly, for various reasons, did not tell Felicia about Dr. Macklin and his odd suggestion. She did, however, mention the visit to Dr. Summers, the boredom, his happy computer novel, and the cold speculum.

To all of which Felicia responded reasonably enough: "I can't think why you still go to that tiresome old sadist. His talking forever is very hostile, I think. I've always had this idea that people are boring on purpose, and it's one of the ways they have of controlling women, God knows it is. If all else fails they'll try to bore us to death. That's one thing I'll say for Sandy, he never bored me that way. But of course he's got his own arsenal of hostile weapons. My father, though! God in heaven!—the jokes, can you believe it? He tells these long, long jokes. These days he gets them off the Internet, he says. Seriously, though, Mol, you've got to quit Summers. No one uses a cold speculum anymore. You should go to a woman, really. They listen, and they know what you're talking about. They've been there too, you know? This Sarah Lowenstein I see now, she's really great. She's very smart and she's sort of shy. I like that in a doctor. It's novel."

Felicia, as she talked, was making pastry dough, cutting butter into the flour in a big brown bowl, with silver knives. And she wore a large white bib-top apron over her jeans and pale-pink (faded) T-shirt. Now she began to laugh, and wiped at her face with the back of a floury hand. "You would not believe this guy I sat next to at dinner last night. Ray Rose? A very hotshot surgeon."

"I've heard of him, I think."

"Well, he's very into art collecting, and that's what he likes to talk about. Philip Guston has gone up, Diebenkorn is up— Matisse is down, can you imagine? Matisse is down. But that's not really the prize. Then he said, he actually said this, he said, 'The trouble with Picasso is that he had no creativity.' Can you imagine? Picasso had no creativity."

Molly laughed in sheer disbelief. "But I suppose you really liked him," she said. "You're going out with him tomorrow."

"I am not. And he didn't like me either—I'm afraid he heard me when I whispered to the man on the other side of me that he was an asshole, Ray Rose was. But Jesus, the big creativity expert—"

"It was that scum prick Freudian Edgar Shapiro!" Dave burst out. "Shrinks! They're the worst, I don't know why they call themselves doctors—black magic is more like it. I always knew eventually he'd make some move, he's always been secretly hot for you—"

"Dave! for Christ's sake, I am not talking about Dr. Shapiro. This has nothing to do with him. He never—"

She might as well not have spoken. As was so often the case with Dave, he chose to hear nothing that she said.

Unwisely, knowing even as she spoke that she was making a mistake, she had asked Dave her allegedly hypothetical question: If you were attracted to a patient— And, as she might have known he would, he instantly leapt—he vaulted, he raced—to his own conclusion: Dr. Shapiro had made some sort of pass at Molly, which he, Dave, had always known that Shapiro would do. And, in a tired way, as she listened to Dave's rant, Molly recognized that literally nothing she could say would change his view. It was less a question of not believing her than of refusing to hear her. On and on he ranted, his anger fueled by years of righteous, obstinate fury at shrinks (they had no *proof,* they charged high fees, no specific results), plus all his current rage and frustration at the sheer, simple, and inexplicable fact that Molly would not love him. He sometimes suspected that she did not even like him very much.

"Fucking shrinks, they're always screwing their patients, one way or another. I heard about one who was charging this poor woman two hundred bucks an hour and having sex with her too—"

"Well she can't have been very poor, and maybe the sex was terrific."

"*Very* funny. Actually they do it all the time—statistics— think they can get away with anything—unscrupulous— ignorant—"

Listening, as she had to do—they were face-to-face, she on her sofa, he on the adjacent leather chair—Molly felt a heating of her blood, and quickening, tightening breath; pure rage is what she felt. The shrieking anger of an overpowered child. Though actually she was neither shrieking nor overpowered.

She stood up. "Dave, now listen to me. Now *listen.* I don't want to hear this crazy stuff. You're just totally, absolutely wrong—" and, as his rant continued—"Dave, just shut up.

SHUT UP! Dave, you have to go now. I'm tired. I don't want to see you. Dave, did you hear me? I'm through."

Very ostentatiously, slowly, Dave looked at his watch, and only then he too stood up. "Lord, I'm running late," he said, as though she had not said anything at all.

"Dave, good-bye."

He smiled, with all his big strong bright teeth, and he said, "I'll call you later."

TWENTY-TWO

"We're seeing a lot of that."

"There's a lot of it around."

"There's not too much we can do about it."

"Plenty of rest and lots of liquids. Liquids are important."

"We're really seeing it a lot."

"No, statistically it's not an epidemic."

Those were the not very comforting or helpful sentences that doctors were saying to their patients during a time in late fall, early winter, when to the patients it seemed that they felt terrible. They could not get well, and nothing helped. They did not get much sympathy from their friends, most of whom felt the same, or worse. Or from the doctors, who were perhaps understandably preoccupied with more serious ailments, notably AIDS—and who did not have a lot to say about what was generally termed "flu." Which everyone seemed to have.

Felicia at last recovered, and Molly came down with it. And she found her symptoms not only uncomfortable, very, but terrifying: she imagined or believed that another large malignant green-golf-ball tumor had grown there, somewhere behind her nose.

It is difficult if not impossible to anatomize fear, but Molly gave it a try, and, if slowly, she came to several realizations, the first of which was that she was now more frightened than when she was first diagnosed and threatened by Dr. Stinger with bad survival statistics. Much more than she feared death, she understood at last, she feared more surgery. Doing all that *again*. The green OR with its ghastly lights and tubes and masked green faces. Going under, despite herself. Waking in the Recovery Room. Prods at her body, insensitive, harsh. Loud voices repeating her name. The protracted bright sleepless nightmare of Intensive Care.

She thought, I cannot go through all that again, I really and truly cannot, and she tried to consider the alternatives. Though she was not sure at all what alternatives there were. There was a long slow death, and then there was a quick exit pill, and somewhere in between there were probably treatments she didn't know about. Alternative medicine.

But in the meantime, she had to remind herself, she had only been diagnosed with flu. She had, definitely and demonstrably, a bad case of flu, that was all—all and also enough to blacken her world temporarily. To summon the ghosts of tumors and surgeons, hospital rooms and light and noise. The nightmare of radiation, nausea, despair.

Paul called. Or, rather, there was a voice on the phone that was Paul's but of course turned out to belong to Matthew. In town, wanting to come by to see her. Molly explained about her flu, although her tone must have told him that she was a little lonely and would like to see him. He would just stand in her doorway and tell her bad jokes, he said. She told him the cleaning woman would let him in.

When he came, Matthew had kindly brought a very large blue potted hydrangea, so big in fact that it was hard to see him behind it. He said, "I hope you like them too. Hydrangeas. I know some people think they're sort of low-class—Paul did as a matter of fact. But I think the blue's really great. Some sea connection, I guess. Maybe I'm just a water freak. I think so, actually."

"Why don't you put it on this table, and come sit down for a minute?"

He did as she said, with a crooked shy smile in her direction—a smile, she noted, that was very much his own, not Paul's. Paul was never shy. Molly noted that, as she had before, and she had too a sudden new thought, which was: Matthew isn't boring, he's just shy and nice, and I'm not very used to either one.

They were talking about the discomforts of flu, Molly's, and were about to move on to those of divorce, Matthew's from Joanne, when a lot of noise from downstairs announced to Molly that Felicia had dropped by. The front door banged open and there followed a sustained burst of animated conversation in Spanish between Felicia and Rosa, the cleaner. And then Felicia's light footsteps, hurrying down the hall toward them.

Molly watched as, at the door, Felicia saw Matthew, whom for an instant she took to be Paul. A quick tiny gasp, and then, still before Molly could speak, Felicia said, "Oh, you're Matthew, I've heard so much." She laughed and went over to him.

As Molly was murmuring, "Matthew—Felicia."

Matthew had stood, and said, "Felicia. I've heard of you too."

They both laughed, and Felicia came to kiss Molly, and to inquire: "How are you, really?"

Then they all talked about the weather for a while: the rains had begun, it seemed very early this year, maybe they would let up sooner than usual? In February, maybe?

Tactful Matthew soon got up to go.

"Amazing, how much alike they look," Felicia observed, once he had gone.

"Yes."

"Very alike, and in a way not," Felicia mused. "I get an idea that Matthew is nicer than Paul is—was?"

"Very much so, actually," Molly told her. And then she began to tell what it was surprising she had not said before—to this close, kind, and trusted friend. She said, "You know in some ways Paul wasn't nice at all, he just looked kind and warm. I never said this before, somehow I couldn't, but we were talking about splitting up when he got killed. I'm pretty sure we would have. So having him die like that was really—" She paused, unable to explain. (Her whole body seemed to ache, and her head.)

"Complicated," Felicia filled in softly. "God. Ambiguous."

"Yes. And then all that money I didn't really think I should have. And even if we were fighting I cared a lot about him, a *lot*. I for sure didn't want him to die. It was terrible."

"Oh, Mol, I'll bet."

"Dr. Shapiro was a terrific help."

"One good doctor."

"You mean I haven't made a match between you and Dr. Macklin?"

Felicia laughed. "No, you haven't. I think he's meant for you, and I'm sure he'd agree."

How did Felicia know that, or why did she think that? But Molly was more or less used to Felicia's witch intuitions, and sometimes she had crazy flashes of her own. "How about you and Matthew?" she said, and she improvised, "He was terribly taken with you, I could tell." On the other hand, maybe he really was.

But, "Oh no," Felicia instantly answered. "If anything, it should be Matthew and you, a sort of Old Testament arrangement. Weren't widows supposed to marry the brothers? Or then there's Henry Starck. Could you see him again?"

"I doubt it. No. Anyway, Paul. I'm just getting to the point where I can think about it a little clearly. I mean accept all the different truths: I loved him a lot, we weren't happy together, couldn't make a marriage together. And I was devastated by his death. And because of it now I have a lot of money. You see what I mean, it is complicated. And then getting the goddam cancer in my goddam sinuses. I almost have to make a connection."

"I would, I'm sure. Connect."

Molly laughed a little. "A doctor wouldn't, probably. That's something they don't do, have you noticed? They don't connect." She asked, "Do you hear from Sandy?"

"No, thank God. But I worry about hearing from him."

"Actually, Raleigh was quite marvelous. So intelligent, and he seemed to me a really kind person. And the fact that everything about Boston that we all took for granted, really everything about us, was so new to him then, that was charming. He seemed very wide-eyed, and at the same time so wise and strong. I was sure he could do anything in the world, and I knew the older doctors were really impressed. He was wonderful. He still is in his way a wonderful man, I know that. Very possibly I'm the one who went wrong—certainly all that drinking. But I'm not supposed to think that way, am I?"

The man on the line, whomever Connie was having this conversation with, made a brief, ambiguous noise of response—ambiguous to Sandy, that is, as he more or less accidentally listened in; he had picked up the phone in his study and there it was. There was so much other noise in the house at that moment, somewhere a vacuum cleaner and out in the garden an extra-loud leaf blower, no wonder they could not hear the click of Sandy's pickup. But who on earth was she talking to in this intimate way, raking up the long-dead past in which he was "wonderful," if wide-eyed? The other person was a man, his one small sound had told Sandy that much. Not that bitch Jane Stinger or some other eager lady listener (like many men, Sandy feared and hated women's conversations, and was consumed with curiosity about them). Could she possibly be talking to a lawyer? If so, he did not see the point in all these intimate, personal details; on the other hand, these days, who knew?

"I've heard good things about him," said the man—the lawyer? The voice was raspy, maybe alcoholic. Harvard? He sounded like it.

"When can I see you?" the man asked Connie, not sounding businesslike but eager. Could they—could Connie, possibly—?

A sudden strong urge to urinate caused Sandy to put down the phone. He hoped the vacuum would drown out that sound too.

Oh Christ, if only he could pee!

He had to see someone, obviously. This prostate problem and now exacerbated by this goddam flu.

He thought, There must be a way to get into Felicia's house without tripping the alarm. And a way to kill Felicia without getting caught—a doctor should be able to do that. He thought, I could be waiting when she comes home, and get her before she goes into the house, before she's turned on the alarm. Maybe I could talk her into letting me in? Say we should try to be friends, be civilized?

He could make what military men call a surgical strike. Only his really would be surgical, or would that be a mistake?—a signature, as it were? A surgical strike indeed.

But would killing Felicia make him feel better or worse? He did not know; he only knew that the very idea made him even more tired and sad than he already was.

It would be much easier, he thought with a small ironic smile, much easier just to stay home and put a knife to old Connie. Which if she is talking to a lawyer, I absolutely will, he thought.

Connie said, "That damn vacuum, it's hard to hear you."

"I said, when can I see you?"

"Was that a click on the line?"

"I didn't hear it. Is your—is Raleigh in the house?"

"I think so, but he'd never listen. He's very honorable, in his way."

"I'm glad to hear it. Look, can we meet tonight? Can you come over?"

"Oh, darling Henry, *yes.*"

Jane Stinger, her divorce from Dr. Mark well under way, moved tidily and very happily to a small cottage on a hilltop in Mill Valley. Built as a visitors' annex by the two men who owned the much larger main house, the little cottage was neat and spare; its living room's big glass wall gave a lovely view of far-off hills and graceful neighboring trees, redwoods, eucalyptus— there was even a palm tree adjacent to the house. Inside, the kitchen was small but handy, her bedroom small and the guest room smaller still, the living room more generous but still quite small. Jane, however, loved this diminution, plus the corre- sponding vast increase in the available outdoors. For one thing it was precisely the opposite of what she had had with Mark in Seacliff; there the large house with its decks and balconies had covered, or almost, the big city lot. How lost she had felt in that house, how lost and alone—and sick; she associated all that space with drinking and subsequent illness. Her fault, of course, no one had made her drink, and certainly Mark had always urged against it. But there seemed no other way to fill such inner emptiness, such spiritual solitude.

In any case, this new arrangement for living, including a long, broad swimming pool, which her generous landlords urged her to use, seemed to Jane a part of the healthy picture that was now her life: a life without drinking and without mean little Mark; an outdoor life of hikes and swimming, and meet- ings. She even planned to get a dog, a big golden, she thought, which Dick and Brian, the landlords, said would be all right, they liked dogs too. Mark hated dogs almost as much as he hated cats (and people, Jane had secretly thought).

Three days a week Jane drove into town to work; on the other days she walked down to the village on various errands. There was an exceptionally pleasant bookstore with a coffee shop attached, where she could sit outside and read and drink herbal tea.

An exemplary life, then, as Jane remarked on the phone to her friend Connie Sanderson. "It's like a reward, something I'd always wanted but didn't know quite how to go about getting."

Therefore, when Jane came down with what she was at length forced to recognize as flu, she was furious, outraged. For a week or so she angrily refused to give in to it, to call a doctor (God forbid a doctor) or to go to bed.

Running into Brian in the market, though, she admitted, "Actually I don't feel too well. I guess some kind of flu."

"You look fairly terrible," he said. "You'd really better call a doctor. We can't have a new tenant dying on the premises. Look, Dick and I have this guy whose office is just down the hill. And so far he seems okay."

That night Dick brought her some homemade chicken-barley soup, and he too encouraged Jane to go to their doctor. And the next day Jane, feeling much worse, called and made an appointment, and went to his office.

Anticipating a doctor more or less in the image of Brian and Dick, a nice intelligent young gay man, friendly and sympathetic—in every way a nice change from mean macho Mark—Jane was a little surprised to find a tall, oldish bald doctor, censorious rather than friendly, but seemingly intelligent. Still, she responded positively, at first, and she knew enough doctors to be suspicious of friendliness, or too-ready sympathy; this man was neither especially friendly nor sympathetic.

He examined her and asked a few routine questions, and she

liked him well enough until his closing speech, when he said, "Well, we're seeing a lot of this, and there's not too much we can do about it. Plenty of rest and liquids—"

At which point Jane boiled over with accumulated years of rage, at Mark and at his profession in general, at most of the doctors she had ever met. Plus which she felt really terrible and was in no mood to hear that nothing, really, could be done. And so she burst out, "What you mean is that you guys still can't do anything about something that happens all the time, like flu. You're great on some kinds of cancer, especially the kinds that most people never get, but you don't do too well with normal, ordinary unassuming misery. Liquids and rest! How come you didn't even mention chicken soup? No Jewish mother, I guess. Or vitamin C, for God's sake. Give me a break! I was married to a doctor for twenty years, I've heard all that crap."

To Jane's vast surprise, this doctor grinned: Was he nuts, did he really go for abuse? His teeth were large and white, forbidding in their brilliance.

"As a matter of fact, I did have a Jewish mother," Dave Jacobs told her. "And, of course, Mark Stinger. I didn't make the connection. If I were you, I'd go home and have a double martini. And then some chicken soup."

"I don't drink," Jane stated, unsmiling (he was grinning enough for both of them). "I'm an alcoholic. Recovering in AA."

TWENTY-THREE

The urologist whom Sandy went to see at last, Dr. Fink, was an unfortunate-looking man. Looks-deprived: would that be the PC phrase? Sandy didn't know; he had to smile, though, at the thought of what he would have said to a patient who complained about a doctor's looks—especially a urologist, for Christ's sake. Some damn-fool dumb broad with a leaky bladder.

Fink had thin red hair, a freckled reddish face, and a big red bulbous freckled nose (did the guy have freckles on his dick too? Probably, thought Sandy, with a secret snicker). Fink's hands were small (small hands small cock, Sandy had heard, and he imagined a tiny, freckled tool). His own hands were long and strong and shapely. Surgeon's hands. Extra-large surgeon's hands.

But Fink was supposed to be the best in town, in urology; all the other doctors went to him when it got down to the nitty-gritty—which is just where Sandy thought he himself was, right then. Well, of course he was, or he wouldn't be here. Still, those hands? Thank God for rubber gloves.

Fink's manner was not so great either. The way he put things. What he said was "Christ, man, you mean you never felt that lump?"

"I don't spend a lot of time with my fingers up my ass."

A pause as Fink continued to probe, which did not feel good. "Try to relax," said Fink (the jerk!).

And then, straightening up, he said, "Of course we could try surgery," in his stupid wheezy voice. As though Sandy had never heard of surgery. Jesus!

"But it's a big one," Fink stupidly, inexorably went on. "You probably know the risks." He gave Sandy a pale-blue, blinking look from behind his bifocals.

Yes, I'll be impotent, you dumb prick. Sandy did not say this, he only grunted. But of course they both knew. And then there's sometimes some degree of incontinence: how come this Fink or whatever he calls himself didn't mention that?

Fink cleared his throat wheezily, and looked away. Still blinking, he murmured, "And then there's the possibility of some degree of incontinence."

In other words, you can't get it up and you wet your pants a lot. Or you diaper up, hiding those things and the stained underwear from the maids and your goddam nosy sympathetic wife, like you used to with the lipstick on handkerchiefs and shirt collars. And, further back, the rubbers you hid in your sock drawer, out of sight of your mom.

To Fink, Sandy said, "I've heard tell."

Fink then leaned back so that his leather chair creaked. Showing off his ugly chest, his wide-striped shirt and purple tie. Purple with red hair? As Felicia would say, Please, gimme a break!

"What I usually recommend," Fink pontificated, "is some time down at Alta Linda. They're doing some great prostate stuff down there."

"Alta Linda! That scumbag hellhole of a hospital from hell? Christ! Have you ever been down there? Ugliest place in the world, full of old creeps in wheelchairs—cancer—"

"But I always—" Fink was weakly explaining.

"So do I! I send CA patients down there all the time. But that's not the same thing."

This fact that he himself would not necessarily go to a place or undergo a treatment that he had often recommended to patients was so obvious to Sandy that he felt no need to explain. And certainly not to this horribly dressed Jewish quiz kid.

The truth was—no matter what he had said to various patients, including Felicia's friend, that Molly Bonner—Sandy would rather die than go to Alta Linda as a patient. And, as Sandy thought this, he further thought, somewhat wryly, It may come to that.

Going down in the elevator, for some reason he found himself thinking intensively about O. J. Simpson. He got off, is what Sandy was thinking. And Nicole did not get by with sleeping around—blonde spoiled bitch. But then he had to remind himself of several obvious facts: One was that O.J. had much more money than he did, although luckily he himself was not exactly poor. Not without resources. But O.J. was black, with a wild black lawyer, lots of lawyers, and a bunch of blacks on his jury. Suppose he, Sandy, had a jury full of doctors—straight, non-Jewish doctors? They'd hang him, they'd love to. He knew that.

Besides, he had no real intention of doing anything so violent and ugly to Felicia.

Jesus, he must be going more than a little crazy, even to be thinking along these lines.

Besides, if he did go after Felicia—or after anyone, for that matter—he would know exactly where to put the knife. Very cleanly, with no mess.

In Felicia's kitchen, she and Matthew West were listening breathlessly to certain sounds from her garden, both familiar and frightening to Felicia. To Matthew, an almost welcome diversion: he found Felicia, her breasts and her eyes, somewhat overwhelming.

Felicia said, "I just don't really know who's out there. I thought I did but now I'm not so sure."

If he had been his brother, if he had been Paul, Matthew thought, he would have rushed out into the dark to see what or who was there, and then rushed back into the house, heroic, to attack this lovely voluptuous blonde with kisses, fierce embraces. Or that is how Matthew always imagined Paul's behavior; Paul had never especially boasted, and was certainly not given to sexual boasts. Also, Matthew depressingly thought, if he were Paul he'd be dead, instead of sitting here half-gassed with this beautiful sexy woman, ogling her breasts like a schoolboy.

The evening had begun very innocently, at Molly Bonner's. Matthew had called to ask if he could come by to see her, and she had said sure, and that there might also be her friend Felicia Flood, whom Matthew had met a few times before. Fleetingly—Felicia seemed usually in a hurry. But they were both very faithful visitors to Molly, it seemed. Felicia, this afternoon, had brought a big pot of fish soup for Molly's supper. But Molly had said, with a small weak apologetic laugh, "Felish, I just can't. I think I'm having an attack of the vapors or something. You know, it comes and goes. But today I just can't eat."

"Should I call Dave?"

Unaccountably to Matthew, they both laughed at this suggestion.

To him the soup smelled marvelous, of fish and garlic and onions, and somehow of lemon. All his favorite smells, and he must have looked hungry for Felicia said, "Well, Matthew, it's up to you. My freezer's almost full and it won't last forever. It's up to you to come and help me out with the soup."

And so Matthew did. He carried the big black cast-iron pot out to her car and he held it steady as Felicia drove down to her house, and when they got there he carried it inside, into the small pretty house, the red-and-yellow kitchen. And while Felicia was heating up the soup, warming bread and bowls and tearing lettuce for a salad, Matthew sat at the butcher-block table and drank some nice chilled white wine.

Too much wine. By the time the food was ready, Matthew had drunk an oversized wineglass full, plus the wine he had already had at Molly's. All in all, a lot more than he was used to. He did not feel drunk so much as very slightly unreal. What was he doing here in this strange, rather disheveled but attractive small house, with this strange and extremely attractive large blonde woman?

She had drunk a fair amount too, and the wine seemed to make her talkative, or maybe she too was a little nervous. She said, "Molly looks so much better, don't you think? She had got so thin and that stupid Dr. Dave kept feeding her steak that she couldn't eat. It's so good that she got rid of him, at last. I thought the way she up and left Alta Linda was marvelous— such fun for us both! But sometimes she sort of regresses, and doesn't feel too great, but that gets less and less often. And I do think finally getting Dave out of her life was a great step forward." She paused to sip more wine, and then to laugh. "It's funny, we both seem to have got rid of doctors at more or less the same moment. Which wasn't easy, in either case."

By now they had finished bowls of soup, some bread and salad, and a considerable amount of wine.

The night outside was dark and rustling, breezy. Full of the sound of leaves, and boughs. But Matthew heard then another sound, footsteps on gravel, slow but definite, purposeful. Still, he couldn't be entirely sure of what he heard, what with all the other night noise—and all the wine.

He looked across at Felicia, and saw that she had heard it too.

Not lowering her voice, she told him, "Almost every night he comes here. At about this time. Now he'll pee."

And so he did. There was the tiny trickling sound of water, or whatever, against dry leaves.

Felicia said, again, that she didn't know, really, who was out there in the dark. "I thought I did but now I'm not so sure," she said. And, in what he felt to be an abbreviated way, she told him about her long and, he gathered, intense involvement with a local surgeon. Specializing in heart surgery, she said. Well known, "prominent." Married, of course. "I was sure it was Sandy out there, sort of stalking. Like O.J. But lately I've wondered. It could be almost anyone, which is a lot scarier."

Agreeing, Matthew added, "It's not necessarily the same person every night either, is it?"

"No." She seemed to consider this. "No, of course not. I'd just sort of assumed that it was. The peeing seemed a sort of signature, you know?"

They were now sitting in a shadowy half-light. Attentive to Felicia, who was staring out the window, Matthew observed that in profile her face was both stronger and less beautiful than earlier, before the dark. Her nose was long and straight, a forthright, purposeful nose, and her forehead straight and commanding, like a prow. Her mouth was strong and firm. But then she turned to him, and she smiled, and everything softened. Her eyes glistened, so blue, and her voice shook a little as she said, "I know this sounds crazy, but would you just stay and sleep with me? I mean"—she looked down, and away—"we don't have to do anything. I just don't feel like sleeping by myself."

Matthew, his heart jumping wildly, spoke as diffidently as he could. "Sure," he said. "Sure."

"I was what they're starting to call an Avoidance Addict," said Henry Starck, with his small dry laugh. "Or that's what Gloria kept telling me. Whereas she was a Love Addict, and so it was hopeless. And fatal."

"I don't think I'm a Love Addict," Connie mused aloud—as

she thought that actually that was a fair description of her old self, with Raleigh. And so she added, "But maybe I was." She also thought, To some extent I still am. In a way. I am crazy about this Henry Starck.

However, even though she had determined to be honest, she did not add that thought. Certainly not. Undoubtedly he more or less knew what she felt, and if he still was at all what they called an Avoidance Addict, her intensity would make him uneasy. She would have to watch it.

But Henry was deeply familiar to Connie, whereas Raleigh had always been somewhat alien, strange. Although much younger (she had to remind herself at times how young Henry was), he still could have been one of the boys she went to parties with a long time ago. Dancing on the Ritz roof, in summer, after an Esplanade concert, or drinking and necking (mildly) in the darkened bar of the old Lafayette. Henry still had the slightly stiff prep-school posture of boys from those days. She was moved by the set of his shoulders, and by his New England vowels.

Henry, true to type, seemed to feel that they should not actually make love. This was not explicitly stated; they just did not. They fervently kissed, and then they left it at that. They rose from the couch, or wherever they had been, and they said good night very lovingly.

Connie was slightly puzzled at first by the fact that she did not find this upsetting, or even odd—unless she gave it too much thought. She was even relieved, in a way, and she very well understood her own relief: sex with Raleigh had been so—so *terrible* for at least the last ten years or so, that she was just as glad not to have to do it.

The words "making love" in fact did not apply to what she and Raleigh did. As he himself put it, he fucked her. In recent years, he did this once a week, punctiliously. She imagined him saying to himself, with mad male pride, I fuck my wife at least once a week. It was usually very quick, on Saturday mornings, the first chore of the day got through early. Sometimes he even whispered complaints, "You're not helping much, how can I come?" But he always did, whether or not she even bothered to pretend.

For a long time she knew that this was all her fault; her "frigidity" was to blame for everything, including Felicia Flood. And then when she started in serious drinking, she knew that she was to blame; who would want to make love to or even to "fuck" a fat old drunken woman? Forgetting the years when she was thin and hardly drank at all, when Raleigh made love to her, although he liked to call it fucking even then, and she never had to pretend, but rather to stop herself from letting him know how eager, how aroused she was. To stop herself from coming too soon, before he did. Although when that happened he didn't seem to mind. He only minded "frigidity."

Connie knew that Raleigh was not responsible for her "low self-esteem," so much mentioned and discussed in meetings. That had evolved over many earlier years. However, she did feel that he had certainly not improved how she felt about herself. For years she had thought that if she had been a really attractive, worthwhile woman he would not have been so often, so flagrantly untrue, although in a textbook way she knew that logic to be wrong; unfaithful men (or women, very probably) were unfaithful for reasons having little or nothing to do with their victims (look at O.J.'s wife, Nicole, the perfectly beautiful blonde, and he was not only unfaithful, he killed her, probably).

To Henry, Connie now said, and the words came from nowhere, really, "I'm sort of afraid of Raleigh, these days. I know it's irrational, but he seems so—so desperate." She did not add, If he knew you were here and that we had been kissing, he'd shoot us both—although she felt that to be true. Instead she said, "He's not supposed to come over without calling first, but then he's never been notably obedient. And he can't stand lawyers."

They were that afternoon having their own version of the

cocktail hour. Connie and Henry, drinking Clamato with lemon. In Connie's highly polished, antique-thronged living room, a room that she no longer liked at all, but she was not quite sure what to do about it. Her lawyer had said that since the furniture came from her family it would be hers, and she had tried giving some of it to her children. "Mom, come on, can you see any of that stuff in Oakland?" Some vestigial New England thrift prevented her from just calling the Goodwill to haul it away. She would simply sell it, at times she decided, and take whatever she could get for it, and donate the money to St. Anthony's, or Open Hand. And if Raleigh kicked up—well, *tant pis.*

But she should not dwell on such problems now. She should take it a day at a time, as she had tried to learn to do, and today she is with this nice young Henry Starck, from Portland, Maine, who is so attractive to her. She would tell him something sort of funny, she decided.

Raising her small pointed chin, Connie laughed a little as she began: "You remember Jane, from meetings, don't you?"

Henry smiled, and nodded.

"You remember, in some of her 'shares' she was talking about leaving her husband, who was this really mean little doctor? Well, it's too funny. She had flu, and went to this doctor in Mill Valley—I think her new landlord recommended him—and the doctor gave her some new antibiotic that cured her flu right away. And then he kept calling to see how she was. And then he told her she didn't need a doctor anymore, and would she go out to dinner. Actually, I've met him. An internist, Dave Jacobs. I didn't like him very much, I thought he seemed mean and bossy, but Jane seems really pleased. Maybe she can handle him. I told her she was addicted to doctors, but I'm not sure how funny she thought that was."

"I think it's very funny." Henry laughed, and he added, "I'm very glad you're not, though."

She smiled up at him. "So am I. Very glad."

TWENTY-FOUR

"You're really lucky to be alive," said Dr. Douglas Macklin to Molly Bonner. "After all that."

"Tell me something I don't know!" But even as she spoke Molly knew that this was rude, and not at all in the right tone for this visit. And so she apologized (she had a definite agenda). "I'm sorry, it's just that I have heard that so much, and in a way you could say it to anyone. Bill Clinton or Magic Johnson. O. J. Simpson. Anyone. And I've especially heard that a lot from doctors."

But despite all her efforts Macklin seemed not to be listening. "Lucky!" he repeated somewhat dreamily. And then, with a big grin, he told her, "I've had some good luck too, you might say."

A quickie divorce, with no trouble? Molly's agile mind had raced ahead to that possible news, which would perfectly coincide with her own plan: she meant to retract her earlier scruple about their going out. The more she had thought about it the more foolish her position had seemed to her. They obviously liked each other; why not? Besides, how many attractive and intelligent, straight, single men did she or anyone know? Plus kind, and funny. Douglas Macklin was all these things, and possibly more; she would be a fool to turn him down completely. She could always find another doctor somewhere. (She would only go to women doctors from now on, she had sometimes thought.) And so she smiled across at Dr. Macklin, Douglas, warmly. Maybe sexily.

He smiled back, warm and friendly. "I knew you'd be pleased to hear this," he said. "As you know, you're really more than just a, uh, patient." Was he blushing a little? And then he said, "I thought you'd want to know"—God, why didn't he get on with it?—"that Claire and I, well, we're not divorcing after all. We got back together."

A simple enough statement, but his delivery had been so laborious that it took Molly several seconds to take it in. Also, that was not exactly the message that she had wanted to hear.

However, she managed to beam in response, and to tell him, "Well, that's really great. Terrific."

"Yes." He continued, smiling, "I think things will be better than ever now. I guess we just needed a little shaking up, you know. But I think once we both faced the prospect of living apart, we were truly appalled. We couldn't do it. Gee, I met Claire back in high school, when I was playing baseball." A triumphant smile. "So now we're going to celebrate with a snow-climbing trip in the Andes. You know it's spring down there, and we've always wanted to do this."

One of the things that Molly thought, on leaving Macklin's office, was, Thank God I don't have to go climbing around in the snow, in the goddam Andes. But then she thought, It's not as though I'd had a choice, actually. He did not exactly ask me, not at all. One chance at dinner was all I got, and even that I'm sure he would have retracted. He wants to be married. To Claire.

The San Francisco day into which she walked out, though, was ravishingly lovely: a clear blue sky, and golden warmth. Later there would be drought alarms, undoubtedly, and threats of water rationing. Dead lawns and slowly dying flowers. But for the moment it was hard not just to accept this beneficent, gorgeous weather as a gift—unless you gave serious thought in a general way to the weather of the world. As Molly tended to do. It seemed to her that every season was unseasonable now, floods in Norway, heat waves in England and Italy. Tornadoes in Georgia, and earthquakes everywhere. Did the fact of global warming explain any or all of this?

And just underneath, or perhaps behind, this local, unnatural warmth was the faintest, slightest chill, like a very pale shadow, a whispered rumor of fall.

In part because of the weather, Molly had chosen to walk to Dr. Macklin's office from her apartment—though in quite a different mood. Then, an hour or so earlier, she had felt a mild excitement, and some small nervousness about her plan: to say, in effect, to Douglas Macklin, Let's do go out, and see what happens. Now, not quite defeated but almost, she was aware of some little embarrassment, as though Macklin had read her mind, had seen or felt her intention. More reasonably she decided that this was impossible. Also, with yet more reason, and sense, she could see that things were better all around for everyone. For Douglas Macklin and his Claire, and for herself; she needed at least one good, reliable, and fairly sensitive doctor. She even further thought, and this was somewhat less rational: I really feel too well these days to hang out with doctors.

But it was true; she did feel extremely well, healthy and strong, walking fast in that euphoric, brilliant air. She did not need to be "involved" with anyone at all. She needed sunshine, and long fast walks in this clean fresh lively wind.

Across the Golden Gate Bridge, in Sausalito, on the other side of all that bright choppy blue bay water, but in much the same weather, Jane Stinger and Connie Sanderson, as they often did after their Mill Valley AA meeting, were discussing their own lives in greater detail than either had offered in the more public "sharing." And they had come to rather different conclusions about life and love from those reached by Molly Bonner.

"Do you really think I'm a doctor junkie?" Jane asked Connie, half laughing. "Don't think it hasn't occurred to me, and sometimes seriously. But I don't think so. God, they're so unlike each other. Mark and Dave. Dave can be irritating too, God knows, but he's just so—so incredibly sexy. I mean, all the time. He says that Molly Bonner used to complain about too much sex. God, some complaint."

Connie smiled, hoping that her expression successfully concealed certain reactions that she felt to be impermissible.

One, she was embarrassed. She was simply not used to that sort of conversation, even after all the AA shares and all the making friends over coffee with Jane, she still was bothered by such personal revelation. No one she had ever known before had talked about her intimate (sexual) life. Nor for that matter had she and Raleigh talked about it, ever. And as a matter of fact Connie had had something of the same problem with Raleigh that Jane had described with Dave Jacobs and Molly Bonner. Hyperactivity. At first—that is, a long time ago.

And, two, she was just a little envious. Hyperactivity in that area was not an accusation that she would make of Henry Starck. He did not exactly conform to the stereotype of the young lover, in that regard—although he had managed to overcome his early scruples about actually making love; now they spent long nights together. But, if anything, Connie was the more eager, the more passionate. Embarrassing to think of it that way, but there it was; she had to be honest and face things, at least with herself. She did not, though, see any necessity for sharing details of her sexual life with Henry—with Jane. She didn't need to, and what good would it really do anyone? She loved Henry in her way, and he loved her in his, and his presence in her life made her much happier than she had been before. As did hers in his, she was sure; he had even said so, in his way.

"Dave doesn't have the greatest manners in the world, though," Jane continued. "I have to admit, he's pretty pushy and he makes a sort of point of saying the wrong thing to people. I've tried to tell him, and I think he really wants to change, and I can help him. I know I can."

Connie reacted to all this in several separate ways, most of which she kept to herself. First off, she thought just a little smugly that Henry was really the least rude, least pushy, and most courteous person she had ever met. She thought too that Jane had certain tendencies toward pushiness herself, and she wondered how this would come out, Jane Stinger and Dave Jacobs, each pushing in opposite directions. She did not think that Jane would succeed in changing Dave, certainly not much. Conventional wisdom, and received opinion would apply, she thought: people don't change. And especially not a rather stubborn older man. A doctor.

But she said, "I used to think Raleigh was a little rude, and he was, by Boston standards."

"Did he change much?" Jane eagerly asked.

"No, really not." Connie could not resist saying this, the truth. Raleigh's manners had not changed much, he had only become so successful that no one minded. She said, "Maybe doctors are like that, do you think? Basically very self-absorbed?"

Jane frowned. "No, I don't think that. Not really. I think Dave's just reacting to such terrible treatment from that Molly Bonner. Talk about ungrateful! You know, she was really sick, and he took care of her, he even took her down to Alta Linda, radiation for her cancer, and she was just—just terrible to him. I think he's hitting out at the world, because of her."

Connie remembered Dave as a rather rude and aggressive young man, many years ago, when he was supposedly happily married. And at that time, since Raleigh was somewhat like that too, she had indeed wondered, Is it being a doctor that makes some men rude? Not wanting to say any of that to Jane Stinger (if Jane and Dave Jacobs made each other happy, *tant mieux*), Connie said another thing that she had not intended; she said, "I'm really worried about Raleigh. I never hear from him, and God knows the children don't. I just hope he's okay."

With a short laugh, Jane suggested, "I could call that Felicia Flood. Dave knows her. She might know."

"Oh, I don't think we have to do that," said Connie. And as she too laughed, she added, "I'm not all that concerned."

Connie was also thinking about the (to her) unknown Molly Bonner. Henry's first wife. Henry had spoken of her almost not at all, and when he had he had done so with characteristic gallantry and restraint. "She's a marvelous woman," he had said, not specifying in what ways—so that Connie had wondered: Did he mean great moral stature of some sort, a marvelous hostess, or cook? Marvelous in bed? "She just doesn't seem to marry very well," Henry had added, with a smallish laugh. Connie asked him, "Paul wasn't wonderful?" "I know almost nothing about him. I meant me."

As Connie and Jane sat there in the briny Sausalito sunshine, though, sipping at innocently unfermented fruity drinks, Connie reflected that what she had said about Raleigh was not entirely true. She did worry about Raleigh; she felt that in some permanent way they were married still.

And so in some spirit of obligation to the truth, perhaps AA-inspired, she said to Jane, "Actually I can't seem to just dismiss Raleigh, just to decide that he's not my worry anymore. I wish I could but I can't."

Jane was more sympathetic to this view than Connie would have expected. "Oh, I know," she said, with feeling. "I worry about Mark too, never mind that he has this beautiful Japanese girlfriend." But she added, in a mutter, "Shit that he is."

"Some curious instinct is telling me that Raleigh's really in trouble," said Connie very seriously. "And I can't do a damn thing to help."

"You didn't cause it, you can't cure it," Jane quoted, and then, with an obvious shift of attention, away from Connie and Raleigh, she began to smile. She said, "I really gave it to Dave last night, though. I guess he thought he was being flattering, but he told me he'd always liked shiksas, his wife and now me. Can you imagine? Of all the ridiculous, racist, sexist remarks. Well, I really let him have it—" And she laughed with pleasure, remembering.

TWENTY-FIVE

Felicia said, "This is terrific! You *never* drop in. And I've got so much to tell you! You won't believe what's happened. You really must have felt me wanting to see you. I called but of course you weren't there."

"Well, I did have this strong feeling that I wanted to come and see you, and it seemed silly to look around for a phone before I did."

They both laughed.

It was true: partly because of the warm and beautiful day, Molly had not wanted to go directly home—where, alone with her cats, she might well be subject to lonely thoughts, even regretful ones, concerning Douglas Macklin. But more strongly than the weather and fears of solitude she had heard an inner voice that urged her toward Felicia. She would find Felicia out in her garden, she knew that she would, and they could just sit out there for a while and talk.

And Molly did just that. Instead of turning off Divisadero toward her own flat, on Pacific, she continued down to Vallejo Street, to Felicia. And she went into Felicia's garden, where the gate had been left open, as though for her coming (but she would have to remind Felicia again, that was really not safe).

However, Felicia was much too eager to tell her news; literally breathless, she had no time for remonstrance, or even for much greeting small talk. "I've got so much to tell you," she repeated.

In brief, what happened was that Sandy, Dr. Raleigh Sanderson, had tripped and sprained his ankle. Right there in the garden. Couldn't move, had to be carted off in an ambulance, which Matthew called. In fact, Matthew had begun the whole process that led to the fall, the sprain, the ambulance.

Matthew and Felicia had had a long, pleasant dinner together in Felicia's kitchen, one of Felicia's richest, most garlicky stews, and a bright crisp salad, a nice wine—very possibly too much wine. And too much food. So that Matthew said, "I've really overeaten. Shall we run around the block?"

"Are you serious? Sounds crazy but it's probably a good idea."

They looked at each other in a smiling but still-testing way, and Matthew said, "You're really the greatest, you know?"

"You're so nice—"

"Well, okay! Let's go." They both stood up.

But at that moment the phone rang, and Felicia made two somewhat odd choices: one was that she answered it at all, and the other was that she did so in her bedroom, rather than right there in the kitchen. Later she was to think: Maybe I sort of knew it was something private, and bad?

Five or so minutes later she came back from the phone, not quite knowing how to tell Matthew what had happened. But she started in. Looking at him very directly as she spoke, she said, "That was about Will. A man I knew in Seattle. His sister was on the phone—she told me he'd shot himself, and she thought I'd want to know. Well, I didn't exactly want to know but I guess that's what people say, they think you'd want to know.

"He had this huge gun collection—we pretty much fell out

over that. He even belonged to the NRA. I knew he was unhappy, that things weren't working out for him, but I guess I
didn't see *how* depressed he was. With all his guns." She shivered a little. "It's scary, you know? To tell you the truth, now I
don't much feel like a walk. I think about guns, and whoever it
is that comes into the garden—"

Matthew said, "Of course," and came over to pat and then
to enfold her in a brief, unsexy, but reassuring hug. "If you don't
mind I'm going out for a little while," he said. "I've got an idea
about this guy in the garden."

She should have been thinking about poor Will, Felicia
thought, in her bathroom, getting ready for bed. But she was
not; she was washing and drying herself, brushing and lotioning,
here and there the tiniest touch of perfume. Silk and lace on her
clean smooth naked skin, and then the cool touch of fresh linen
sheets. She was thinking of Matthew, thinking happily of love,
and pleasure.

Matthew came back into the house, and he too was thinking
of love, but first he said, with a small pleased laugh, "I think I've
fixed that guy. But good." And then, "Oh God! what a lovely
woman—everywhere—lovely."

About an hour later, half dozing in the happy aftermath of
love, they were awakened by a shout—a scream of surprise and
pain from the garden. Terrible, and to Felicia identifiable.

"Jesus!" she whispered to Matthew. "It's Sandy."

" 'Embarrassing' is barely the word for it," Felicia told
Molly. "Except that all three of us were more than a little out of
focus. Matthew and I were still a little—well, you know, half-
asleep—and we had had a lot of wine. And Sandy was really in
pain. Matthew'd grabbed up his shoes and pants and sweater,
and I just had a robe and slippers, so it was all pretty obvious.
Jesus! I had to introduce them. Of course they didn't shake
hands or anything, just sort of grunted, both of them—and

Sandy stuck out his elbow and he said, 'Don't touch me,' or something like that. 'Just call 911.' Matthew asked if he wanted a brandy or anything, and Sandy said no, and then he said, 'I'm a doctor.' As if that explained anything."

"Actually explains quite a lot," said Molly.

They both laughed.

"When I think of how we looked!" Felicia went on. "Remember that fancy pink silk robe that Sandy brought me from New Orleans? Well, it sort of matches the nightgown I'd uh, started out in, put on after my bath, and so that was what I just grabbed up. Oh, I forgot to say that Sandy was in *black tie*. God knows where he'd been, some fancy doctor do. But there the three of us were in our costumes. And poor Sandy, really in pain. His face all screwed up. But he insisted on just lying there until the ambulance came, he wouldn't let either of us touch him. God, talk about glowering. And then when the ambulance pulled up and the guys got out, you would have thought he was R. Milhous Nixon, with his troops. Giving orders. In fact that's what he said, 'Take me to the General.' It was a minute before I realized that he meant San Francisco General, the hospital. That's where he always said you should go for emergencies. Well, anyway. What a night!"

"Indeed," agreed Molly.

"So odd," Felicia mused. "If it hadn't been for that terrible phone call, poor Will's sister, I would have gone for the walk with Matthew, and Matthew wouldn't have set the trap that made Sandy trip and sprain his ankle."

"What kind of a trap was it?"

"Really simple. Just one of my little gardening benches across the path. But actually it's lucky he didn't get hurt worse. Poor man, lying there in his fancy clothes. His black tie. I guess I should call and see how he is."

"Maybe," Molly reluctantly said.

"Matthew's gone to some sort of diving meet out at Ocean

Beach. It's interesting how unlike they are, isn't it? Matthew and Paul."

"Yes," said Molly, hoping this to be the truth.

As she walked up the hill toward her building a little later, Molly reflected on several not quite related topics. One, on the whole she felt that she was pleased with the way things had worked out with Dr. Macklin. He was a very nice man and a very good doctor, and his wife was obviously what he most wanted, so it was good that he should get her back. Also, good doctors were not all that easily come by—she guessed.

She thought too that she was much more tired than she should be, and for just an instant a familiar panic touched her. *Had* her green-golf-ball tumor come back, or maybe a new one, more virulent, more aggressive?

But then she thought: It's only a year since all that surgery. In fact, as she recalled the date, which was also that day's date, she saw that this was the anniversary. And, as a present, she let up on herself a little, assuring herself (as she might have a friend), You've been through a lot this year. It's not surprising that you're not entirely recovered. It's okay to be tired.

Knowing she should not, though, Molly imagined that time a year ago. The weeks and days just before surgery when she had thought that any change, even death, would be an improvement.

She remembered the anesthetist in that frightful green OR saying to her, "Good night, now, sleep well," heavily ironic. The Recovery Room, then Intensive Care. The doctors, including Dave, saying over and over, "The size of a golf ball, how lucky you are!" Doctors asking the other women in the room, who was really only one poor crazy woman, "Do you know where you are?" The double clock.

And then radiation. Nausea, endless nausea—thinking again

that any change would be an improvement. And Alta Linda, the bottom of the world.

There in the brilliant, clear winter sunshine, Molly shuddered a little; she tried to reassure herself that none of that could happen again, not ever. And in the meantime she stopped for a minute to rest, halfway up that very steep hill, with its glorious view of water, and boats, and farther hills of promising bright grass.

She was struck by a vision, or a fantasy: for a euphoric moment she imagined that she and Felicia would rent some space down in the Tenderloin, say (or even buy a building; with all this money Molly could afford to do that), and make it into a warm bright clean new shelter, with beds and food and baths and privacy for homeless people, men and women, children, anyone. A crazy idea (she imagined what Dave would say), impractical, probably, but nevertheless it made her smile with pleasure. She would call Felicia right away, when she got home. At least Felicia would be enthusiastic. Forgetting fatigue, Molly began to hurry up the hill.

TWENTY-SIX

Dr. Raleigh Sanderson wheeled along expertly in his chair, his injured, bandaged ankle riding ahead like a banner, a signal that he was of a breed apart; he was not related to all the other men in wheelchairs who, less skillfully and less aggressively, maneuvered the long corridors, often with the help of attendants, or who sat about in the bright self-consciously cheery waiting rooms. Just as Dr. Sanderson's bright-white hair signaled otherness: although he and many of these men were about the same age, and some were even younger, he had the best head of hair in the bunch, white but strong and full. Alive, and vigorous.

The other men, the patients, had looks of defeat and shame. (Of impotence.) They were embarrassed to be in this place at all; they had let it get them down. Even, this morning one old guy in cords and one of those old-timey camel-hair cardigans—this bald guy actually asked, "Does this here particle stuff work on ankles too?"

Jesus H. Christ! Laymen. Sandy started to explain but then he thought, Oh, why the fuck bother? Let this stupid prick assume whatever he wanted. So he just said, "Sure, these fifty-million-buck machines can do anything." And he laughed, as though he had paid for them himself. (Come to think of it, he wouldn't mind owning a piece of this action, not at all. He wondered who did—he would have to investigate. Even post-divorce he'd have a few bundles around.)

"You headed for the room?" this jerk asked next.

"Oh no, I'm heading out. I've got a car coming." Not saying, I've already been to the room, I've had my jolt for the day.

And he certainly did not tell the story of how he had been railroaded down here. How he went to the General in the ambulance, thanks to that slut Felicia and her boyfriend. His terrible attack of groin pain, and the smart-ass resident who said, "That's sure a long way from your ankle. Sounds like a prostate problem to me. Should we call your regular doctor?" And so on, until he, Raleigh, had been convinced that at this place, this Alta Linda, he might, just might, get radiation that would shrink the tumor. Avoid surgery. If only what he had said to that stupid guy (and impotent: Sandy could tell from his eyes) turned out to be true, that these fifty-million-buck machines could do anything.

The car he had ordered turned out to be a limo, an old one, not a stretch; still, it looked long and sleek and black and conspicuous among the old clunks or new Jap cheapos that most of these people, these *patients* drove or were driven in by relatives, not chauffeurs. Moving toward the car—of course it was his—Sandy wished he did not need crutches. But his ankle did furnish a kind of disguise for him; no one would guess that he too had the big P problem. He might even be just a visiting doctor—which, in a way, he was. Or a big investor, looking things over.

The driver was dark and fat—Mexican, probably—and not in uniform, but what can you do? He could call the company and complain about sloppiness (maybe even refuse to pay); on the other hand, why bother?

And the streets they were driving through looked like Mexican slums, and probably were. Ugly bright small stucco houses, lots of small failing businesses: auto parts, computer parts, dirty-looking restaurants. Sandy's pure Cedar Falls Presbyterian soul revolted, and he tapped on the glass. "Couldn't we get more out into the country? Leave the city?"

"Yes sir. As you say!"

Well, the guy was black, no Mexican, but how in hell could you tell? They're all so dark, those people.

Then, very quickly, they were actually up in some mountains, large rounded bright green ones, bulbous, like something diseased. The ugliest scenery, ugliest countryside Raleigh had ever seen. He closed his eyes and thought of New England. He remembered driving to Maine with Connie about a hundred years ago, the narrow twisting bad black roads, back then, the fields and stone fences. Birches and lakes everywhere, and how beautiful Connie said it was. But then silly Connie even thought it was beautiful in Cedar Falls; she loved the river and the falls, all that. Felicia too was always saying how beautiful something was, her garden, her flowers (even, he smiled briefly to remember, his cock). Were all women basically superficial and silly, after all? And, except for screwing, did he really not like them much? Oh shit, he thought as he looked at the monstrous swollen extrusions of earth, these mountains—oh shit, who cares? Who cares if anything is beautiful or not?

Sandy did wonder if either Connie or Felicia, those scenery-enthusiasts, would have anything good to say about these hills, this horrible landscape. God, probably they would.

Quite suddenly, then, Raleigh Sanderson, who did not believe in intuition, nor certainly in visions—suddenly he knew with a terrible clarity that all these treatments would not work for him; he would have to have the surgery, and after that he would be—useless. No more Felicia, no more nurses, no more even Connie.

Horrible! but also unreal, *untrue.* Layman's superstitious thinking.

He forced himself to concentrate instead on the idea that he had earlier had about investments, investing in particle therapy (of course it would work for him; it would shrink—if not re-move entirely—his prostate tumor). Those guys with money in dialysis really screwed up, did a lousy job and let it get out pub-licly that they owned the fucking machines.

He tapped on the glass. "Turn around, I want to go back."

With a quick screech the driver did just that—Jesus, lucky they both weren't killed right here.

He would call his brother Durham, the stockbroker, first thing when he got back to the hotel. With that thought Raleigh thought too, for the thousandth time, what a total jerk their mother had been. Raleigh and Durham, good Christ! What a re-ally dumb broad. *Belle.*

Back in his room, Sandy ordered a martini, which he did not really want but he thought that if he could at least get it down he might feel better. More like himself.

Waiting there, looking out the room's long narrow window, he observed the scruffy palm trees, ragged, tattered fronds that rattled in the ominous November wind, which also swung the large black creaking hotel sign: SUNDAY CHAMPAGNE BRUNCH, ALL YOU CAN EAT. $18.95.

And he thought, as Molly Bonner had before him, This is the worst place I've ever been. This is hell.

A Note on the Type

The text of this book was set in Simoncini Garamond, a modern version by Francesco Simoncini of the type attributed to the famous Parisian type cutter Claude Garamond (ca. 1480–1561). Garamond was a pupil of Geoffroy Tory and is believed to have based his letters on the Venetian models, although he introduced a number of important differences, and it is to him that we owe the letter we know as old-style. He gave to his letters a certain elegance and a feeling of movement that won for their creator an immediate reputation and the patronage of Francis I of France.

Composed by ComCom,
an R. R. Donnelley & Sons Company,
Allentown, Pennsylvania

Printed and bound by Quebecor Printing,
Fairfield, Pennsylvania

Designed by Dorothy S. Baker